THE DEPTH OF DARKNESS

MITCH TANNER BOOK ONE

L.T. RYAN

LIQUID MIND MEDIA

ACKNOWLEDGMENTS

Special thanks to Amy, Gail, Helen, Keith, Nikki, Marianne, Melanie, and Steve.

CHAPTER ONE

<blockquote>
"The depth of darkness to which you can descend and still live is an exact measure of the height to which you can aspire to reach."
- Pliny the Elder
</blockquote>

I closed the grill lid over three plump hamburger patties and leaned back against the sliding glass door. The fire hissed every time fatty juice dripped between the grill grates. Wispy smoke escaped through the slots on the side and wrapped around my head. The heat from the grill felt comforting, despite the lingering eighty degree temperature.

I watched as Ella Kate leaned forward and brushed the first fallen leaves off of the round patio table. She rested her elbows on the blue and orange mosaic glass tiles. Her gaze drifted from the trees behind our house to the dull pink sky. For a six year old, Ella didn't talk much. Of course, all I really had to compare it with was my son Robbie. I knew that the reason she didn't speak much was because of Robbie and her mother, my estranged wife, Marissa. When Marissa left in the middle of the day twelve months ago, she took Robbie with her, leaving Ella and me behind. Which really meant that Ella was without both of her parents most of the time. Being a homicide detective in Philadelphia didn't leave much time for family, I'm afraid.

People died at the oddest hours.

But I did the best I could and made every moment count. And so did my mother, who always seemed to be around.

I rapped on the glass door to get Momma's attention. She set her cell phone down on the kitchen island and slid off the barstool she had been perched upon. The sliding glass door screeched open and she stuck her head out.

"What?"

"Could you tear yourself away from that conversation long enough to bring some plates, buns and the ketchup out here?"

"I'm going to tear you away from something if you talk to me like that again, boy."

"Don't forget pickles, Grandma," Ella said.

"Sure thing, sweetie," my mother said.

I held out my hands and acted offended. "What's with the preferential treatment?"

Momma scowled at me like she was a pit bull, then she winked at Ella and went back inside, closing the door behind her. I looked over at Ella, who now had a sizable smile on her face. It was enough to make my heart skip a beat. Although she smiled more frequently now than she did a year ago, the moments were still too far in between.

It took my mother five minutes to return with the plates. I lifted the grill lid as she stepped outside. A rush of smoke greeted me. Using a stainless steel spatula, I flipped the burgers over. A fresh stream of fat juice coated the fire below. Flames rose up a good eighteen inches. I reacted a second too late and wound up with a couple of knuckles full of singed hair. The smell of burned hair momentarily overpowered that of the burgers.

Closing the lid I said, "Momma, would you mind grabbing me a beer?"

"Get it yourself," she said while placing her feet on an empty chair and crossing her legs at the ankles.

"I'll get it for you, Daddy," Ella said.

"Thank you, honey." I turned toward my mother. "At least someone around here appreciates me."

She waved me off and went back to playing a game on her cell phone.

"You just stay seated, Ella," I said. "I'll grab it myself." I reopened the grill lid and turned the burners down to low. The burgers were about ready, and if I got caught up in the garage a minute too long, they'd burn. I went inside, through the living room and the kitchen, and into the garage. That's where I kept my beer fridge. I flipped on the light. My 1969 Boss 429 Mustang was parked in the middle and took up most of the usable space in the two-car garage. I'd resurrected it from the dead eight years ago. Lately I'd had little time to tinker with it, so it remained alone in the garage. I traced a finger along the fender. It turned dark with dirt and dust. Time to give the Boss a bath.

I grabbed a beer out of the fridge and closed the door. I stood there for a moment admiring Robbie's artwork, held there by magnets. I pulled out my phone and flipped through my contacts list, stopping when I came to Cassie's number. Cassie was a woman who had helped me out in the past. You could say she had a knack for finding information in places others couldn't. I pressed the little phone icon next to her name and brought the phone up to my ear.

"Mitch?"

"Cassie, sorry to bother you. Hadn't heard from you in a while and I was wondering if you'd uncovered anything on Marissa and Robbie?"

"Mitch, as I've told you, when it happens, if it happens, I'll let you know. You can't press this. I'm doing what I can."

"I know you are. Just keep me posted." I hung up and slipped the phone into my pocket and returned my attention to the beer in my other hand. I had managed to twist the cap off when my phone rang. My heart leapt at the possibility that my call to Cassie had jarred some new piece of evidence loose. I glanced at the caller ID. Sam Foster, my partner, was calling.

Sam and I had been friends as little kids, then enemies from fourth through most of ninth grade, and then best friends as we formed an All-State duo on the right side of the defensive line on Bonner's state championship team. He played defensive tackle. I was lined up as defensive end next to him. We still hold the record for most combined sacks in a season, I think. Neither of us headed off to college after high school. He enlisted in the Army and I became a cop. We remained friends through it all. He joined up after his second stint, and now we're partners.

"What do you say, Sam?"

"We got one, Mitch."

"Ah, you're kidding me. I'm about to sit down to dinner with Ella and my mother."

"Good," Sam said. "At least you already have a babysitter in place."

I stood five feet from the sliding glass door that separated my living room from the back deck. Momma must've said something pretty funny. Ella was in stitches. I could hear her laughter through the door.

"You at home?" I asked.

"Yeah."

"I'll be there in fifteen."

I stepped outside, avoiding eye contact, and turned off the burners and cut the gas. I plated the burgers and set them down on the table. Ella looked up and smiled at me. I placed a hand on her shoulder. "Sweetheart, Daddy's gotta go to work."

CHAPTER TWO

The uniformed officers did a good job of securing a perimeter around the house. *Woman Found Dead by Husband* didn't get the media off, so tonight we were lucky on that front. The less I had to deal with them, the better. One of the guys suspected foul play. They said that the husband, a man named Roy Miller, acted a little like a weasel. Why a weasel? The officer couldn't say. Just said that's what Miller reminded him of.

Inside we met our victim, one Dusty Anne Miller. She was thirty-eight, blond, and attractive if you could overlook the gash and dent in her forehead. Her silk bathrobe was cinched at the waist, but had fallen open during her supposed accelerated descent down the stairs. In addition to the possibly fatal wound on her head, she had a fractured arm and femur. The broken bone in her leg nearly penetrated the skin, which had become discolored. Both appendages were bent at odd angles. Shards of glass littered the back of her body. Whiskey had mixed with the blood that pooled around her body, creating a brownish tint. The bottom step had bits of hair and skull and brain stuck to it. I wondered which injury occurred first, and had the head injury done her in, or in addition to the fractures, had she broken her neck as well.

Roy Miller seated himself at the kitchen table. He wasn't a big guy, but not little either. Average described him best. His brown hair looked disheveled. It matched the scruff on his face. Not quite a beard, but a bit more than stubble. He was too distraught to talk to us, but the responding officer told us that he'd said he came home and found his wife at the bottom of the stairs. The shower had been running. He figured she'd got into the shower, realized she'd forgotten to bring her new shampoo upstairs, then slipped at the top of the stairs due to a combination of wet feet and hardwood floors.

Her matted hair suggested that she had indeed been in the shower, and there was a paper bag from one of the local stores on the table. Inside the bag was a receipt time stamped from earlier that day. On the receipt were several personal items, including the shampoo that Dusty Anne never reached.

"Looks pretty cut and dry," Sam said in a low voice.

I glanced up at him, arching an eyebrow. "You know what they say about looks."

"Yeah, they get better with beer."

I started to smile but managed to catch myself before it spread too far. Last thing we needed was for either of us to be seen laughing while hovering over a dead woman's body. Most people wouldn't understand, and when you said things like coping mechanism, they rolled their eyes.

Sam motioned for one of the officers to come over. I walked away as he told the young cop to bring Roy Miller down to the station and set him up in one of the interview rooms. Meanwhile, I walked the perimeter of the downstairs. Nothing stood out to me. Sometimes you get a sense about a scene that tells you something happened. I didn't get that here. Like Sam said, cut and dry.

By the time we went back outside, the sun had set. We got

inside my city-issued Chevy and headed toward the station. Neither of us spoke. We were like an old married couple in that sense. After knowing one another for going on thirty-five years, we didn't have to fill the void with useless banter. That didn't mean we didn't at times. It just wasn't required.

It didn't take us long to reach the station bordering 61st, Thompson and Haverford in Carroll Park. I stood in front of the mirrored glass outside of the interview room where Roy Miller waited. Sam had set off in search of fresh coffee. Most of the time you wouldn't find it at nine-thirty at night. But this was Friday. And Fridays in Philly were crazy.

As I waited, I saw Roy go through a myriad of emotions. He slammed his fist against the table in anger. He paced the room in frustration, tearing at his tangled hair. Tears and sobs expressed his sadness. I tried to imagine being in his shoes and wondered whether it was harder to come home and realize your wife had left you or that she'd taken a nasty spill down the stairs and died.

I smelled the coffee before I heard Sam. For the first time, I glanced down and saw he was wearing tennis shoes. He handed me a lidded cup. A tiny wisp of steam slipped through the lid. Station house coffee. Nothing beat it. Maybe I could retire and franchise it one day.

"Ready?" Sam asked.

"After you, my man," I said.

Sam opened the door and stepped inside. He walked to the far corner of the room, crossed his arms and leaned back against the wall. I stepped in, closing the door behind me, and took a seat opposite Roy.

"Mr. Miller, if you recall I'm Detective Tanner, and that's Detective Foster. We don't want to take too much of your time, but we do have some questions we'd like to ask you."

He made eye contact with me for the first time and nodded. He cleared his throat. "Anything you need."

Turned out anything we needed was a rehashing of what the officer back at the Miller's house had told us.

"I walked home from work, stopping off to have a few beers. When I got home, the door was unlocked. I opened it, stepped inside, and saw her at the bottom of the stairs. I ran up to her. She wasn't breathing. I called nine-one-one and tried to do CPR, but her body was at such a weird angle and I remember reading that you should never move a body that was injured, so I waited. But, like I said, she wasn't breathing and I couldn't find a pulse. So I..."

"Waited," I finished for him.

He nodded. His gaze dropped from mine and fell to the table. Tears tracked down his cheeks again.

We waited for him to stop and asked the same questions in different ways. He never altered his answers. Finally, Sam left the room and I followed him out.

"What do you think?" he asked me.

"Story sounds legit, if not a little forced. Then again, could be 'cause he's telling the truth."

Sam nodded. "Want to keep him overnight and work on him some more in the morning?"

I studied Roy Miller through the mirrored glass. I didn't see a killer. I saw a man grieving over the loss of his wife. "Send him home. We can pick up again tomorrow at his house."

CHAPTER THREE

The following evening I went back to the Miller residence. The wind had picked up. A tropical storm had made its way up the east coast and was poised to strike our area the next day. As long as it didn't interrupt my cable signal, it could do whatever it wanted. The regular season started tomorrow.

I rapped on the door and waited. The porch light flipped on, casting a yellowish hue across the front of the house. The door opened and Roy Miller's head poked around the edge.

"Detective Tanner?" he said.

"Evening, Roy," I said. "Just wanted to ask you a few more questions."

He chewed on his cheek for a moment, lowered his head a notch and said, "I've got nothing else to say."

He tried to close the door. I wedged my foot just enough inside the frame to keep him from doing so. "It'll only take a few minutes, Roy."

He relented, opened the door and invited me in. The smell of chicken wings loomed. I glanced toward the kitchen and saw a yellow and white striped bucket on the table. A bottle of ranch dressing had been set next to it. On the other side of the bucket were two beer bottles. One looked empty, the other halfway there.

"This is interrupting my dinner," he said.

"Yeah, well, mine too." I took a look around, paying attention to the furniture, the floors and the walls. If the fall had been staged and the death had been due to other reasons, there might be some evidence that had been overlooked. Seeing none, I turned to Roy and gestured for him to head over to the kitchen.

He took a seat at the table and glared up at me. His demeanor had changed considerably in the past twenty-four hours. Another step in the grief process, or just tired of acting?

"Mind if I eat?" he asked.

"Yes, I do mind," I replied. "Now, take me through what happened once again, Roy. I want you to start from the beginning."

He sighed and watched me for a minute. Finally, he relented. "I was walking home from work."

"Which is where again?" I interrupted, pulling out my notebook to jot down his answer.

"Kessler's Auto Detail. I mostly handle the window tinting there. Anyway, I stopped off and had a drink." He stopped and picked up the bottle and took a drink. From there, he recounted the story in minimal detail. It was either the truth or he'd rehearsed it enough times to sound convincing.

When he was through, I asked, "Did Dusty Anne have any enemies?"

"Enemies?"

"Anyone who she might have angered, or who had an issue with her? Maybe she owed someone money and hadn't paid it back yet. It could be something that was trivial in your mind, but blown way out of proportion to someone else, Roy. So I need you to think about it."

He leaned back in his chair. His head dropped back and his eyes scanned the ceiling as if the answer might be there. He crossed his arms over his chest and returned to a normal sitting position. "No, nothing like that. Why do you ask? Do you have a witness who saw someone coming or leaving?"

There was something about the way he looked at me just then. It went beyond surprise. His face held a look of intrigue, or perhaps suspicion.

"Roy, did you ever wonder if Dusty Anne cheated on you?"

He placed his hands on the table and pushed back in his chair. I gestured for him to move no further. "Who've you been talking to?" he said. "I want to know who."

"That's none of your concern, Roy. At this time, I'm here with you and I'm the one asking the questions. Now, you might not have had anything to do with that fall, but if someone else did, and you have information that you are withholding, that'd be obstruction of justice and you'll do jail time."

The clenched muscles in Roy's jaw stood out on his shaven face. His breathing had turned heavy and ragged. It seemed he was either going to lash out at me or have a stroke. Finally, he settled down and said, "I have no information other than what I've told you, Detective Tanner. Now, I'd appreciate it if you'd leave and let me eat my dinner."

I rose from the table and took a few steps back, keeping my gaze fixed on him. "I'll be in touch with you soon, Roy."

He followed me to the front door. "Don't bother. I'm getting a lawyer."

"You certainly can do that, but it'll just make you look guilty."

"I'm not getting one to defend me, Detective. I'm getting him so I can go after you assholes for harassing me."

I laughed as I stepped off the porch. Then, something caught my eye. I'd missed it the night before, perhaps because the lighting had been different, or maybe because I was out of touch with the surroundings. On the hedges I spotted a few drops of what appeared to be blood. I stopped and turned around. By the time I swung my head around to say something to Roy, he'd taken off.

I crossed the porch in two large steps and kicked the door wide open. It hit the wall and bounced back at me. I kicked it again. I heard a door slam from the back of the house. I went to the right around the stairs, which led to a bedroom with no exit. I cursed and turned around and headed to the other side of the house. A mudroom led to the backyard. The door hung open on the hinges. The wind blew it further open for me.

My feet hit the ground in time to spot Roy hopping the back fence. He went over it quickly and gracefully. I'd underestimated the guy. I gave chase, hopping the fence with almost as much grace. For five minutes, I followed behind him as we passed through a half-dozen of his neighbors' yards.

We came to a clearing and Roy broke into a sprint. I did my best to keep up. He hurdled a chain covering the driveway to the old water tower. I did the same. My ankle felt unstable as it hit the ground, but I kept pushing. Roy ran right to the tower, put his shoulder into the door and busted it open. By the time I made it through, he was a quarter of the way up the spiral staircase. What the hell was the guy doing?

I stopped, took a moment to collect myself, then called Sam. He figured his ETA to be around ten minutes. He also said he'd get help out there. Fine by me. One less call I had to make. I hung up with Sam and made another call to let forensics know about the evidence. We needed them there before the storm hit. I stuffed my cell in my pocket and continued up the staircase. The metal door at the top whipped in the wind, banging into the wall. The sound echoed through the hollow body of the old tower. The higher I climbed, the tighter my stomach felt. When I finally reached the top, I wasted no time stepping through the open doorway.

Then I froze.

CHAPTER FOUR

I'd been told to wait for the negotiator. But I knew that guy was playing poker tonight, and he wouldn't respond until at least the third page. By this point, they'd paged him once, maybe twice. So it was up to me. Now, staring out into the open sky, I realized I should have waited.

I balanced on a two-foot wide ledge that surrounded the old water tower. I don't think it had been used since the '80s. I was a bit busy, so I didn't bother to call the town historian to find out. The wind blew in from the south. Fortunately, I was on the north side. Unfortunately, while the circular contraption protected me from the full thirty-mile per hour gust, I found myself being pelted by two razor thin wisps of wind that followed the gracious curve of the tower and met precisely where I stood.

I had a moment of clarity, during which I questioned my sanity by blurting out, "Fuck me."

I suppose I could have tried to say something to Roy, who had climbed over the waist-high railing about thirty seconds ago.

There was the temptation to let him jump. The sooner I got off that tower, the better.

I watched him release one hand, then the other. He leaned back against the railing, sometimes jerking forward and back because of the wind that whipped around and pelted him, the same as it did me.

I knew I should have said something to the guy. Sanctity of life and all that bullshit. That's the reason I got into homicide to begin with. To give a voice to those who could no longer speak. This guy could still speak though. And it wasn't like someone was taking his life here. He was prepared to do that by himself.

I could no longer hold my tongue. I was hot and sweaty and starting to have a panic attack, dammit.

"Well, then jump you bastard," I said.

He looked over his shoulder. The only light up on that tower came from the moon, and while it was full on this night, wispy clouds raced by and at that moment, they covered the entire white orb.

I couldn't get a read on the guy. His eyes looked black as coal. I could tell his mouth hung open from the dark hole in the middle of his face.

"Look, man," I said. "I'm cramping up here. So either you jump, or you get back over that railing and we go downstairs, and then I kick your butt on solid ground."

Roy turned his head forward and tucked his chin to his chest. He said nothing back to me.

Pissed me off.

I reached out for the railing and leaned forward. It was amazing I was up there in the first place. I'd been scared of heights since the age of eight or nine, when I climbed higher in a tree than I ever had. The reason? To save a one eyed tabby cat for the cute thirteen-year-old girl next door. Her name was Victoria. The cat, that is. I don't remember the name of the girl anymore. Maybe if she had thanked me, I would. It hadn't been the fact that I was higher up in the tree than I'd ever been before. Hell, that had been kind of cool to my eight or nine year old self. What did me in had been the branch that snapped when I was twenty feet off the ground. I've been told that it doesn't matter whether you weigh eighty pounds or eight hundred, twenty feet passes pretty quickly when you fall out of a tree.

And that's why I felt my stomach higher in my throat with every step I took forward. Those boards below my feet were old and splintered. At least, I imagined they'd be if I had a light to shine on them. Not that I'd look. Hell, it could have been plastic wrap under me. No way I was looking down. Not a hundred feet or so up in the air.

"Don't come any closer," Roy said.

"Oh, now you can talk?" I said, my panic at an all-time high as I realized I stood more than ten feet away from the door that led back to sanity.

He eased along the outer edge, further from me. I glanced down and saw that only his heels remained on semi-solid aboveground ground. Big mistake. Not him on the ledge. Me looking down.

A doctor might say it's impossible for a stomach to turn, but I swear mine did at that moment. My knees went a bit weak. A lot weak, as a matter of fact. Next thing I knew, my armpit collided with the metal railing.

"I got five bucks you hit the ground first," Roy said.

His words jostled me forward. "You don't know your physics," I said. I stopped before explaining any further. It would have been lost on him.

The episode I suffered through a moment ago seemed to cure me, at least temporarily, of my fear of heights. I rose and let go of the railing and walked toward him. This time he grabbed the railing with his left hand and spun, stopping so that his right leg hovered out in the air while the tip of his left foot balanced on the ledge.

Crazy SOB, I thought. "Get back over here," I said.

Red lights bounced off the trees. I saw the same lights reflected off the water tower. I looked down, twisted stomach and all, and saw a ladder and engine pull up to the tower. A moment later a flood light shone up at us.

I got a good look at the man who stood in between life and death. I'd just upgraded him to person of interest in his wife's death. Thus far, we'd labeled Dusty Anne Miller's death as accidental. But I didn't believe that now. Roy's actions on this humid, windy night only served to convince me that he was guilty as sin. Maybe more so.

"C'mon, Roy. Let's go downstairs, have a Starbucks, and talk this thing through."

I wasn't a fan of coffee I didn't make myself, but since I seemed to be in the minority, I thought it a good line to use.

Then Roy said something I don't know that I'll ever forget. He said, "Coffee? It's almost midnight."

Did dead men care about such things?

Roy looked down for an awfully long time. He eased his butt to the railing again and placed both hands on it. His stare remained focused on one of the fire trucks below. I wanted to look over, too. I'd never been involved in a jumper situation and found myself wondering if they pulled out one of those circular bouncy things like in the old cartoons. Might be fun, for the right person.

I didn't look though. With Roy distracted, I reached out and grabbed hold of his collar. He yelled something indecipherable. I pulled back as hard as I could. He toppled over backward, landed on his head. I hovered over his body, leaned forward.

"Roy?" I said.

Roy said nothing. His eyes were shut, his mouth open a bit. I felt for a pulse. Found one. I pinched his hand and he winced in pain. A good sign, I thought. If his neck was broken, he wouldn't have felt that.

Roy came to somewhat and said, "What the hell, man?"

I grabbed him by the shoulders and dragged him around the water tower until we reached the door. The wind had blown it shut. Luckily, it hadn't been locked.

Now, that tower ledge was at least a hundred-fifty feet off the ground. There was no way I was going to carry that guy down the stairs. So I pulled out my radio and called in for back up. Soon, the firefighters' flashlights lit up the corridor.

Jerry Haynes appeared first. Jerry and I go way back, before he was a firefighter and I was a cop. Together, with Sam, the three of us raised some hell as kids.

Jerry said, "You OK, Mitch?"

"Yeah, just remind me to check my shorts when I get back on solid ground."

CHAPTER FIVE

"We'll take it from here," Jerry said, pulling Roy from my arms. He laid the guy on the ground and began to assess his condition. "Where's this blood coming from?"

"His head," I said. "He did a reverse endo over the railing and his skull broke his fall."

Jerry tossed me a thumbs up. I suppose he was telling me he got the info, but I like to think it was one of those congratulatory thumbs up for a job well done. After all, I hadn't killed the guy and I didn't let him take his own life. I deserved a pat on the back for that.

I relinquished my control of Roy over to Jerry and his firefighter buddies and then started down the spiral staircase that ran along the water tower's outer wall, inside of course. Overhead light bulbs encased in black metal cages cast a yellowish glow that seeped over the railing. They probably would have provided me with a view to the bottom. I didn't look to verify that. With every step my adrenaline level dropped. I certainly hadn't overcome my fear of heights up there on that balcony. Temporary insanity helped me through it.

Two uniforms passed me at about the halfway point. Fresh faces. I didn't know either of them. We needed someone on this side of the law to watch over Roy now that he'd been upgraded from person of interest to suspect. I sure as hell wasn't going to do it. That's what we paid the young guys for.

"What's the scene like down there?" I asked.

"Sam's out there," the baby faced guy said. His red cheeks gave away his Irish ancestry. That or he'd been drinking on the job. Judging by the look on his face, his sack hadn't dropped enough for that. I glanced at his nameplate. Jennings. Didn't ring a bell with me.

"Did he light into that woman from Channel 3?" I asked. Sam couldn't stand that woman. Attractive, yes. Even more of a pest, though. She was always the first to the scene of a homicide. Everything else, too, I suppose. I wondered how this young guy knew Sam. Didn't ask.

"Oh yeah," Jennings replied. "And that douche bag from Seventeen."

"Hey, I like that guy."

The smile dropped from Jennings's face faster than his body would have fallen to the water tower's ground floor. Or a ton of bricks, for that matter. Eighty or eight hundred. Laws of physics.

"I'm just messing with you, Jennings," I said.

"You're a douchebag, Tanner."

Hey, look at that. The left one dropped. I couldn't help but shake my head, laugh, turn, and continue on my way down that spiraling staircase. Their footsteps faded as mine echoed off the surrounding walls.

As I stepped off the metal stairs onto the concrete bottom, I noticed Sam standing right outside the doorway. At six-four and built like a linebacker, he blocked most of the artificial light from outside. He leaned against the frame with his left elbow propped up next to his head. His right leg was straight while his left leg crossed over the other at the shin, all casual and relaxed. Did anything faze the guy? Guess that's what the Rangers does for someone. He had the door propped open with a red brick. I recalled seeing several of them on my way inside. At the time, I had thought about grabbing one to use on Roy.

Sam glanced over his shoulder, did a double take. "You look like ten-day-old garbage."

"Thank you," I said.

"That your blood?"

I hadn't realized that Roy had bled on me. I had the sudden urge to strip down and find the nearest shower. I resisted looking down. "How bad is it?"

He pointed at my chest. "Just on your shirt. Your hands, too, I guess."

"Dammit. Have to get tested again." AIDS, Hepatitis, and any other blood borne pathogen — these guys out here carry all of them and don't give two craps about warning you about them. In Roy's defense, he didn't have the faculties available at the time.

Sam laughed and punched my shoulder. "It's not that bad, man. Come on, let's go deal with the hyenas."

Hyenas, Sam's pet name for the media, wasn't that far off in Philadelphia. Or most places, I suppose. Normally, Horace "Huff" Huffman, our Lieutenant and esteemed leader, would handle them for us. Not tonight. He was at the same poker game as the negotiator. Huff would ignore his pager no more than two times. Then he'd take his time getting down here and ream us for a job not well done. So Sam and I were on our own. Two sacrificial lambs wading through a pack of trained, vicious hyenas. There was only one thing to say.

"No comment," I said.

"No comment," Sam said.

The leader stepped ahead of the pack. Her dark wavy hair and eyes black as coal gave us reason to pause. Behind the beautiful facade something evil worked, though. "Detectives, do you think—"

"I think we said, no comment," Sam said. "Now kindly get out of our way before I charge you with tampering with a crime scene."

Sam had a way with words. He could say in two sentences what would have taken me two paragraphs. Or one obscenity laden sentence, which would do me no favors when the evening news ran the clip repeatedly.

The news crews backed up past the point where the tape should have been strung. They moved slowly, dragging their feet. I thought hyenas were a hyper bunch?

"Are Jennings and that other doofus the only two uniforms out here?" I asked Sam.

"Saturday night, that's all we get this far out. Half the precinct's on loan downtown for that festival."

"Which festival is it this weekend?"

"There's so freaking many, Mitch. I can't ever remember."

"Just another excuse to get loaded."

"That's right. So how's about we finish up here and get down there?" He threw his thumb over his shoulder for emphasis.

I looked up at the pale blue tower and shook my head. Had I really stood next to that railing? "We gotta question this guy tonight. Hopefully forensics got a good sample of that blood spot and can tell us something new. If anything, we can BS our way with Roy. Maybe get him to open up."

At that time, the firefighters emerged with a still unconscious Roy. Two medics met them at the door and loaded the guy onto a gurney. Jennings and his partner followed the group out. Sam headed toward them.

"What the hell were you two thinking going up there without

cordoning off this area? Every one of them reporters trounced around in front of the entrance. What if that guy had dropped something? Now it's pounded in the damn mud."

I laughed at the tirade. For as smooth as Sam could be with the media, he could light up a rookie cop. He would have made a hell of a drill instructor if he'd stayed in the Army. I left Sam to the discipline and jogged over to Firefighter Jerry.

"Did a number on him, Mitch," Jerry said.

"Kept him from jumping," I said. "So, when do you think we can get at him?"

"He's going to the hospital."

"Evaluation, then we can bring him back to the station?"

Jerry laughed and hiked his thumb in the air toward Roy. "Guy's been out of it for, what, fifteen minutes now? He'll be under observation all night."

"Dammit," I said, looking toward the ambulance as they hoisted Roy up and inside.

"He might not even remember what he was doing up there to begin with."

"Oh, he'll remember once forensics processes that blood."

"You mean those guys?" Jerry pointed over my shoulder.

I turned around and saw Sandusky leaning against his black crime scene investigation van. His arms were crossed over his chest, and his legs spread wide. A lit cigarette dangled from his mouth. I supposed that, to a man in his line of work, no one dies of natural causes.

"Hey, cookout tomorrow," Jerry said. "You wanna come over?"

I started to move toward the van. "It's supposed to rain all day tomorrow, Jerry. Tropical storm something or another."

Jerry cursed and said something else, but I ignored it. I hollered for Sam. Together we jogged over to Sandusky's van.

"Fellas," Sandusky said.

"Get that evidence?" I asked.

"What evidence?" he asked in reply.

"At the house," I said.

"Ain't been to no house, Tanner."

"Are you kidding me, Sandy? Roy Miller's house. I called it in and gave the address. Found a spot of blood outside. We need that processed."

Sandusky jerked his body forward and started toward the front of the van. "Hey, all I heard was water tower, Tanner."

A crack of thunder roared overhead. I looked up and noticed that the clouds no longer raced by the moon. They had consumed it. I felt the first drops of water hit my face. "Hurry, before this rain washes it away." I opened the passenger door of the van and hopped inside. Looking back over my shoulder, I said, "Sam, get your car and get over there."

Sam took off running. I watched him skirt behind the reporters who were still bunched up around an imaginary crime scene line. I hoped they wouldn't see us. Last thing we needed was one of them following us back to the Miller's residence.

Sandusky shot me a curious look.

"Just floor it, asshole."

He dropped the van into drive. The tires spun in the dirt and kicked gravel everywhere.

"Go easy," I said. "Gonna attract attention that way."

He waved me off and ignored the narrow road that led to the street, instead choosing to drive through the grass.

"You know where we're going?"

"I spent all day there yesterday, Tanner."

Had it only been one day since Dusty Anne's death? The episode atop the water tower felt like it lasted at least a week. How long till the calendar caught up with my brain this time?

"What do you think?" I asked.

"About what?"

One thing about Sandusky, the guy is incapable of giving a

straight answer after one question. If I hadn't been trained to go through this process, I'd have knocked him out and stole his van right then and there.

"Dusty Anne and that crime scene?"

"Who says it's a crime scene?"

"That's what I'm asking you, man."

"Why would you ask me that?"

"Because you've processed thousands of crime scenes, so I'd like to get your opinion."

"On or off the record."

I'd almost had it by then. "Whatever, man, I'm just fishing for opinions, gut feelings, intuition. If the Holy Spirit came down and gave you any clues, I'd love to hear them."

He cleared his throat as he turned the steering wheel and navigated toward the Miller's house. "On the record, it looks like a woman, mid-thirties, fell and hit her head."

"And off the record?"

"Signs point elsewhere, but you'll have to wait for the ME to confirm that."

Sandusky, despite his shaggy outward appearance and aloof mannerisms, had a tendency to be right on the money.

So he pulled the van up to the curb on the opposite side of the road. I heard Sam brake hard and stop on the other side of the street. I hopped out of the van and held my hand above my eyebrows to shield my eyes from the rain. That cursed rain. I said as much, too. We all met on the sidewalk in front of the Miller's residence. Sam held his windbreaker over his head. The rain hit it with a dull, hollow sounding *thump.*

"Where's this evidence?" Sandusky said.

"Follow me." I walked up to the gate and lifted the latch, then kicked it open. The porch light was still on. That's how I noticed the blood earlier that night. I headed right for it.

I stopped a foot from the hedges, and Sam and Sandusky came

to a halt behind me. I frantically searched for the blood I'd seen earlier. My head jerked side to side, bobbed up and down. I probably looked like the world's worst dancer at that moment, hands on my hips, doing some weird version of the Chicken Dance.

"Well?" Sandusky said.

"Just hold on a minute here," I said. It didn't matter though. The rain had washed it away. "Son of a..." I kicked my foot across the ground, breaking a few of the lower branches.

"Just point to the general area," Sandusky said while fishing through his pockets. He pulled out a multi-tool and held it up in the light. In his other hand, he held a plastic evidence bag, upside down. "I'll clip the branches and we can see what we find."

"Will that work?" Sam said.

Sandusky shrugged. "Can't hurt."

I felt Sam grab my collar and tug me backward. It came as a surprise. Nearly took me off my feet.

"Let's get out of the man's way," he said to me.

I took a few steps back and turned and started walking with Sam toward the gate. Our work was done.

"Want to go back to the office and look over the pictures?" he asked.

I did, but doing so would remind me of the blood trail we had just lost. I needed a distraction. "No."

"How about we grab a beer?"

"Now you're talking."

I followed him through the gate. We passed in front of the black crime scene van. Both of us stopped when we saw Carla. She leaned against Sam's Camaro, holding a large golf umbrella. It protected that fine, dark wavy hair. Her eyes still looked blacker than the night. To what did we owe the pleasure of a visit from the local news superstar?

"How's it hanging, fellas," she said.

"We've got nothing to say," Sam said.

"You sure about that? It's the day after an apparent accident, and I find you two, Philadelphia PD's top homicide detectives, back at the scene with forensics. This after chasing the corpse's widower up a water tower and then knocking him out?"

Neither of us said anything. Sam opened his door and got in. I walked around the trunk, past Carla.

She reached out and grabbed my upper arm. "Come on, Detective. Something's up. At least toss me a small bone."

I looked over at her. Our eyes met. She smiled.

"Least you can do for an old friend," she said.

I broke free from her grasp, pulled my door open and stopped before getting in. "Go to hell, Carla."

Her mouth dropped open an inch. I think I saw her smile. It was hard to tell in the darkness.

"And you can run that sound bite."

CHAPTER SIX

A little after two in the morning, Sam parked the car in front of my house. I stared out the window at the yard leading up to the two-story colonial. The weeds had been bad this year, and my failure to get them under control had drawn the ire of the neighborhood HOA. My fault, I suppose, for letting Marissa convince me to buy the place half a decade ago. I'd been happy living next to Sam in the old neighborhood. Sure, it was a bit run down. But anytime I wanted to have a beer with a buddy, he was right there. And if he was out, Jerry lived across the street.

"When you gonna ditch this place and move back home?" Sam asked.

I hadn't sold the old place. My cousin lived there. I could kick him out any time I wanted. Not that I would.

"The memories inside there gotta drive you crazy, Mitch."

I nodded. They did. "I can't leave until Robbie comes home. It's the only home he remembers. You know that."

Sam nodded, reached over and grabbed my shoulder. "Go on inside now, my man."

"I called her the other night."

"Who? Marissa?"

I shook my head. "Cassie."

"Man, you know I'm not crazy about that woman."

"She gets results."

"Half the time, if that. The rest of it, she's just crazy."

I shrugged and said nothing.

Sam took a deep breath. "She have anything for you?"

"Nah, still nothing."

Sam reached out and squeezed my shoulder. "Go inside, man."

I opened the door and stepped into a puddle that had formed in the gutter between the street and the curb. Cold water rushed inside my shoe and soaked my sock. I cursed the rain again. Then I started toward the front porch. In my mind's eye, I could see both my kids playing on the porch. I knew that only Ella would be inside. It still hurt.

Before I reached the screened-in front porch, I glanced toward the garage. Maybe once Dusty Anne Miller's case was wrapped up I could take the old 'Stang out for a spin.

I pulled the screen door open and shuffled across the front porch. Experience had taught me that if I tried to walk at a normal clip, I'd likely trip over a toy fire truck, or a doll's stroller, or a play shopping cart. I'd almost made it to the front door when I banged my shin against the all-weather sofa I kept out there for those evenings when the humidity was low and the temperature somewhere around sixty-five. I glanced down and saw that someone had moved the sofa a good twelve inches to the left. I grunted and groaned as I reached for the door handle. The knob turned, but the deadbolts were locked.

I tapped my fingertips against the window while freeing my keys from my left pocket. The deadbolts slid and clicked as Lana turned them. I waited for her to open the door. The door cracked open and her perfume enveloped me. She greeted me with a smile, then a soft kiss. Her eyelids opened and shut slowly over her golden brown eyes. She wore one of my pinstripe button ups, top two buttons undone. There weren't any pants to speak of. The shirt hid the curve of her hips and came to about mid-thigh. I admired her mocha colored smooth legs.

Lana Suarez and I had been dating for a tad over four months. Ella had taken to her pretty quickly, and now Lana gave my mother a break every now and then and watched Ella for me when I had to go out at night. Most nights she was happy to do so. She had been tonight. Until she realized why I was so late.

"You smell like beer," she said as her eyes narrowed and her lips drew tight. I'd ignited her Cuban temper.

"It was a rough night, Lana." I reached for her hand. She pulled away and stepped behind the door, pulling it open a few feet. I stepped inside, and said, "Sam and I hit up Schmitty's on the way over for a couple beers. I needed an alcohol laden detox."

"What happened?" she asked as she walked past me, avoiding contact at all costs.

We stopped in the great room and I said, "I stopped by the house from the day before—"

"The woman who fell or something like that?" The anger eased from her face.

I nodded. She knew all the details. I'd stayed up half the night telling her about it. "And on my way out tonight, I spotted something. When I turned to say something to her husband, he took off like a bat out of hell. I chased after him. He led me up inside the water tower, out onto the ledge."

"You went out there?" She slipped into the kitchen and disappeared behind the refrigerator door.

"Yup."

"What about your fear of heights?"

I shrugged and then fell back into my recliner. "We have the power to overrule our minds, especially when the situation dictates our beliefs to be something other than what they truly are. Truly, as defined by ourselves, for those of us who want to hang onto old habits, whether good or bad."

"That's deep, Mitch." She twisted the top off a Bud Light and handed it to me.

I grabbed the cold bottle and took a deep long pull. "I know. I've been taking guru classes online."

She rolled her eyes and then pointed at my bottle of Bud. "You're almost forty, you should upgrade from that swill you like to drink."

"I'm in my late mid-thirties, and I enjoy this swill just fine, thank you." I took another pull and held the bottle up to the light. Half-full, at least tonight. Any other day it'd be half-empty.

I watched her as she retreated into the kitchen area and pulled the cork out of a bottle of red wine. She reached up for a wine glass. The shirt lifted as she did so, but not far enough so that I could catch a glimpse of what she had on underneath.

"You sure you want to do that this late?" I asked.

"Tomorrow's Sunday. No school. Might not have school on Monday. Principal Bennett said it depends on what kind of damage this tropical storm does." She came back into the room and stopped in front of me. I noticed her shirt had loosened around her chest by a couple of buttons. A tiny drop of wine had slid along the curved glass and dripped from the glass's stem onto the cream-colored carpet. She followed my eyes and saw the red spot on the floor. "Shit, I'm sorry, Mitch."

"It's no problem."

She set her glass down on the table next to me and went back to the kitchen to grab a towel, which she ran under the faucet. "I'm so careless," she said when she returned.

"It's no biggie," I said. "Like I told Marissa when she chose this color, we got little kids, it's bound to get dirty and stained."

Lana looked up at me, eyes big and brown. I knew why she

watched me. I'd said Marissa and kids in the same sentence. That never led to a happy moment.

"I'm OK," I said, taking another drink from the bottle. I set it down next to her wine glass and slid out of the chair and onto my knees on the floor. The plush carpet felt like a foam mattress. I grabbed her hand and stopped her from wiping the floor. She rose up on her knees and pushed her breasts into my chest. I wrapped my arm around the back of her waist and pulled her in even tighter. Our lips met. I rose and pulled her up to her feet.

"You want another beer?" she asked, her mouth less than an inch from mine.

"You want to finish your wine?" I asked.

She reached for the glass, took a sip and set it down. "I'm good."

"Then so am I."

She grabbed my hand and turned and pulled me toward the stairs. We climbed, stopping every fourth or fifth step to kiss, and then we crept past Ella's room. By the time we reached my room at the end of the hall, she had her legs wrapped around my waist and I supported her with my hands on her buttocks. I grabbed the handle and kicked the door open, then reversed the direction of my leg and pushed it closed. We fell onto my bed, leaving the lights off. The lightning outside provided all the ambiance we needed.

CHAPTER SEVEN

The storm whipped up something fierce throughout the night and into the early morning hours of Sunday. I lay in bed with Lana draped across my chest until about eight in the morning. Her breath was hot and soothing against my neck. I lifted her arm and slipped out of bed, then went downstairs and cooked up a batch of chocolate chip pancakes for the three of us. Ella had been in the kitchen waiting for me. She helped mix the batter. I did the rest of the work. She took all of the credit. Nothing new there. The storm didn't let up all that much, so getting out of the house was pretty much a wash. I phoned the hospital throughout the day, but Roy Miller remained unconscious.

So we stayed on the couch all day. Watched cartoons in the morning, pre-game shows until one, then football the rest of the day. Opening weekend. Every team with a blank slate with no wins and no losses. There was hope yet for my Eagles. Lana left before Sunday Night Football started. I put Ella to bed at halftime. By the end of the fourth quarter, I was asleep on the couch.

Monday started for me at five a.m. A whole hour before my

alarm was set to go off. My cell phone started ringing and vibrated across the coffee table. I grabbed it and put an end to the ruckus. With my eyes closed and my mouth dry, I said, "What?"

"He's gone."

The words hung there for a minute until I placed the voice. Sam. Shouldn't have taken so long, but it was five a.m.

I licked my lips and swallowed, and asked, "Who's gone?"

"Miller."

This caused me to sit up. "Roy Miller? Our suspect?"

Sam paused for a beat, and then said, "Yeah, that Roy Miller."

"Son of a..." I rubbed my eyes with my left hand, kicked my legs over the side of the couch and rose. My knees popped like cap guns. "How the hell did this happen?"

"No one can tell me." I could feel the anger in his voice. It matched my own.

"Didn't we have someone watching over his room? Please tell me we had him on twenty-four hour watch."

"Affirmative."

"Okay. And?"

"Working on it, man." Sam's voice sounded hushed, like someone was nearby he didn't want to hear this conversation. "Someone else is laying into the guy that screwed up right now."

"Huff?"

"You know it."

I didn't envy the recipient of Huff's tirade. Good boss? Yes. Grade-A prick? Hell, yes.

I said, "Why am I the last to know about this?"

Sam had no answer. I imagined him with his lips drawn tight, shaking his head at me.

"Where you at now?"

"On my way to the hospital."

"I'll see you there."

I leaned my head back and stared up at the ceiling. There was a dark spot in the corner. Rain had seeped through again. I'd had the roof patched there a year ago. It never ends.

I stepped into the kitchen and refocused. Where would Roy have run off to? Not home. Our files said he had no family in the area. Maybe a friend's house. We could check that. The only chance we had at getting to the true cause of his wife's death remained with him. If we didn't find him, her voice wouldn't be heard.

I started the coffee, which I'd wisely prepared before falling asleep during the fourth quarter of last night's game. For a second I wondered who had won the game, then I remembered I didn't care for either team. I could Google it later if I felt that I needed to know. I found my way upstairs and into the shower. Ten minutes later I was downstairs, pants on, shirt half-buttoned and untucked, shoulder holster unbuckled, socks and shoes by the front door.

I drank my coffee black while scarfing down two eggs fried in butter to the point where the yolk was intact but no longer runny. A bit of salt added all the flavor I needed. The doorbell rang as my laptop hung on that stupid start up screen. Five-year-old piece of crap. I thought about replacing it with one of those new laptops and giving this one to Ella. Maybe someday. Roof repairs and all were still hanging in the balance.

"Hi Mom," I said as I opened the door.

She had on her blue robe, cinched tight at the waist. I presumed the plastic bag in her hand contained the clothes she intended to wear later that day. She yawned and stepped inside. "Coffee?"

"Already poured you a cup."

"Two sugars and milk?"

"Two packs of Splenda and half-n-half."

"I don't like that stuff." She pulled her graying hair back in a ponytail as she walked past me. She smelled of smoke.

"When did you start smoking again?" I asked.

She waved me off. "Get off my case."

"Someone has to be on it, or you'll be digging an early grave."

She went to the kitchen and sat at the island. I'd set a plate of eggs on it next to her coffee. She held the mug up to her face, then took a sip.

"Well?" I said.

"It'll do."

There, I had my mother's approval and could now go about my day.

"Is school closed?" she asked.

"Don't think so. Let me check." My laptop was waiting and ready. The school's website said that school was on. This pleased my mother.

"Where are you off to?" she asked as I headed toward the door.

"Hospital."

She got a funny look on her face. "Why?"

"To see Sam."

Her expression changed to worry. "Oh, he's not hurt is he?"

I shook my head and offered her a slight smile. "Nah, someone else."

"Anyone I know?"

"I hope not, Momma."

I stepped onto the front porch, stopped to slide the sofa back to its regular place, and picked up the toys and magazines that the circling winds from the day before had strewn about. At that moment I realized that my car was still parked at the Millers's. I pushed open the door and called for Mom.

"I need to borrow your car."

"No way. I've seen cop movies. It'll come back demolished."

"Just for a few hours, Mom. I'll get Sam to follow me back as soon as we leave the hospital."

She shook her head and tossed her keys to me. "Someday you'll grow up."

I ignored the shot and closed the door behind me. Her car was old, but kept up. When I sat down inside of it, it smelled like I was deep within a pine forest. The radio was tuned to the local soul station. Not an easy station to get the dial to pick up as I recalled. I wasn't in the mood to shake my money maker, so I turned the volume down and drove to the hospital in relative silence. No getting rid of the road noise, though. I rolled the windows down. The wind rush created a sort of white noise that drowned out my thoughts.

The roads were empty at six a.m. Perhaps parents slept in a little later today, hoping that school would be closed. That would give them a welcome excuse to stay home. Little Billy and Annie can't be home alone. Not with all the crazies out in the world.

If they only knew.

Fifteen minutes after pulling out of my driveway, I found a parking spot at the hospital. I called Sam on my cell and met him at the entrance. We showed our badges at every desk along the way. No one bothered to ask questions, they just said, "Mornin' officers," and, "Go right ahead officers." That's a right good start to a cop's day. Better than bullets whizzing by. And water tower ledges.

I recognized Roy's room by the empty chair positioned outside the door. That's where our guy would have been last night. Question was, had he been there when Roy escaped? I peeked through the open doorway and saw Huff standing there, looking out the window.

"Huff?" I said, stopping inside.

"Come on in, guys." He didn't look back at us. There wasn't much of a view that I could see, so I had no idea what he was entranced by.

We stood there a minute or two before Huff finally turned around. He placed his hands on his expanding waist. He hadn't dressed for the occasion. He wore dark blue sweatpants and a hooded sweatshirt with the logo of that rival team just up I-95. He hadn't shaved all weekend. I bet the hair on his head would have been a mess if he had any.

"What'd our guy say, Huff?" Sam asked.

"Said he sat in that chair outside the door all night. He got here at eleven, pulled double duty with Jennings till twelve, then took over. He slept a good six or seven hours he claims, not bothering to watch a single game all day."

"Who was it?" I asked.

"Ramirez," Huff said. "Know him?"

I didn't know any of the new guys these days. "Nah."

"Baby-faced kid two months out of the academy. Got a baby on the way, and he wanted the overtime. Didn't react too well to being placed on admin leave."

"Imagine so," I said. "You believe him?"

"Doesn't matter what I believe. Hospital has security footage, and we're in the process of procuring that. But most important to me is what the hell happened to Roy Miller."

"Me too," I said.

Huff turned back to the window. He grabbed it and tugged. It slid open with a tiny squeak. "Hear that?"

"The squeak? Yeah."

Huff spun around and nodded. He hiked his thumb over his shoulder a couple times. "Ramirez says he recalled hearing that a half-dozen times or so. When he checked, Roy was sound asleep."

"He attribute it to a mouse or something?" Sam asked.

Huff shrugged.

"And then he stopped checking," I said.

"Yup," Huff said.

"How long did he wait to look?"

"He says right away. Until he stopped."

"What's outside that window?" Sam asked.

"Have a look," Huff replied.

So Sam and I crossed the room and Huff stepped out of our way. I opened the window wide enough for both of us to stick our heads out. Though we were three floors up, a fire escape was bolted to the building. Roy wouldn't have even had to drop to reach it. All he would have had to do was stick one leg out, then the other, and he'd have been on it.

"Someone was out here," Sam said, pointing at the painted black metal platform.

I nodded. "They opened and closed the window to see how Ramirez would react."

Sam turned around and shook his head, pointing past the open doorway. "Well, look at that."

Huff and I followed his gaze and his finger. Across the hall was a wall of tempered glass. The kind that gives off a nice reflection.

I said, "Whoever was out there could see Ramirez's reaction."

Sam took three long steps, placing him near the doorway. He turned and said, "And look, you can't see out the window from here."

"So whoever was out there waited until Ramirez got complacent, and then left the window open."

"And Roy Miller climbed out to freedom."

"Huff, did anyone try to come by and see Roy at all yesterday?" I asked.

"We'll find out," Huff replied.

"Come on, Sam," I said. "I need to drop my Momma's car off at my house."

CHAPTER EIGHT

L il' Debby Walker hated her nickname. She didn't mind it so much when she was five, but now that she was nine, she resented the H E double hockey sticks out of it. She wasn't a darn pastry. Speaking of pastries, the Cheese Wagon came to a stop ten feet in front of her. Since Billy moved away, she was the only one at the bus stop in the morning. Katy rode the bus home, but her mom took her to school.

The bus driver looked over at her and nodded. She checked the street both ways before crossing to the other side. Good habits ingrained deep. She had lots of them. Her mother told her she was neurotic, whatever that meant. Her brother teased her that she was something called oh sea dee. Gibberish. To her ears, at least.

So Debby looked left, then right, then left again. She tapped the fingers of her left hand to her thumb twice each. She counted her steps from the curb to the bus. On the seventh step, she stopped and looked down to see where her feet were. If not even with the bus's front left tire, she'd have to start over again. The bus driver didn't like it when she did that, but he's not the one who'd have to live the consequences of her getting this wrong, so she'd start over. The fate of the world could be at stake.

Lil' Debby Walker thought so, at least.

Today her feet lined up perfectly. A smile beamed on her face as she rounded the front of the bus and stopped in front of the open sliding door. Three steps up, one forward, a quick smile for the driver, turn left, then the fourth row on the right. Her seat. Window seat. Lil' Debby's seat every year since kindergarten.

Not today, though. Two boys in the fifth grade had decided to take her not-so-assigned place on the bus.

"Get up," she said.

"Go away," the brown haired one said.

She tucked her blond curls behind her ears and slung her backpack over her right shoulder. "Get up or I'll tell everyone how you wet the bed that weekend my mom watched you. You remember that, don't you? It was only two months ago."

The boy's friend started laughing, which drew a punch to the shoulder from the brown haired boy.

"Let her have her stupid seat," the brown haired boy said, pushing his friend toward the aisle.

Debby took a step back. She looked over her shoulder and saw the bus driver watching her and laughing to himself. He winked and gave her a quick nod.

The brown haired boy bumped her with his shoulder as he passed and said, "Stupid little freak."

She didn't care. She had her seat. She'd won, as she often did. While she might be neurotic, or oh sea dee, a stupid little freak, or any other number of things the kids called her, she was also smarter than them all.

A state certified genius, her mother had said.

You mean certifiable, her brother had said.

Oh hush, Ronald. Lil' Debby's gonna skip two grades. She might graduate high school before you. Definitely college.

Ronald had blushed and given her the middle finger when her mom wasn't looking.

Debby didn't like the sound of skipping grades and going to college at the age of fifteen. She wanted nothing to do with it. It had been hard enough for her to make friends with kids her own age. Imagine the way she'd be treated if she jumped from third to fifth grade. The Boy Who Wets His Pants would be relentless toward The Stupid Little Freak. And so would his friends. And probably all the other kids.

So she begged and pleaded to remain where she was. Her mother agreed, reluctantly, and with the caveat that they'd revisit the subject after the fourth grade. She didn't know the word caveat, but she got the meaning from context. Surely, at the ripe age of eleven, Debby would be more than mature enough to skip junior high and go right to high school.

Puh-lease.

The bus turned right into the next neighborhood. Even at her age, Debby could tell that the houses were nicer. So were the cars. That meant the parents made more money than her mom. Not hard to do, she supposed, considering how little she had. And everything she did have had been given to her second hand.

Lil' Debby, charity case.

Seven kids got on the bus. Six walked past her without so much as a glance. But the seventh stopped, smiled and tossed his bag to her.

"Hi Beans," she said.

Bernard "Beans" Holland hated being called Beans as much as she despised Lil' Debby. That didn't stop her from using his nickname loudly and often.

"Can you at least call me Bernie?" He pushed his thick glasses up his nose and fell onto the seat.

A cloud of dust shot up and fell back down through the rays of sunlight that slipped in between the giant two story houses.

"Glad that storm passed," she said.

He glanced at her over the rim of his glasses. "We're talking about the weather now?"

She gave him a cross look. "What's that mean?"

"No idea. Something my mom said to her boyfriend." Beans grabbed his bag off her lap and pulled out a tube of lotion. He squeezed a dime-sized circle on the back of his hand and rubbed it in.

Debby held out her hands, palms facing down, in front of him.

"What?" he asked.

"Can I have some?"

"You don't need it."

"Why not?"

"You know why."

"Just because I'm not black doesn't mean I don't like putting your pretty smelling lotion on my hands."

"I don't wear pretty smelling lotion," he said to a chorus of laughter behind them. "I've got dry skin."

Debby glanced over her shoulder and narrowed her eyes at the brown-haired boy. A slight shake of her head was all it took to make him stop. And what he did, the others did. She kind of relished the power she now had over him.

"Here," Beans said.

"Why thank you, Bernard," she said, smiling at him as he handed the tube over. They were two oddball peas that had fallen from their original pods and made one of their own out of the scraps the world threw at them. Without each other, school would have been a miserable experience. Together, they could take on anything and anyone.

The bus completed its tour through the fancy neighborhood and hit the main road to school. Five to ten minutes, on average, is all they had before being forced to put up with a day confined behind their desks. To Debby, it was so boring. To which her mother would respond, skip those grades and you won't be bored. On so many levels, Debby was sure that would be the case. Spending half a day crammed inside one's own locker had to be a rush, right?

The old stinky Cheese Wagon clanked to a stop in front of the gymnasium. Debby and Beans waited their turn and exited. Once on the sidewalk, they turned right and walked toward the back of the bus, through an invisible cloud of diesel fumes.

"That stinks," Beans said.

"You stink," Debby said.

He pulled out his inhaler and took a puff. "It's not good for my asthma."

"You say that about *everything*." And he did. Running, jumping, climbing, standing, squatting, peeing (she wasn't so sure about that one), playing video games. They all gave him asthma attacks.

"I do not. Those fumes are—" His body lurched forward. His knees and elbows scraped the pavement. His glasses flew through the air and landed a few feet in front of him. The sunlight fractured as it passed through the broken lens and cast several golden beams of light of varying sizes on the ground.

Debby spun around. The brown haired boy stood there with a broad grin on his face.

"You ever do that again you little freak, and I'll beat his four-eyed face into the ground."

She dropped her bags and shoved him in the stomach. "Get out of here, piss pants!"

The boy spat in Beans's direction, then turned and jogged off. Debby looked around. No one paid any attention to the situation. It didn't surprise her. To most of the world, she and Beans were invisible. She extended her right arm, then her middle finger and shook it in the boy's direction.

"Don't do that," Beans said. "You'll get suspended."

"I don't care," she said, turning around and offering him her hand. All fingers extended this time. He reached up and she pulled back until he was back on his feet. "Besides, none of them wanted to help, so it was meant for all of them."

The school bell rang. Lingering kids ran through any available door.

"Shoot," she said.

"Is that the final bell?" he asked.

"I think so."

"We better go."

She scooped up both of their backpacks. It was better for Beans not to run with any extra weight. Together, they raced through the main entrance. Principal Bennett stood outside the office. His perfect brown hair was perfectly brushed back and his beard perfectly manicured. He shook his head, the hair bounced and then settled back down, and he held out his hand in a stop gesture.

"Please," Debby said. "Beans... I mean, Bernard had a bad fall. He tripped on the pavement, then he had an asthma attack, and no one would stop and help us. So that's why we're late."

Principal Bennett cocked his head to the side and leaned forward. His eyes traveled up and down and back up Bean's short frame. "Mr. Holland, it looks like you should head over to the nurses' office." He angled his head in the other direction a couple times. "Ms. Walker, hurry on to class now. If your teacher has an issue with you being tardy, you tell her that you were talking with me, and I'll be happy to take the matter up with her."

This was why Debby liked Principal Bennett. He treated her like an adult, not a kid. He didn't use little kid words with her. He showed her respect.

"Yes, sir," they answered in chorus.

So Beans headed left and Debby turned right. She hurried to class. The halls were empty. Her footsteps bounced off the walls that surrounded her. She thought she heard her name. When she looked over her shoulder, Beans and Principal Bennett were gone. But a man she did not recognize stood outside of an open closet. He leaned on a broom or mop handle and watched her. She'd heard the phrase "a chill went down my spine" spoken before. She never knew what it meant. Until that moment.

Room one-twenty-two couldn't come fast enough. She ran, holding the straps of her backpack tight. She hoped the door would be unlocked when she arrived. If not, she was prepared to scream as loud as she could. That turned out to be unnecessary, though. The handle turned with no resistance. She burst through the open doorway, and slammed the door shut behind her.

"Ms. Walker," the teacher said.

"Sorry, Ms. Suarez. I was speaking with Principal Bennett. He said if you need to discuss my tardiness, take it up with him."

"That'll be okay, Debby. Go ahead and take your seat."

She did. And she watched the window in the middle of the door. And when the guy passed by, he stopped and made eye contact with her. And that chill went down her spine again.

CHAPTER NINE

B y the time we reached the house, Ella had left for school and Mom had changed into her clothes. She insisted that Sam come inside for a few minutes and catch her up on his life. They hadn't talked in about six months. Sam held back, which was good, otherwise we'd have been there a long time. Mom had a follow up question for every answer he gave. It got to the point that I texted another detective and asked him to call in pretending to be Huff just to get us out of there.

It worked.

We took off in Sam's Camaro and went straight to the station. We could pick up my police issued Chevy later that day. The Homicide Detectives' room wasn't much to look at. Two sets of four desks butted together to form two big squares. Some called the room the Block. An old timer named Anderson who was on his way out when I was on my way in referred to it as the Square.

"The only person you can trust in this city is the guy sitting across from you, Tanner. And once he moves on, forget about him. He won't have your back anymore."

I'll never forget his advice.

I simply called it the office. It didn't need a nickname. Wasn't like we were on some network TV show.

Sam's desk was across from mine. That's how we did it. Partner across from partner to promote discussion amongst each other. That'd never been a problem for Sam and me. Even when we were pissed at each other, we found a way to talk. The benefit of being boyhood friends, I suppose.

Sam opened a manila folder. His shoulders slumped forward and he placed his head directly over the images. He looked up at me. His face looked bleak and drawn.

"What you got there?" I asked.

"Dusty Anne."

I swiveled in my seat and rolled my chair around the block of desks. Sometimes we played hockey or football like that. I stopped next to him. He scooted over a few inches and shared the view. Seeing the digital images blown up in high resolution did nothing for Roy Miller's case.

"Doesn't look like a fall to me," he said.

I nodded in agreement. "No more so than it did in person."

Sam pulled a piece of paper from the back of the folder. He laid it neatly on the table. The Medical Examiner's report. "The ME agrees with our assessment."

I used my finger to scan the document. There I saw it. Written in Karen Dempsey's unmistakable handwriting.

Homicide.

"We should have kept him here Friday night," I said.

"We had no choice," Sam said.

"Bureaucratic BS, Sam. We should call the shots."

"I'm not disagreeing with you, man. But you know as well as I do that he would have called his lawyer and been out of here. Shoot, he's still got a solid alibi."

"And yet he ran. Twice. Now he's roaming free doing God knows what and who knows where."

"We'll find him, Mitch. Trust the process, man."

"Process my ass." I got up and kicked my chair. It rolled into the wall and tipped over. Perhaps I put a little too much leg into it. I walked over and righted the chair. The impact had dented the drywall. I'd have to find a new poster or process map to hang there. I rolled my chair back to my desk and took a seat.

"I'm gonna make us some copies," Sam said, getting up and heading to the door on his side of the room.

"Triplicates," I said.

Sam nodded and left the office, leaving me with the memory of finding Dusty Anne, half-dressed and dead at the base of the stairs inside the Cape Cod house. A shattered bottle of Jack spread out around her. Shards of glass stuck in her buttocks and thighs and back. Whiskey mixed with blood surrounded her body. Her hair was coated with the stuff, more blood than whiskey, though, due to the gash on the side of her head. The bottom step had also been covered with blood, hair, and bits of skull. The final conscious stop on her trip down the stairs.

If Roy Miller's story was to be believed.

I had the sudden desire to smoke. I hadn't done that since I was a rookie cop pounding the 26th District amid the historic buildings.

Sam came back in the office, dropped a folder on my desk, then went around to his side. He pulled out a drawer and placed a second folder inside.

"I suggest you do the same, partner," he said.

So I gave the file a quick once over and dropped it into my middle drawer. And just in time.

Huff stepped in and said, "You two, my office, now."

Horace and Fairchild made childish sounds and said something stupid. Nothing new. The guys were as mature as fourth graders, if that. Sam kicked Fairchild's chair on the way out. The guy nearly fell to the floor. That would have almost made up for the crap start to the day.

Huff waited for us in his office. He sat in his high back leather chair with his ankle crossed over his knee. He'd ditched the sweats and now wore a navy blue suit, white striped shirt, and a paisley tie.

"What's up?" Sam asked.

"Have a seat, guys," Huff said, gesturing toward the seats in front of his desk.

We both sat down in the less than comfortable chairs in front of Huff's desk. Though we both towered over him when standing, he now had the high-level view. He seemed to enjoy looking down on us.

"We got a lead on your boy," Huff said.

"Which boy is that?" Sam said, playing along. Huff liked to talk younger person lingo when around us. For fifty-something he didn't do too bad.

"The asshole who escaped from the hospital this morning."

"Oh, that boy. Sorry, Huff. Just needed a little clarification."

I bit my tongue to keep from laughing.

"Yeah, well," Huff said. "Whatever."

"Where is he?" I asked, cutting through the thickening BS.

"He was spotted outside of Quakertown."

"That's just a pit stop on 476," I said.

Huff nodded and uncrossed his legs. He leaned over the desk, resting his right forearm on his oversized calendar pad. "At a gas station."

"So he's headed north and filling up a gas tank," Sam said.

"When was this?" I asked.

Huff glanced at his watch. "About an hour ago."

"Why are you just telling us now?" I asked. "An hour's a long time to waste."

"I just found out a few minutes ago," Huff replied, holding his hands out toward me.

"So an hour ago," Sam said. "He's about thirty miles away. That means he could be up to a hundred miles away now."

"If he stuck to the interstate," I added. "And there was no traffic."

"That's right," Sam said. "Or he could have picked up 76 and headed to New York from there."

"Or gone west," I said. "Using back roads."

"How'd we find this out?" Sam asked.

Huff said, "They knocked around the cashier and took a couple hundred out of the register. Didn't pay for their gas either. Filled up two tanks on a tan and white F-250."

"Plates?" I asked.

Huff shook his head. "Negative there."

"Dammit," I said.

"Dammit," Sam echoed.

"So what now?" I asked.

Huff leaned back in his chair. He crossed his ankle over his knee again and placed his hands in his lap. "You two go up there and interview the kid. I don't trust those hick cops to have done it right. They might have missed something that will help us find them."

"You know that's out of our jurisdiction," Sam said.

"Yeah, I know, smart ass." Huff picked up his paperweight and tossed it between his hands. He stopped and pointed at us. "That's why you keep this quiet. If I get any further leads, I'll reach out and we'll go from there. Otherwise, I expect you two back here in about three hours."

CHAPTER TEN

W e took Sam's Camaro. It was fast and it drew more smiles from the ladies than the police issued Chevy I drove. A quick trip through the city and we were on 95 heading north. Traffic was thick, but moving. Conversation was sparse and fell out of our mouths like molasses. Typical, given the circumstances. Our minds were elsewhere, yet at the same place. We filled the first few minutes of that half-hour drive by surfing radio stations. We settled on a jazz station. With the windows rolled down, the tunes were nearly sucked out of the car before they hit my ears.

We reached Quakertown a half hour later. Once a pit stop for travelers, it had tripled in size in the last decade. To the west were farmlands, remnants of the once rural community. To the east, new residential subdivisions established for those who wanted to work in Philly or Allentown, but not live in either of the cities. Plus, they could get more for their money out here. Big houses, three to four thousand square feet, which cost a fraction of a thousand square foot place in one of the historic districts. There was a small downtown area. The only ones who frequented it were the locals. An uncommon blend of farm folk and suburbanites, like mixing coffee from Belize with a Turkish blend. Surely not frequented by those who broke up the monotony of their five hundred mile drive with a filling of the tank, an emptying of the bladder, and a sandwich or bag of chips.

"What gas station did he say?" Sam said as we pulled up to the red stoplight at the end of the exit ramp.

At the stoplight the open windows provided the oppressive humidity an opportunity to envelop us. I felt my forehead grow damp with sweat. I used the edge of my thumb to clear my brow as I looked out the window and surveyed the scene. "That one, over there."

Sam turned right, drove a hundred yards or so, and pulled into the Quik-Pit parking lot. A dark red overhang covered the empty bay of gas pumps. Yellow police tape secured the perimeter of the pump area and the entrances to the store.

That's how you do it, Jennings.

"They're losing more in revenue by not pumping gas than Miller and his accomplice took off with," Sam observed.

"Most likely. Not our business or our choice though. These cops have their own protocol."

"Think it was the state police?"

"No idea, Sam. Don't know much about how they operate out here." While I had experience working with detectives in various police departments in the tri-state area, this area was a mystery to me.

"Come on," Sam said. "Let's go check this place out before that police tape gets cut in two."

We both exited the Camaro and walked up to the front of the store. A painted striped line covered two-thirds of the glass. Sam could see over it easily. I had to rise up on the tips of my toes. The area in front of us was where the clerk would have stood. They had to work all day with their backs to the pumps. Not a great idea in my experience. The cash register hung open, no one behind the counter to close it. The aisles were barren. So we went around to the left side of the store. The doors there were locked. I knocked on the glass door while Sam headed around back. No one answered or appeared from the back of the store. I knocked again. A minute later I saw Sam through the glass, on the other side of the store. He gave the door there a yank and then shrugged his shoulders. We met in front of the building.

"I'll call Huff," I said, pulling out my cell phone.

Huff answered on the second ring. "You guys there?"

"Yeah, Huff, but the kid's not."

"Where is he?"

"How should I know? Ain't no one here, man."

"Sit tight for a few. I'll make a few calls and get back to you."

I wrapped my hand around my phone and stuffed both in my pocket. I stared over the hood of the Camaro at the fast food joint across the street. A line of cars wrapped around the side and back. A little early for lunch, I thought. Perhaps the late breakfast crowd.

"What's the deal?" Sam asked.

"He's gonna call us back."

"Sounds promising." Sam shook his head and looked at the ground. He kicked a cigarette butt off the sidewalk.

"Sounds like we're wasting an hour of our time."

"At least we get paid no matter what."

"Screw the paycheck. I want Roy Miller in custody."

"I know, Mitch. Just giving you a hard time."

"Every minute we stand around here, Miller gets that much farther away."

"He'll slip up. Don't you worry about it. The guy ain't that smart. Before you know it, he'll make a mistake and we'll have him in custody. Someone'll have him in custody."

Sam, my ever-optimistic partner. I never understood it. With all the crap he saw in Afghanistan as an Army Ranger, how could he be so positive? He'd always said it was because he came home alive. Many of his friends didn't. But I knew there were thoughts he did not share with me. Memories that were too painful. I could see it in his eyes and that distant stare out to nowhere.

"He should have never escaped our custody," I said. One of us had to be pragmatic.

We fell silent. The rolling tide of vehicles filled the void, like at the beach. As soon as one wave headed back into the ocean, another broke. By this time of day, the morning commuters were already at work. These cars belonged to people heading from one far off destination to another. Truckers making that long haul up and down good old I-95. One long boring strip of highway that would take you from Miami to the Houlton–Woodstock Border Crossing, just east of Houlton, Maine, at the Canadian border.

My phone vibrated in my hand. "Yeah, Huff," I said.

"Trail's dead, Tanner. Lost my lead on the kid and nothing new on Miller."

I paused and exhaled into the phone. "All right." I ended the call and looked toward 95.

"Well?" Sam asked.

"Wasted our time."

"Nah, we got to bond. Never a waste of time." I didn't have to look to know he had that boyish grin spread across his face.

"Think we should try to track the kid down on our own?"

"The security footage will tell us all we need to know once we get our hands on it. No need to waste any more time up here."

"Wanna get a drink?"

Sam looked at his watch. "A little early for that."

I shrugged. "Maybe you got a point. It's five o'clock somewhere, though."

Sam rolled his eyes. "Get in the car and cut the cliches."

And so I did. We got back on the interstate, heading south. I spotted a sign for a Cracker Barrel and told Sam to take the exit.

"Place is always packed," he argued.

"That's 'cause it's good," I countered.

"Look, there's a Waffle House, two more exits. We can get in and out and be back in town in time for lunch." Good 'ole Sam, planning with his stomach.

"I want pancakes."

"You can get them at Waffle House."

"No you can't. It's not called Pancake House. It's the Waffle House for a reason."

"I bet you twenty bucks you can get pancakes there."

"Twenty bucks?" I said.

He nodded.

"Show me," I said.

He stopped at the light at the end of the exit and unfolded an Andrew Jackson in front of me.

"Shoot, keep on going," I said. "We're going to Waffle House. You might as well hand that over to me right now."

It turned out that Sam knew there were no pancakes served at the establishment. He was willing to part with twenty bucks if it meant not waiting a half-hour or more in those stiff wooden rocking chairs that line the porch of every Cracker Barrel in the U.S. of A.

We slid into a booth just past the counter. A good seat, I noted. Not held together with duct tape like some diners I'd been at in the past. I ate my waffles, not leaving a single piece behind. Not pancakes, but they were good. A side order of sausage rounded out my meal. The coffee was better than I had expected. Good enough that I'd consider coming back. I had two cups, black. After I finished I licked the grease off of my fingertips and leaned back in the booth, stretching both arms out along the vinyl top. It didn't take long for my stomach to feel like it contained a thirty-five pound kettlebell.

"Aren't you glad we came here?" Sam asked, tearing a corner from his over-buttered toast and stuffing it into his mouth.

I nodded. At the same time, the waitress came by and asked if I wanted anymore coffee. I declined, as did Sam.

"Just the check," he said to her. Then he turned his head toward me. "You've had some time to think and eat and drink that coffee."

"I have."

"What do you think?"

"I think Waffle House makes good waffles and great coffee."

Sam smiled. "You're easy to please, but that's not what I meant."

"I know, man, I know."

Sam mirrored my posture and waited for me to give him an answer. I knew he wouldn't agree to leave until I did. We'd been through this a time or fifty before.

"This guy's a bit odd," I started.

"That psychology degree tell you that?"

"It's a minor, which means I took about four classes. And yeah, it does. So does my common sense. And don't you go ragging on me for getting some kind of education."

"Hey, I got my education out there in the 'Stan."

I nodded. While not college, spending a year or two in Afghanistan should qualify any soldier for a degree. At least an Associate's in ass-kicking and bullshit-bureaucracy.

"So give me a diagnosis," Sam said.

"On you? We don't have enough time for that you philandering fool."

Sam smiled as he used his last piece of toast to soak up the remaining egg yolk on his plate. "On Roy."

"I'd have to go look at those old textbooks." Which wasn't exactly true. I remembered what I had learned. But I also wasn't qualified to be making any kind of determination about the man.

Not without talking to him in the proper setting first. And even then, I couldn't call myself a psychologist. I knew enough to be dangerous. The degree helped in the sense that a wet dishrag helps when you run out of toilet paper. It creates a mess you can't just flush away.

"Best guess, Mitch?" Sam's expression turned serious. He thirsted for knowledge on what we were facing.

"This cat's got no family that we're aware of. Just his wife and now she's dead. He's only got a couple of friends that we've found. Born and raised in the city. Never served in the military. Never spent time abroad or anywhere else in the U.S. of A. He's a loner. He's suicidal, based on his actions the other night. He might have killed his old lady. Would he do it again? He's on the run, he's alone or with one other person. If cornered, or in the right situation, he'd kill again. Especially if the person he's with is so inclined. He might have taken his wife's life, someone he cared about, at least at one time. If he did that, he probably won't hesitate to take another life that means less to him. As for all the other stuff, we'd need a profiler to give us some help."

Sam nodded and said nothing.

"We might need to dig a bit deeper. Who was the other guy? Maybe there was a childhood friend who moved away that he's kept in touch with."

Sam nodded again, remaining silent.

"He's not that old. We should dig up his elementary school and see if any teachers remember him."

Sam nodded. "Good idea."

"Let's also find out what happened to his parents."

"I got part of that," Sam said. "Deceased."

"Yeah, I got that, too. But how?"

He nodded again. He pulled a notebook from his inside pocket and jotted on a blank page.

"I see this guy killing himself before going to jail," I said. "I say that with one caveat though. One that could lead to him making us take him out."

Sam looked up from his notebook and lifted an eyebrow. "Do tell, partner."

"Huff said there were two of them. Now, we still don't know if the ID was good or not, but—"

"Strength in numbers. We find the childhood friend, we probably find the guy Roy's riding with, and maybe find where they're staying."

I snapped my fingers and aimed my forefinger at him. "You got it, bro. Let's get the hell out of here."

CHAPTER ELEVEN

I was on my cell phone before we got back outside. I spoke so fast that Huff told me to slow down at least ten times.

"Okay, Tanner," Huff said. "I got some of this in the works already. Expect to have the parental history on my desk by the time you get back. I like the childhood friend angle, but don't get your hopes up there. I'll get a couple guys on it once we find out which schools he went to. Then we can see if any of his old teachers are still present at the school or in the area. Some of them might be retired by now. I sent Horace and Fairchild out to act on a tip we received after you left."

"You did what?" I shouted.

Sam turned his head, dipped his chin to his chest and looked at me over the rim of his sunglasses. I waved him off.

"Set your huge ego aside, Tanner. We need to get this guy and bring him in. Besides, it's not a tip on his location, rather about him. A friend stepped forward, said he had some information that could help us. I figure, at the least, he'll lead us to Miller's social circle."

"Speaking of that, let's get his PC."

"What?"

"His computer," I said, leaving out the words *dumb* and *ass*.

"Oh, yeah, good call. I'll get forensics on that. Maybe we'll find some dirty pictures on there."

"Not quite what I was thinking, Huff, but have at it."

"Shut up, Tanner. You know what I mean."

I wasn't going there.

"All right, Tanner. You two get back here ASAP."

I hung up and adjusted the vent so the cold air hit me in the face. The temperature had risen past eighty degrees with the humidity even higher. Oppressive was the word to describe it. I shifted in my seat so I could look at Sam without twisting my neck. A kink had developed that ran from my right shoulder to the base of my skull. The result of sleeping on the couch all night. And for what reason? Because I'd been too lazy to climb upstairs.

"What's up?" Sam asked.

"He's already working the parent angle." I rubbed my neck and shoulder. "Said he should have a history worked up for us by the time we get back."

"Why'd you yell?"

"He brought Horace and Fairchild in on this."

"Gotta be kidding me."

"I know, right."

"Why?"

"Acting on a tip," I said, shaking my head. "Supposedly one of Roy's friends made a call and said he had some information."

"The damning kind?"

I hiked my shoulders an inch. "Dunno. But the hope is that friend A might lead us to friends B through E."

"Assuming he has that many friends."

"Right."

"And the teacher thing?"

"He's gonna have the records pulled, then check with the city to find out if any of those teachers are still working and/or living in the area. But you know, even if we find one or two, they might not remember him."

Sam nodded as he reached for his blinker. He tapped it up with his left hand and swerved the Camaro a lane to the right.

I glanced at the speedometer. We were going one hundred and five. Without lights and sirens.

"I bet we get pulled over," I said.

He laughed. "Wouldn't that be some shit?"

"We could have them give us an escort."

"You know these pricks, Mitch. They'd be happier if they took us in for reckless."

"What's this us crap? You carrying a gerbil up your ass?"

Sam laughed and eased up on the gas. "Guess I can drop down to about eighty-five. Ain't no point in getting pulled over."

"That's why we should take my car at all times."

"Your car smells."

I looked at him, paused, then said, "Like your sister after a night out."

The banter went on for most of the ride. It was silly and pointless and it distracted us from the mess we would have to face when we reached the office. If only I'd known that the situation was going to get worse, I might have told Sam to turn the car around.

CHAPTER TWELVE

Ms. Suarez dismissed her class of third graders for recess. Debbie and Beans were the last to leave the classroom. Even Ms. Suarez had left before them. They took their time walking down the hall. Ms. Suarez waited at the corner, waving them forward.

"Come on, Beans," Debby said.

"Bernie," he said.

"Whatever," she said.

She wrapped her hand around his wrist and pulled him forward. She expected him to complain about his asthma. He didn't. He jogged along beside her. She heard his ever-present wheezing increase a notch. Recess was their time to get outside and away from the rest of the kids, most of whom tortured poor Bernard Holland. Debby knew that one day her friend would show them all. He'd grow up to program computers to run faster and bigger than they ever had. He'd build planes that would cross the globe in an hour while riding amid the stratosphere. Or maybe he'd invent a stove that could cook dinner in a minute or two instead of thirty to forty. That's what he'd told her one time, at least. A snap of the fingers, he'd said. Mac and cheese as you please.

"You two," Ms. Suarez said. "Always lagging behind."

"He has asthma," Debby pointed out to the teacher.

Ms. Suarez smiled and offered a knowing nod. She ushered them past the tinted glass door. They stepped outside, his wrist still in her hand, and walked toward the outer edge of the recess area. While the other kids turned into four-foot tall savages, Debby and Beans found a shady spot under an old oak. He went to sit down in the grass.

"Stop," Debby said.

"Why?" he asked. "Did you see a spider?" Beans was terrified of spiders. One time Debby had stuck a fake but realistic looking spider in his cereal. He screamed so loud and so long that he nearly passed out. She wished she had it on video. Not that she'd ever share it with anyone.

"No," she said. "The ground is wet from that storm this weekend."

Beans bent over and placed his hand on the ground to verify this. When he straightened back up, he nodded. "Let's go over to the bench."

They walked along the back fence toward the other side of the recess yard. There was no shade to protect them from the bright sun. The air felt heavy, like they were walking through a cloud. Debby's gaze traveled from one kid to the next. Most of them played on the large play set in the middle. Swings and slides and ladders and some kind of half-circle geometric plaything. Fun, she thought. But not for Beans.

"Come on," she said, taking his hand. "Hurry up."

"I'm already hurrying, Debby," he argued.

They reached the corner and turned right. The bench was close to the school building, just off to the side a few feet in front of the gate. Debby once again turned her head and watched the kids having fun. She felt a slight urge to join them. She never did, though. Not even on the days when Beans had been absent from school.

She felt Beans's grip on her hand tighten, and she looked back at him.

He stared at her with a serious look on his face. "You should go have fun, Debby."

"I am having fun. Nothing is better than hanging out with you Beans. Besides, those kids don't like me."

"No, they don't like me. If you ditched me, they'd like you just fine."

"Nonsense and gibberish, my good man."

"What?" He smiled and let out a single laugh.

She smiled back and tugged on him in an effort to get him to pick up his pace. When they'd almost reached the bench, she cast one last gaze toward the kids. Sometimes she wished that Beans wasn't there to occupy all her time. Those thoughts were fleeting and she chastised herself for thinking such things. There was no kid she'd ever met who spoke to her or understood her the way he did. She'd be lost in the third grade jungle without him by her side.

By the time they reached the bench, Beans looked like he wanted to collapse. He sat down in a huff. His hand reached into his pocket. She imagined that he wrapped his thin fingers around his inhaler. But he didn't pull it out. No, Beans sat on that bench and took a deep rattled breath or two. He looked like a fish who'd escaped from a hook after dangling over the water for a minute. He glanced up at her and smiled.

She felt relieved.

So she reached behind her back and stuck her fingers through the chain linked fence. The metal felt damp, like it had been sweating. Everything else had been. Why not the fence? She didn't watch the kids playing and having a good time. Instead, she looked up and stared at the clouds for a long moment. A cool breeze passed. It had the same smell her yard used to have when her dad was around and he mowed the grass on a Saturday morning. She remembered lying on her belly, watching cartoons and hearing the sound of the mower buzzing by the window. Those stinky gas fumes would always follow, but they'd soon be replaced by smell of freshly cut grass.

Beans said something that she didn't quite hear. She started to look down at him when she noticed the strange man from earlier. He was on the other side of the gate, maybe fifty feet or so away. He leaned against the side of the school and watched her. That shiver went down her spine again. Three times in one day. That, as her mother might say, was a sign.

The guy narrowed his eyes and then lowered his head. He reached inside his pocket and pulled out a set of keys.

Debby watched on in horror. Beans said something again. Maybe he repeated himself. She wasn't sure. His words sounded like they came from a hundred miles away. Or a few feet through the water. It was all the same to her.

The guy turned and stuck the keys into the side of the building. He leaned forward into what she supposed was a closet of some kind.

Along the outside of the building?

It made no sense to her, but she had to trust what her eyes were seeing. Besides, she'd never walked along the outside of the entire school. He returned a moment later, holding a brown bag. Not like a trash bag, but something else. He began walking in their direction, his gaze fixed solely on her.

Debby said, "Come on, Beans." She didn't wait to see if he followed along. The tone of her voice should have told him that she meant business.

One of the boys from her class ran up to her and blocked her path. His name was Peter. His red hair and freckles always made her think of a pepperoni pizza. Strange? Yes, she admitted that. What was stranger was she couldn't look at him for long, otherwise she'd get hungry. When she tried to go around him, he held out his arms and stopped her.

"Let me alone, Peter," she yelled.

He stepped to the side so that he was in front of her again. "Go back to your little black boyfriend, dweeb."

She threw her arms forward and pushed him back. Peter's cheeks turned as red as the hair on his head.

"I ought to kick your little freak butt." Peter also rode the same bus as her. Everybody copied the red-haired boy.

She shrieked and bulldozed her way past him. By this point, Ms. Suarez had started toward her to see what in God's name was going on.

"What in God's name is going on?" Ms. Suarez said.

"She hit me," Peter said. A few other kids added their two cents to confirm this.

"Go away," Debby said to him. Then she grabbed Ms. Suarez's hand and started to pull. "There's a—"

"What are you doing, Debby?" Ms. Suarez freed herself from the child's grasp and placed her hands on her hips. Her thin eyebrows angled downward in the middle. She tilted her head to the side and leaned over a bit. "Are you okay?"

"There's a strange man on the side of the building, and he—"

Ms. Suarez straightened up. Her tone went from caring to fast and serious. "What does he look like?"

"Old."

"What's he wearing?"

"A blue suit."

"Like Principal Bennett wears?"

"No, like a trash man."

"What color is his hair?"

"He has none."

Her expression eased up and her voice relaxed. "That sounds like our new janitor."

"What happened to the old janitor?"

Ms. Suarez shrugged. "He stopped showing up."

Debby pulled away from Ms. Suarez and looked toward Beans, the bench and the gate. The gate swung open. She screamed. The man was coming for her.

Ms. Suarez said, "Wait here," and she started walking toward the open gate.

At that moment the bald headed man who had seemingly been stalking Lil' Debby Walker throughout the day burst into the recess yard with a brown burlap sack. He pulled a rifle from the bag and aimed it in the direction of Ms. Suarez.

"Don't move, bitch," he said.

It caught the teacher off guard. She had picked her pace up to a run when the guy appeared, and now in the presence of the rifle she tried to turn around. Her feet didn't cooperate with the rest of her body. At one point Ms. Suarez's body was parallel to the ground and three feet in the air. She hit the ground with a thud and made a painful gasping sound.

Debby looked from Ms. Suarez on the ground to where the man had been standing. He wasn't there. She shifted her gaze to the left. The man reached for Beans and yanked him off of the bench. Debby tried to scream. She couldn't. Neither could Beans. So she did the next best thing. She started running after the man who had Beans hanging over his shoulder.

CHAPTER THIRTEEN

S am and I sat in Huff's office, in the little seats, while he lorded over us from his deluxe office chair. We looked at copies of the papers that were spread out in front of him. According to the documents, Roy Miller's parents, Susan and Robert, died when their Taurus sedan clipped the rear fender of another vehicle and went over the side of a bridge. The reason they ran into another car? The brakes didn't work. And the reason for that?

The line was severed.

I noted that the words "was" and "severed" were used. Not "had been" and "cut." That's an important distinction. There was a line crossed when the word cut was used.

"So they both drowned," Sam said, looking up.

Huff nodded.

"Any insurance?" I asked.

"Life?" Huff asked.

The man had come up through robbery, not homicide. I reminded myself to be patient with him. "Yeah, life."

"You mean like a reason why someone might have severed the

brake line?"

Sam and I stared at him and did not reply. At least Huff was on the right track.

His face reddened. Those veins on the side of his head stuck out around his temples. "You two are looking at the same information I am. Find out for yourself." He rose and walked to his door and kicked it open. "I'm going for some coffee."

"I'll take," the door slammed shut, "some." I looked at Sam and laughed. "Guess not."

"You always giving that man a hard time. Gonna give him a coronary one of these days."

I shrugged. My cell phone rang. I pulled it out and looked at the display.

"Who is it?" Sam asked.

"Lana."

"*Kuh-cha*," he said while snapping his wrist.

"Shut up," I said and then I sent the call to voicemail. "There, now. Would a whipped man do that?"

Sam laughed, then stopped abruptly. He pointed at a spot on the paper in front of him. "There it is. Seems that elder Mr. and Mrs. Miller had a twenty-five thousand dollar life insurance policy."

"Not all that much." I drummed my fingers on the edge of the desk. "We should check bank records for the following two months and see if Roy made any large purchases or had any debts, legal or otherwise, to pay off."

"And check to see if Dusty Anne had a life insurance policy taken out recently with Roy designated as the benefactor."

I nodded. "Three deaths in two incidents that appeared to be accidents."

"Follow the smell to the barbecue."

My phone rang again and I pulled it out and looked at it and said, "Lana again."

Sam held his hand in the air holding an imaginary whip. His arm twitched. He wanted to snap that whip real bad. "Come on now, answer it." The smile on his face broadened.

"Come off it now," I said as I sent the call to voice mail again.

Huff reentered the office carrying three cups of coffee. Steam slid through the tiny slits in the lids. Maybe he felt bad for his childish outburst. "You geniuses figure anything out while I was gone?"

Not that bad, I guess.

"As a matter of fact," Sam said. "We did. Turned out mom and pops had a small life insurance policy."

"Only problem is," I said, "this happened over ten years ago. Banks are a pain about giving up records from that long ago. Turns out some guy actually has to get up and search for a physical file. Can you imagine?"

Sam grinned.

Huff sat down and said, "Don't worry, fellas. I got this one. One of my old contacts can get that for us by tomorrow."

Sam and I looked at each other. He lifted an eyebrow and nodded. We had a running bet on whether or not Huff would ever be useful to us. Looked like Sam won. There goes that twenty from earlier.

I opened my mouth about to thank Huff for finally coming through for us, when my phone rang. "There's gotta be some kind of crisis going on."

"Go on man, me and Huff got this," Sam said.

I gave him a look.

He held his hands up in retreat. "No whips this time."

I stood up, walked toward the door and pushed it open.

"*Kuh-cha,*" Sam said to his own laughter. "See Huff, like a whip, 'cause his girl has him whipped. You know what I mean?"

I let the door close behind me and reached down to answer the call.

CHAPTER FOURTEEN

Debby rushed toward the edge of the recess yard. She hurdled Ms. Suarez's body. Her teacher whimpered and coughed. Debby reached out and grabbed the metal post. She used it to whip her body around and through the open gate. The man had a head start on her and was already close to halfway to the front of the school. But she was fast. It was one of her powers. Brains and speed. Watch out world, here comes Lil' Debby Walker. Super version.

"Let him go," she yelled.

The guy looked back. He had Beans draped over one shoulder. Her friend reached out toward her. His mouth draped open and his eyes wide. In the man's other hand, he held a cell phone to his ear. He stuffed it in his pocket and seemed to pick up his pace.

A van pulled up to the curb at the other end of the long strip of grass that ran parallel to the school. The rear door slid open. It was dark inside. She thought she saw a guy in the back who then moved to the driver's seat. White teeth and whites of the eyes. That was it. Black, but not in skin color. She saw his white hands. He wore a mask though.

Why didn't the guy who grabbed Beans wear one?

"Hey!" Debbie yelled.

The guy ignored her. He started to jog toward the van. Debbie sprinted. No way would he get away with her friend. Beans had always told her he had her back. Well, now she had his.

"Son of a bitch," Debby said. It was the first time she ever used a cuss word outside of her own head. She kind of liked it. Well, she would have if the situation wasn't so dire.

The guy couldn't move fast enough and Debby caught up to him. Without thinking, she launched herself head first into him from a couple feet away. Whatever results she had been expecting, they weren't what she received. The guy turned to the side right before she reached him. Her head slammed into his hip. Pain shot through her head, neck, shoulders and back. She fell to the ground. Grass clippings stuck to her face and found their way inside her mouth. Her world went sort of black.

CHAPTER FIFTEEN

"Come on, Mitch. Answer!" Lana shouted into her cell phone. She crawled along the ground, dragging her left leg. It didn't seem to want to move when she willed it to. She reached the bench and pulled herself to her feet. Using the metal railing atop the chain link fence, she dragged herself forward.

Debby had flown past her seconds prior. She tried to tell the girl to stop. A lack of air in her body prevented her from doing so. Now not one, but two kids were in danger. That shouldn't have happened.

Lana looked back and saw the rest of the kids on the ground. Some had their hands over the backs of their heads. They'd all been through the drills. A reality of life these days.

She couldn't support her weight on her left leg, so she hopped forward using the fence for support. Pain radiated from her calf, through her knee, to her hip. Was it broken? No time to worry about that. A child needed her.

"Get off of me," she heard Debby scream.

Lana moved as fast as she could, ignoring the pain. Past the fence, she had to hop on one foot. Pain shot through her body every time she landed.

Debby screamed again. No words, only pain. Lana pushed forward. She saw the man lift Debby by her waistband and toss her inside the van. Then he pulled Bernard off of his shoulder and threw him in too. The van door slid shut and the guy got inside the van through the front passenger door.

And like that, the van was gone.

"Lana!" Mitch's voice called to her through her cell phone, which she held down by her waist.

CHAPTER SIXTEEN

"Lana!" I yelled into the phone for the fourth or fifth time. I heard doors opening all around me. I looked up and saw Sam and Huff standing in the hallway outside of Huff's office. Up and down the corridor, cops stared at me.

"Everything all right, Mitch?" Sam asked.

I ignored him. The only thing I wanted at the moment was to hear Lana's voice instead of the sounds of chaos.

"Mitch?" she finally said.

"Lana, what's going on?"

"Mitch, you have to get down here now," Lana said. She was in hysterics.

"Hold on," I said, stepping into the empty break room in an effort to find some privacy. "Lana, what's going on?"

"The kids, Mitch."

"What about them?"

"And there was a man with a gun and he shot it and he took them, Mitch. The bastard took them both."

"Took who?" Ice went through my veins and I swore my heart stopped. I prepared myself to hear the name Ella.

"Debby Walker and Bernard Holland," she said. The names did not spark recognition. "Two of the kids in my class. We were outside. I..." She paused, during which time she choked a few sobs down. "I couldn't stop him, Mitch. I tried, but I couldn't." She gasped, then groaned. "My leg, it hurts. I think it's broken. But that doesn't matter. Those kids are gone, Mitch." Her voice broke down into sobs at the end.

"Listen to me, Lana. Are they still on the property?"

A second passed and she composed herself enough to resume speaking. "I don't think so."

"You don't think? This isn't the time for that, Lana. I need a decisive answer."

"I don't see them. I think they left. Why would they stay around?"

Unless the men intended to take anyone else, she had a good point.

"Okay. Listen to me, Lana. You need to get the rest of the kids inside. The school needs to go on lock down. Do the officers there know what happened?"

"I don't know. No one has come back here yet." There was a pause, then Lana screamed.

"What is it?" I said, worrying that they'd come back. Panic began to fill every inch of my being.

"There was another gunshot, Mitch. Oh my God, they're still out there."

"Get those kids inside. Now. I'm on my way." I waited for a response, but didn't receive one. Glancing at the display, I saw that the call had been disconnected. I jammed my cell inside my pocket and ran out of the break room. Sam and Huff stood a few feet outside the door. I grabbed Sam by his coat and said, "Come with me, Sam."

"What's going on?" Huff called out.

Every eye in the building was on me at that point. They looked as worried as I felt. My voice had been loud, and I had no doubt they overheard my side of the conversation. Most of the men and women in the precinct had kids and some of them attended Ella's school.

"Huff, get every available cop down to my kid's school."

"Why?"

"Shooting and kidnapping."

"Oh, Jesus. You sure, Tanner?"

I didn't answer. There wasn't time. The door was a couple yards away. I hit it with my shoulder and pressed the release. The sunlight blinded me as we stepped out into the hot and humid air. The thin sheen of sweat on my forehead doubled.

"My car," Sam said.

"We need lights," I said.

"Fine," he said. "Your car, but I'm driving."

"Okay with me." I didn't want to drive. My nerves were beyond on edge. Lana sounded hurt. Not just emotionally wounded, but physically. Something had happened to her, maybe beyond the injury to her leg. She said there had been a gunshot before the man took the kids. Had she been shot? It'd be just like her to put off her own welfare so that we focused on stopping the men from getting away with the kids.

Sam and I got inside my car. Me in the passenger seat. Him in the driver's. He fired up the engine and hit the gas. I swear he had it to the floor before shifting into drive. The car lurched forward. The tires smoked and left a set of long black tracks on the parking lot asphalt. He turned on the lights and the siren and cut down the middle of the road. We were about four miles from the school. A straight shot, though. No turns. Traffic parted as if one of us held some kind of mystical staff. The drive normally would have taken eight to ten minutes this time of day. We got there in three.

Sam pulled into the parking lot, laying on the horn. Anyone within fifteen feet of the car ran. He pulled to a stop past the main door. We knew the fire department and ambulance service would need those spots.

I stepped out of the car and surveyed the parking lot, then the front of the school. Puddles left behind by the tropical storm soaked the parking lot and spots along the lawn. There were dozens upon dozens of cars around, but I saw no vans. There were no men with guns, aside from the cops that started to fill the area. Scanning the front of the building, I saw a crowd huddled around something at the school's entrance. Sam and I ran toward the group.

"Police," I shouted.

A few heads turned. Their faces were pale. They looked shocked and saddened.

"Help," a teacher said. I recognized her from a barbecue I'd attended with Lana back in July. I couldn't remember her name. Blond lady. Good looking. I remembered thinking that at the party, too.

"What is it?" I asked.

Like the traffic a few minutes earlier, the crowd separated. I'd say it was the nightstick that held the power, but I hadn't carried one in years. As the group shuffled and stepped to the side, my jaw went slack at the sight of the man on the ground fighting to gasp his last breath of air.

"Is that...?" Sam said.

"Yeah, Principal Bennett." I stepped over the man's body. "Move aside, people."

A woman spoke up. "I'm the nurse."

"Then help him," I said. "Don't just kneel there."

She looked up at me. Tears rolled down her cheeks. She shook her head. She didn't have to say anything. I understood. Principal Bennett had no chance. That should have been obvious to me by the gunshot wound to his chest and the amount of blood he'd lost. I guess sometimes I'm the optimistic one.

"Make him comfortable," I said.

She nodded and choked back her sobs as she cradled his head in her arms.

"Did anyone see what happened?" Sam asked.

The teacher spoke up again. "I was out here with him. We were close to the front door. Heard a gunshot. Both of us ran outside."

"Is that what you're supposed to do?" I asked.

Sam grabbed my shoulder. I'd slipped up. Should have never said that. The teacher looked at me, confused. Maybe a little betrayed.

"Sorry," I said. "Go on."

"It all happened so quickly." She lifted her arm and wiped her eyes with the cuff of her left sleeve. The right one was covered in Bennett's blood. "A van pulled up. The side door opened. You know, the sliding one?"

We both nodded.

"I saw a guy inside, sort of."

"How do you mean, sort of?"

She gestured to her head. "He had on a mask."

"Okay."

"Then another man appeared from behind the school over there." She pointed in the direction that we had entered. "He was carrying a kid over his shoulder."

"Who was the kid?" Lana had told me, but I wanted to see if this teacher knew.

She shook her head. "Don't know. But listen, after that a little girl came out of nowhere and attacked the man."

"Attacked?" Sam asked.

"Well, ran into him," she said. Her hands animated her retelling. "She bounced right off of him. He picked her up, tossed her into the van. Then he tossed the boy inside. He spun around and aimed that rifle at someone."

"Who?"

"I didn't see."

"How do you know it was someone then?"

"I just guessed it was."

"You guessed?"

"I couldn't see. They were behind the school. But why would he stand there like that?" She mimicked the stance. Legs spread wide, shoulders hunched, arms out and hands supporting a large weapon. "He had to be aiming at someone."

"Okay," I said, figuring the 'someone' meant Lana. "And then?"

"The guy slammed the side door shut, opened the front passenger door and sort of got in."

"Sort of?"

"He kept the door open. Half-stood, half-sat, aimed the rifle at us. And then he..."

"Got it. Thank you, Mrs.?"

"Gladstone."

"Mrs. Gladstone," Sam said. "You said you got a good look at the man who had the kids."

"I said that?" she asked.

Sam glanced at me. "Well, did you?"

She nodded.

"Can you tell us what he looked like?"

"Sure, that's easy. He's been around here the last couple of days. He was the new janitor."

CHAPTER SEVENTEEN

The sounds of over a dozen sirens approached. Police, fire, rescue. Red and blue lights circled and reflected off cars in the parking lot. The proverbial cavalry had arrived.

Too damned late.

Amid the wail of the sirens, Sam stepped closer to the blond-haired teacher and said, "We need to see the personnel records. Can you show them to us?"

The teacher's gaze settled in between us, fixed on the wave of emergency rescue personnel that had descended upon the elementary school.

"Miss?" Sam leaned forward.

She shook her head.

"Who can?" Sam asked.

She glanced at Principal Bennett's almost lifeless body.

"Anyone else?" Sam asked.

"The Vice Principal."

"Which one of you is the Vice Principal?" Sam asked.

No one spoke up. Everybody stared back. Shock had most definitely set in.

"He's not here," the teacher said after a long pause. "Maybe out to lunch?"

I glanced at my watch. "A bit early for that, isn't it?"

I looked over and saw two paramedics running toward us. An EMT and firefighter pushing a gurney followed, trying to keep up. Those who remained around Principal Bennett were ordered to step back a good distance. The medics needed room to work, not that it would make much of a difference. I took one last look at Principal Bennett. I hadn't had the chance to get to know him that well. Pretty much nothing more than a 'hello' in passing. I figured this would be the last time I'd see him alive.

Sam tugged on my sport coat. I turned and saw cops swarming the area. Plain clothes, uniformed, and even some of the upper brass. They all were here. They entered the school as well as surrounded it. Those kidnappers couldn't come back for seconds.

I saw Huff park his car. He got out and walked toward us.

"Oh, Lord," Sam said. "Can we hide?"

"Good luck with that," I said, looking around at the crowd. "We're in munchkin land, and I'm not talking about the kids. Come on, pretend like you didn't see him and we'll go inside. Grab Blondie and bring her with us."

Sam asked the teacher to walk with us. She was non-responsive to his request, so he threaded his left arm around her right and guided her along.

"Not so fast," Huff said, catching up to us.

"Boss," I said. "What's up?"

Between labored breaths, he asked, "What do you two think you're doing?"

"Investigating."

He took a moment and fanned his red, sweaty face with his hand. "This ain't a homicide."

I glanced down at the dying principal. "It will be. And the sooner we get started, Huff, the better."

He wagged a finger in my face. "You can't dig around the kidnapping angle on this."

I resisted the urge to slap his hand away. It wasn't good for me to hold in my anger. It'd only come out ten times worse later on. I hoped that Huff would be around then.

Sam said, "I think the two are connected."

"You know the Feds are gonna want in on this," Huff said.

"I don't care what they want," I said, knowing that Huff had a point and that we might be cast aside once the Feds arrived.

"Just be prepared," Huff cautioned.

"For what?"

"To be removed."

"What are you talking about?" I had to argue against the possibility, if only to get Huff on our side.

"I know you date one of these teachers," Huff said, looking around the crowd of lost faces. "Might be a conflict of interest."

My patience ran out, and I snapped. "You listen to me you good for nothing piece of crap. Those kids that were taken were under my girlfriend's care and protection. By extension, that puts them under mine. I don't care where this leads or who it goes through, you are not pulling me off this investigation. I'm not going to rest until those kids are found. You got that? If that means I find Bennett's killer, so be it. But don't you stand there and tell me what the hell I'm gonna do and what I'm not gonna do, you pencil pushing flabby excuse for a cop."

I had the distinct feeling that all eyes were on me. A quick survey of the area in front of the school confirmed that.

Huff's face reddened. He took a step forward, pointed at me, stopped, turned and walked away. He erupted into a tirade of obscenities after he stepped off the curb.

"Let's go inside," I said, pushing through the front door.

The teacher led us down a short stretch of hallway that ended at the administrative offices. The area was empty both inside and out. Everyone had cleared the room and were either out front or in the auditorium. We had a team of uniformed officers that went through the school and escorted teachers and students, room by room, outside and into the auditorium. No doubt they would have done the same for the front office employees.

"When did you say this guy started?" I asked.

"Last week," she said. "Mid-week maybe? That's the first time I recall seeing him."

"The principal and assistant are the only two who have access to personnel files?"

She shrugged. "I really don't know. I'm a teacher, not an office worker."

"We need to start tearing this office apart," Sam said.

"Wait," she said. "Let me go find someone." She started to walk away. Before I could look away she turned around. "Where did everyone go?"

"Besides out front?" I said. "The auditorium."

She left the office. I looked over at Sam.

"You want to go find her?" he asked, referring to Ella.

"More than anything," I replied.

"Go."

"No, not yet. I can't leave this yet. I know she's safe right now." My words almost convinced me of this. "I'll find her before we leave and let her know I'm involved and she's going to be okay."

Sam nodded and went back to pulling open drawers, searching for the personnel file. I walked around the office and took a few steps into a narrow hallway with glass walls. From there, I saw the offices of the principal and vice principal. They were on opposite sides of the hall, facing each other. The principal had the better of the two, in my opinion. Bennett had a view of the outside. He could look up from his computer and gaze out a nice wide window. Not too far away was a fenced in lake. The fence must have been put there to protect the children from getting too close and falling in. I imagined my little Ella standing in front of the fence, little fingers wrapped around the chain links, watching ducks on the pond. She had a fascination with water and everything that lived in it and on it. Half the books in her room were on turtles, sharks, whales and dolphins. The rest were on birds, mostly sea faring birds. I read two or three of them to her every night at bedtime. If I was home, of course.

On Principal Bennett's desk were several framed pictures. His kids and his wife, I presumed. It looked like his kids ranged from age five to fifteen or so. There were four of them, all girls. His wife was fit and attractive. They looked like a happy family. No longer.

I heard the main door to the office area click open. I set a family photo back on Bennett's desk and left his office. When I reached the end of the hall, I saw the blond teacher standing there with an older woman with dyed brown hair. She wore a brown pants suit and no makeup.

"I'm Barbara Winder," she said. "You need access to our personnel files?"

"Yeah," Sam said. "In particular those of a janitor you just hired."

She nodded and walked around the long counter that divided the room. "I know where that is. If you'll just give me a minute." She slipped behind the desk and logged into a computer. A printer came to life a few moments later. Its fan whirred into action and then it began spitting out paper.

Sam walked over to the printing station and waited for it to complete the job.

"His name is Michael Lipsky," she said. "D.O.B. is August 19th, 1974. He came to us—"

"What the hell?" Sam said. He held the paper in front of him, shaking his head. "Get over here, Mitch."

"What is it?" I asked, crossing the room in a couple steps.

"Look." He held the paper out for me to inspect.

I nearly fell over right then and there. "Are you kidding me?"

"Who was responsible for hiring this man?" Sam asked, crossing the room with me close behind.

"That's what I was about to tell you," Barbara said as she scooted back in her chair and rose. Her lips quivered. I imagined that Sam and I were an intimidating duo. "He's childhood friends with Vice Principal McCree. Apparently he had a bit of tough luck and Ben stuck his neck out for him."

"And Ben McCree hasn't shown up for work today," I said. "Is that right?"

"I...I suppose he hasn't. What's this you're getting at?" She paused and drew in a long breath. "You don't think?"

"What kind of car does McCree drive?" I asked.

"A truck of some kind."

"Color?"

"White, I think."

Sam and I stared at each other.

"We need his address," I said. "Now."

"I'll get it for you."

The teacher and Barbara Winder shared a tense exchange. Had a killer and kidnapper been in their midst all this time? Barbara printed off another piece of paper. Sam grabbed it off the printer. He nodded at me and we left the office. We made quick work of the short hallway and then headed toward the school's entrance. He stopped and placed his arm in front of me. I skidded into it.

"What about Ella?" he asked.

I looked over my shoulder and said, "You're right. Come on. This won't take a minute."

We found the auditorium and Sam pushed the door open. I

passed through the open doorway, cupped my hands to my mouth and shouted, "Ella Tanner. Come over here."

Hundreds of small faces turned my direction. I scanned the sea of children and saw my daughter get up and wave at me. She picked her way around the tangle of kids until she stood in front of me. I scooped her up and gave her a big hug.

"I'm scared, Daddy," she said.

"I know, baby," I said. "You're safe in here. Nothing's gonna happen to you. You know that, right?"

She shrugged. Her eyes watered. Her bottom lip trembled. She bit it to keep it from doing so. "I want to go home with you, Daddy."

"Daddy can't go home yet, Ella. I've got to go catch a bad guy."

"Please, Daddy."

"Look around, baby. See all these men with uniforms? These are Daddy's friends. His co-workers. They're gonna take real good care of you."

She nodded and let her weight drop. I let her down to the floor. Before she took off, I leaned over and gave her a big hug. She squeezed my neck extra tight. I took one last look around the room in search of Lana, but didn't spot her. I figured she wasn't in there or she would have come over at the same time Ella did.

"Ready to go?" Sam asked.

"No," I said. "But we should anyway."

"Let's go get this bastard."

I didn't need for Sam to tell me twice. I stormed down those halls with a purpose. I heard Sam get on his cell phone and call Huff. He filled Huff in on what we found and gave him McCree's address, telling him to get a few cars to meet us nearby.

Sometimes things move fast. This appeared to be one of those times. But if there's anything eighteen years as a cop had taught me, it was that appearances weren't always what they seemed.

CHAPTER EIGHTEEN

News trucks lined the main road beyond the school parking lot. The entrances had been blocked off by a couple police cruisers. Good call on someone's part. A few reporters who were hell bent on getting the story first made the rest of the journey on foot. It seemed every ten feet they encountered another line of cops whose purpose was to keep them away. Our forces on site had doubled since Sam and I went inside the school building. Philly's finest were all on site. The killer and the kids were anywhere but here.

We used the fire trucks to shield us from view as we made our way to my car. Once I had it in sight, I said, "Toss me my keys."

"I'm driving," Sam said. "You're too worked up."

I felt my blood boil. My ears burned. Maybe he had a point. "Fine, whatever. We need to get there before those other pricks do."

He glanced at me through narrow eyes. "Horace and Fairchild?"

"Yeah. Got a feeling Huff has some kind of deal worked out

with them. Notice how they get all the gravy assignments, and then how he brought them in on the Miller murder?"

Sam stood on the other side of the car. He shrugged and said, "You worry too much about that stuff, Mitch. Everyone is not out to get you, man."

Perhaps his words were meant to provide a moment of clarity amid a chaotic situation.

If so, they did not have the intended effect.

Sam got in, fired up the engine, turned on the lights and hit the sirens. It took us longer to get out of the congested parking lot than it did to travel the next three miles. The traffic again parted for us as best as one could expect near lunchtime. Sam still had to dodge the odd vehicle or pedestrian. Ignorance never failed to show its face.

McCree's house was in Drexel Hill, a few miles to the west. He lived in a single story ranch with a brick front and gray siding around the side. The yard looked well maintained with trimmed shrubs and a few remaining flowers in the flowerbeds. We drove past the house and parked a block away. The squad cars couldn't do that. Be a dead giveaway to anyone inside.

Huff walked up to our car and waited without saying anything. A couple minutes later Horace and Fairchild pulled up and got out of their city issued Chevy, identical to mine.

"What the hell are they doing here?" I said to Huff.

"You want to go in there alone?" Huff said. "Be my guest. Get your head shot off playing hero."

Either Horace or Fairchild laughed. I couldn't tell. By the time I glanced over at them they'd stopped and both had serious looks on their faces. I'd gotten into it with both of them at one time or another. They quickly learned they wanted no part of me, especially with Sam at my back.

"We lead," I said. "And we go now." I started down the sidewalk toward the house.

"What the hell are you doing?" Huff called after me. "We don't have anyone in back to cut them off if they escape."

"Send those two assholes," I said.

Now, deep down I knew I had acted irrationally. The most important thing at that time should have been the kids. And by walking up there and announcing our presence, I risked putting them in danger. If they were there, of course. We still didn't know that. There was no van, no big F-250. Just a '90s model red two-door Honda Civic parked in the driveway. The passenger side of the car looked beat to hell. Tint peeled away from the edges of the rear windows.

Sam caught up to me. "What the hell you doing, Mitch?"

"Forget those guys," I said. "This goes down, it'll be their faces in the papers, not ours."

"Is that what this is really about, man?" He grabbed my shoulder and turned me toward him. "You want some recognition? Really?"

He knew I didn't. Truth was we were in the middle of a turf war. Since the arrival of Huff, our turf had been shrinking by the week. At least, that's how I felt.

"No," I finally relented.

"Okay, then. Let's be smart about this. Wait until those guys are in position and we have some backup squads positioned at the end of this street as well as the parallel streets."

I started to walk back toward Huff and the other two detectives. "How long till the backup squads get here?"

"En route now, Tanner," Huff replied in a subdued manner while avoiding eye contact. "Be in position any minute."

"Okay," I said, and then I pointed at Horace and Fairchild. "Get those two in position."

Huff nodded and gestured toward the street that ran behind the house. "Get going you two. Let us know when you're about to breach the backyard."

Both men shot me a look that said they wanted to argue, but they bit their tongue and did what Huff told them. Those guys weren't dumb enough to bite the hand that fed them. I, on the other hand, made it my goal in life.

"Get going," Huff said to us. "You know the drill from here out."

We did, so we started moving. We didn't bother with the sidewalk, instead cutting across lawns to stay out of view of the house. Angry faces watched us through drawn blinds and open front doors. I could read their minds. *What are these two big dudes doing running through my lawn!*" Imagine their surprise when we pulled our Glocks from our holsters.

"Stop," Sam said, extending his arm out in front of me like I was a little kid and he'd hit the brakes too hard. "Wait for confirmation."

"You know what I think of confirmation, Sam?"

"I know, man. Doesn't change anything though. Be patient. Be one with the—"

Huff's voice came over the radio, saving me from the Tao of Sam. "Sam, Tanner, go now."

"Works for me," I said. I'd reached the porch before Sam began moving. I wrapped my hand around the knob and gave it a turn. To my surprise, I found it unlocked. I turned it all the way and then pushed the door open an inch.

"Got you covered," Sam said from behind me.

I squatted and pushed the door open a bit further. My pistol led the way from that point on. Working as a team, we cleared the first room. From there we had two choices. It looked like the kitchen was to the left, through the dining room. In the open space before us was an empty great room with a hall that I figured led to the bedrooms.

We heard a scream that came from the hallway. Sounded

female. A little girl had been taken. We didn't bother to check out the kitchen.

Sam relayed the development over the radio. I expected Horace and Fairchild to burst through the sliding glass door at the back of the house at any moment. They didn't, at least not at that point. We rushed down the darkened hallway. There were three open doors and one closed one. We quickly cleared each room in search of the children. I hoped we'd find both, and that they'd be abandoned. Let us end their ordeal. All the rooms were empty, though. We were faced with one final room. The one with the closed door. Sam and I stood in front of it, shoulder to shoulder.

"On my count," I whispered.

Sam nodded.

"One, two," I didn't get to three. Sam cut me off and kicked the door open.

We found Assistant Principal McCree inside the room. There weren't any children in there, though. It turned out the source of the scream had been a woman in her mid-twenties. The owner of the Civic, I presumed. She laid on the bed, spread eagle, naked, with McCree hovering over her.

CHAPTER NINETEEN

"What the friggin' hell!" McCree shouted as he rose up and the woman rolled away from us toward the far side of the bed.

"Stop right there!" Sam yelled.

The woman froze in place. She'd managed to get herself tangled up in a satin sheet that covered half her round ass. She burrowed her head underneath a pillow. Tufts of brown hair stuck out and covered her neck and shoulders. McCree didn't heed Sam's warning. Instead, the vice principal—and wouldn't the parents of the students love to know why he was absent on this of all days— rose up and lunged toward Sam.

Bad move.

Former Army Ranger and all that.

McCree was about the same height as Sam, although half the weight judging by his concave chest, narrow shoulders and stringy arms. Sam nailed the guy in the solar plexus with a left uppercut. McCree collapsed to the floor and balled up into a fetal position.

His face turned dark red, almost purple, while he struggled to pull air into his lungs.

Sam knelt down beside the man and said, "One single breath, man. Bet that's all you want."

I leaned out through the open doorway and said, "We need a female officer in here now."

A young female cop by the name of Marcy Wiggins entered. I'd worked with her before on a handful of occasions. Smart woman, very perceptive. Kind of lady that could go far if she kept applying herself. She stepped over McCree and walked around the bed. Her dark hands contrasted with the naked woman's pale skin.

"Bring her to the other room, Officer Wiggins," I said. "And find a robe or something for her to put on."

After Officer Wiggins and the woman had left the room, Sam reached down and pulled McCree to his feet.

"Where are they?" Sam barked.

McCree had resumed breathing, although the forced and ragged action left him unable to speak. At least, that's the way he made it seem.

"Answer me!" Sam pushed the guy down onto the bed. McCree fell back, arms waving, overly dramatic.

"What are you talking about?" the man asked.

Sam pulled his shoulders back. He towered over McCree in this position. Quite intimidating. "I'm gonna give you to the count of three and then you had better answer my question."

McCree started to pull himself backward on the bed. He dug at his sheets and pushed his feet along the floor. Sam took a step back and drew his pistol.

"Don't you freaking move!" Sam shouted. He was so good at this part. I knew that this wasn't an act, though.

McCree threw his hands up over his face. "Please, I don't know what is going on here." The man started to cry, and I believe he pissed himself.

"We need some gloves in here," I said to Officer Jennings. The baby-faced cop had just stepped into the room. He shot me a nervous look before taking off down the hall in search of the gloves I requested.

Sam took a deep breath. He shrugged his shoulders and rolled his neck side to side. Part of this was for show. I'd seen him do it before. But I knew that he was also trying to calm himself down. We were all worked-up over this one. Anything that led us one step closer to the children.

"Where are those kids, McCree?" Sam asked in a subdued tone.

McCree pulled his hands to the side and looked up at us. "I don't know what you're talking about."

Sam leaned forward and placed his hands on his knees, then said, "This morning, two children from your school were abducted at gunpoint."

"Oh my God." McCree's face went pale, maybe even a little green. "No, not..."

"Not what?" Sam asked.

McCree shook his head and pressed his lips tight. The color drained from them, too.

"Why didn't you show up to school today, McCree?" Sam said. "Where you been all morning?"

McCree looked between the two of us, but said nothing. I shifted my gaze from the man to the wall behind him. A framed Jack Vettriano painting hung there. I always wondered why the artist never let you see the lady in red's face.

"This is going to be easier if you cooperate," Sam said.

"Eat shit," McCree said.

Sam lunged toward him. I noticed in time and managed to get

my hands on his shoulders. I wrangled him through the bedroom door and out into the hallway.

"Keep an eye on him, Jennings," I said. Then I pulled Sam into the great room. "What the hell are you doing?"

Sam looked away and said nothing.

"C'mon, man. It's normally you keeping me in check. I know you're pissed. I am too. Believe me, I want nothing more than to put the barrel of my Glock to his head and pull the trigger. But that ain't gonna do those kids no good. We need to get some answers out of this guy. Breaking his jaw isn't going to help."

Sam still said nothing, but he made eye contact. His nostrils flared wide with each inhalation. I let a few more seconds pass and he seemed to come down a notch.

"You got it? You ready to go?"

He turned his head toward the dim hallway and nodded. "Let's go back. I'm fine now."

I stepped into the hallway first. Officer Wiggins stood in the doorway of one of the other bedrooms. She held up her hand and gestured for me to speak with her as we approached.

"What is it?" I asked.

"According to the woman, her name is Laura Weaver, they've been here since late last night. They never left. Got drunk, slept in. Got up around seven-thirty. Made love. Napped. They were at it again when you two barged in."

"Who is she?" I asked.

"She's a student teacher at the school."

"Interesting." I nodded and saw Sam do the same.

"And they've been here all night?" Sam said.

Wiggins nodded. "That's what she says."

"Nobody move," I said, nodding at Sam. "Come with me."

"Where're we going?" He asked as we stepped through the great room toward the kitchen.

"Garage."

"His truck?"

"Yeah."

The first door I pulled open led to the pantry. It was stocked with sugary cereal, bags of chips, and four cases of soda. How the hell did that guy stay so thin?

Sam pulled the other door open. "In here, Mitch."

The smell of motor oil and gas reached me before I turned around. I expected to see the single car garage filled with a truck. Instead, it was empty. I stepped into the room and looked around. First thing I noticed was a thick pool of oil in the center of the floor. There were posters along the walls, girls in bikinis on the hoods of cars or straddling motorcycles. A pegboard mounted to the interior wall held his hand tools. It appeared they were organized by size and purpose. Beneath the pegboard was a custom workbench with a solid steel top and plenty of drawers. I started looking through them, but found nothing of importance.

"What you think?" Sam asked.

"I think we need to ask McCree about his pickup truck."

CHAPTER TWENTY

The smoothness of the road had given way to bumps and bouncing. They must be on a dirt road or gravel driveway. Debby didn't dare open her eyes to verify. The *ping* sounds she heard beneath her led her to believe it was gravel. Although, dirt with rocks was a close second. She and Beans had been told to keep their eyes and mouths shut. One peep out of them, and they'd have hoods over their heads. That wouldn't stop her from listening, though. She'd seen a cop show or two on TV. Right now was about the clues. And the clues would come from the men. Unfortunately, the men didn't speak at all aside from the occasional direction of turn right or turn left.

They didn't stay in the van for long. She wasn't sure where it happened, because there were no windows in the back of that van, but they had pulled off the road. When they opened the door, the bright sunlight blinded her. She stepped out and saw tall bushes and trees surrounding them. There were empty beer cans and cigarette butts on the ground. A couple dirty magazines sat atop a bench made from a fallen tree. She thought it might be the kind of place teenagers came to hang out. Maybe her brother had frequented the area.

The men had led her and Beans to a big truck. The entire passenger side of the cab opened up wide like a whale ready to devour her. It was like a car in there, with a full backseat. Nothing like the trucks she had seen before. One of the men picked her up and placed her on the floor, then put Beans next to her. They were to remain there for the rest of the trip.

Eyes and mouths shut.

What could she have seen from down there?

Now, Beans cried softly. She reached out her hand and found his. His whimpers stopped. She heard him wheezing. He needed to take a puff on his inhaler soon. She had to speak up and tell the men, or Beans might die.

"He needs his inhaler," she said quickly.

"Shut up," one of the men said.

"He has asthma. He'll die if he doesn't get his inhaler."

"I'm gonna beat you," the other man said.

Debby started to cry. "Please. Just let him use his inhaler. He's having trouble breathing."

The man driving the car slammed on the brakes. There was a soft skidding sound. Definitely dirt, she thought. Her momentum shifted as the car stopped abruptly. She rolled one way, then whipped back the other. A pain traveled through her shoulder.

One of the front doors opened. She pressed her eyelids together even tighter. A burst of air swirled around her as her door opened. She felt hands on her legs, pulling her from the truck. Next thing she knew, she was placed against the frame of the vehicle. She felt tiny knives penetrate her eyes through shut lids. She figured she faced the sun. Her feet dangled in the air.

"Look at me!" the man shouted.

She opened her eyes. After she got past the sun-blindness, she realized that she sort of recognized the man. It wasn't the guy who'd taken Beans from the recess yard. She figured this guy had been the one driving. He'd had on a ski mask when she first saw him. But now without the mask and in the light, he looked familiar, although she couldn't place him. She noticed a dull ache behind her eyes and on her head around the spot where she had hit the other man's hip earlier that day. The edge of her vision felt watery.

Focus, Debby.

The guy said, "When I say keep your mouth shut, I mean keep your damn mouth shut."

She struggled to talk. "He has asthma."

The guy slapped her across the face. "Shut up!"

Debby began to cry. The tear tracks felt cold as the wind pelted her face. She struggled to turn her head to the left. The other guy sat in the passenger seat. He watched her in the side mirror. Their stares connected. He narrowed his eyes then looked away. She noticed a tattoo that started behind his right ear and ran down his neck. A weird, spiky design.

"You and I reached an understanding?" the man holding her said.

She turned her head, nodded and didn't say a word.

He let go, and she fell to the ground. "Okay, then. Get your butt back inside. We're almost there."

The door swung open and missed her head by inches. She pulled herself up using the running boards and then slipped inside, taking her place on the floor, head to head with Beans. The vehicle didn't start moving, though. The men were speaking to one another. Their voices were so low that she had trouble making out what they were saying. A minute later the front doors opened, then the rear ones. She felt hands on her body, pulling her out. Beans gasped. She opened her eyes and saw him being pulled from the cab.

"What are you doing?" she cried.

The guy said nothing. He slipped a black bag over her head and tied it loosely around her neck. Then he said, "If you struggle, that's going to cinch tighter and you'll strangle to death. You got that?"

Debby said nothing. She didn't even nod out of fear that the string would draw tighter and she *would* suffocate. She had no idea where they were going or why they were going there. She didn't want to think about where this was leading. She'd seen similar events on TV shows. Rarely did they work out for the people that were kidnapped. The only thing she knew at that moment was that she had no intention of dying in the back of the white truck.

CHAPTER TWENTY-ONE

W e reentered McCree's bedroom. The man sat on the edge of the bed in a pair of shorts. His shoulders were slumped over. He draped his left forearm across his knees. In his right hand he held a lit cigarette.

"Where's your truck, McCree?" I asked.

He looked up at me, then at Sam. He took a deep drag on his cigarette. Exhaled through the corner of his mouth, away from us. The smoke drifted toward the window, which was cracked open a couple inches. I found myself appreciating the gesture. I hadn't smoked in ten years, but the urge came around every once in a while. This wasn't one of those times.

"Well?" Sam said, taking a step forward.

McCree took another drag and said nothing.

I lunged toward the guy, knocking the cigarette from his hand, and grabbing his arms. "You listen to me you piece of crap. We need to know where that truck is, and we need to know five minutes ago."

McCree looked over at the cigarette burning through his satin sheets. "These are five hundred dollar sheets." He said it so matter-of-factly that I forgot he worked in a school.

"They can burn and so can you." I let him go and took a step back.

A red-ringed circle spread out along the blue sheets. McCree knocked the cigarette to the floor and used his palm to put out the embers. Once they were extinguished, he looked at the palm of his hand and brushed away the gray and black ash. "I loaned my truck to my brother."

"Roy Miller," I said.

"What?"

"Is he your brother?"

"Who the hell is Roy Miller? My brother is Brad McCree. His truck's in the shop. He's in construction. Can't work without a truck. He needed mine for a job, so I lent it to him."

"What kind of job?"

"Whatever kind of job guys in construction need a truck for, man. I don't know. I'm not his boss. He needed my truck, and I had a ride available if I wanted it." He jutted his chin toward the open doorway and I imagined the half-dressed woman with Officer Wiggins.

"And the name Roy Miller?" Sam asked. "What does that mean to you?"

McCree shrugged and held out his arms. "Never heard that name in my life. Can I light up again?"

"No," I said. "What about Michael Lipsky?"

McCree looked toward the window. He clenched his jaw. The muscles at the corner of his face rippled. After a moment, he said, "What about him?"

"You hired him to be a janitor at the school. Correct?"

He nodded.

"They told us that you two were childhood friends. Is that correct?"

He nodded again.

"Did you ever meet his wife?"

This time he turned his head toward us. He looked confused. "Wife? He told me he was single. Said she left him some time back."

"Are you sure you never heard the name Roy Miller?" Sam asked.

"Jesus Christ," McCree said. "I told you, I have never heard that name."

"Not even on the news?"

"I don't watch that crap. It's depressing."

"Looks like you've got a nice antidepressant in the other room," I said.

He smiled and his face lit up. "Fresh faces every year. I even let some come back around time to time."

Sam cleared his throat, stepped forward and leaned over so he was face to face with the guy. "Roy Miller is believed to have killed his wife, Dusty Anne Miller, this past Friday night."

McCree reached into his pocket and pulled out a cigarette. He flipped it between his fingers. "Sucks for her. But I have no idea what that has to do with me."

"Had you kept in regular touch with Lipsky?" I asked.

McCree shook his head. "Nah, not since high school. He called me up out of the blue. Said he'd been through the ringer since his old lady bailed. He asked me for a favor. I pulled some strings, got a few things waived and brought him in as a janitor at the school. Didn't think it'd be a permanent position, just something to get the guy back on track. Told me he lost his programming job a few years back and been out of work since. He'd taken to living in shelters and on friends' couches and stuff like that. I thought if he could get an apartment, some decent clothes, a regular shower... who knows, you know? Maybe he could get a job with one of the companies downtown."

"What kind of things did you get waived?" Sam asked.

"Background check, credit check, things like that. They make the process take forever, and I didn't want the guy on my couch disrupting my...extracurricular activities. Besides, I knew him from way back. Decent guy."

"Like you, huh?" I took a moment. "So, aside from the fact that you were friends as kids, you know nothing about the guy?"

McCree shrugged. "He's a good guy. What's to know?"

Sam dropped the picture he had taken from the school's administrative office on the bed. It landed face up. "That's Lipsky?"

McCree nodded.

Sam shook his head. "We have reason to believe that Lipsky is Roy Miller."

CHAPTER TWENTY-TWO

McCree straightened and looked Sam in the eye. "Say again?"

"You heard me. He bolted from custody early Sunday morning at the hospital. We got a tip this morning that he held up a gas station about thirty miles away. He was with another man. They drove off in a white Ford F-250. What do you drive?"

"A white Ford F-250," McCree said after forcing himself to swallow.

"And where is that truck right now?"

"I told you, I loaned it to my brother."

"And how well did your brother know Miller, or Lipsky?"

"They were the same age. The two of them were best friends. He was over a lot, that's how we became friends."

"You and your brother were friends as kids?" Sam asked.

McCree shrugged.

"What's your brother like, McCree?" I asked.

McCree shook his head.

"Telling me that you don't know?"

McCree locked eyes with me. "You should have access to his record."

"His record? You mean he's a felon?" Sam asked.

"Yeah."

I took a step back, turned and left the room. Sam followed me out. We stopped in the middle of the hallway. There were several more cops combing through the house.

"What do you think?" Sam asked.

"I don't know what to think," I said. "We've got a murder suspect with two names. A vice principal with an ex-con for a brother, who also happened to borrow the man's truck. A truck spotted thirty miles away carrying our suspect and maybe the ex-con. And now two kids missing, presumably taken by the suspect who was hired a few weeks ago by the ex-con's brother."

I assume Sam followed along judging by the way he nodded.

"Let's get these two down to the station and get this house processed. I don't think those kids were brought through here, but we might find Miller a.k.a. Lipsky's prints in here. McCree might not have been down at the school, but that doesn't mean he wasn't involved. We treat him and the woman as a suspect for now."

Sam started toward the room. Officer Wiggins stepped into the hallway to cut him off.

"What do you want me to do with her?" she asked.

"Get her dressed and bring her back to the station," Sam said. "We want to get her isolated and ask her some questions."

Sam went into McCree's bedroom. I turned and walked into the great room. I looked at everything in a different light. This had come about so quickly that I hadn't had time to ask the most important question. Why? Why had this happened? Why those two kids? Thinking back on what that blond haired teacher told me, Miller a.k.a. Lipsky had been carrying the boy toward the van. The girl ran after them. Attacked the man, as the teacher had put it. Had she been defending the boy? I needed the kids' names, addresses and parental information. I had to find Huff and find out if anyone had notified the parents yet. If not, I wanted to do it personally. The boy had been targeted, and I had to find out why.

As I looked around the kitchen, I heard McCree shouting from the bedroom. Bad idea to shout at Sam. If McCree didn't shut his mouth soon, he'd find that out firsthand. From the kitchen, I went back into the garage. I recalled seeing the crawl access in there. It had been closed then. Someone had already opened it. I squatted and rocked forward. I placed my hands on the dirty concrete floor and peered into the opening. Beams from flashlights lit up sections of the crawlspace. I saw lots of spider webs.

"What've you got in there?" I called out.

"Nothing," a voice called back. "It's empty other than a couple snake skins and some spiders."

I fought off a quick bout of the shakes. I hated both snakes and spiders. Crooks I could deal with. My 9mm gave me the upper hand there. A black widow or a brown recluse didn't care about what kind of gun I carried. Neither did a cottonmouth or a rattlesnake. I hoped I'd never encounter any of them. I rose, walked back inside, through the kitchen, to the opened sliding glass door. Horace and Fairchild hung out on the back porch, smoking.

"You two find anything out here?" I asked, trying to remain as polite as I could.

They shrugged and said nothing to me.

"Guys, we've got two kids who need our help. This isn't the time to act on our grudges."

"Get lost, Tanner," Fairchild said. "We were told to hang back and stay out here unless ordered inside. We can't do nothing to help out here."

"Guys, look, I don't mean—"

"Oh, crap! Look, Tanner," Horace said, hopping up and down and pointing to the corner of the fence. "See those bricks over there? I bet that's a clue." He jogged to the edge of the yard. "I'm gonna get these processed ASAP."

The two men fell out laughing. A couple of hyenas. They'd fit in nice with the media. I waved them off, then turned and stepped back inside while muttering a few choice obscenities under my breath.

By the time I reached the hallway, Sam emerged with McCree. He'd handcuffed the man. McCree did not look happy about it.

"Wait till you two hear from my lawyer," the guy said.

"Hey, he struck me. I got Jennings to back me up on that."

"Is that right?" I said.

"Both of you can blow me," McCree said. "When I'm done with you, your pensions will be mine."

I resisted the urge to stick my leg out in front of the guy, sending him sprawling to the floor with no way to break his fall. Instead, I grabbed his left elbow. Sam had his right. Together, we led him outside the house, where things took a turn for the worse.

CHAPTER TWENTY-THREE

H uff stood at the edge of the front lawn, waiting for us. We tried to avoid him, but did not succeed.

"Detectives," Huff said. "Come over here."

I glanced around and saw Jennings close behind us. I got his attention and relinquished control over McCree to him. "Get him to the station. Don't put him in the room with Wiggins. Separate rooms, close together. I don't want to have to run up and down that hall. Got it?"

Baby-faced Jennings nodded and led McCree to one of the patrol cars. I heard the man fussing about the cuffs and police brutality and unlawful arrest. I guess he figured his complaints would be addressed by the rookie cop.

Standing close to Huff were two men and a woman. They wore dark suits and dark Ray-Ban-like sunglasses. They all looked to be in shape. The men were clean cut and fresh out of the academy. The woman looked to be in her mid-thirties. She had her long hair pulled back in a tight ponytail. She had a slender face with a figure to match.

"Detectives Tanner and Foster," Huff said. "These are Special Agents Vinson, Braden and Dinapoli." He pointed at each of them in turn. The woman was Dinapoli. "They're with the FBI."

"Surprise, surprise," Sam said.

I glanced at each agent. Their sunglasses hid their eyes. I wondered if they even bothered to look at us.

The woman spoke first. "We're not here to take this case away from you, Detectives. From talking with Lieutenant Huff, we understand that there are multiple facets involved here, including two homicides and a potential suspect linked to both of those, as well as the kidnapping. We're going to work together as a team on this. We'll take point and you two will be kept in the loop the whole time. We'll rely on you as much as you rely on us. If you cooperate with us, things will go smoothly."

"This is our case," I said. "We started it, we should be point on this."

Huff stepped forward and cut me off. "What Detective Tanner means is that we're happy to help in any way we can, but we want to be there every step of the way."

"Like hell that's what I mean," I said. "I'm not giving up control of anything."

She lifted her sunglasses revealing eyes that reflected gold in the sunlight. "I understand your frustration, Detective. I really do. But we have a protocol to follow. I'm serious about us being a team now. There's no Feds versus Locals here. Not with me. Not with my two agents here. You two will be working with me while Special Agents Vinson and Braden are sent to notify the families and do some—"

"I want to talk to the families. There has to be something there, and I don't trust those two kids to figure it out." The guys probably weren't that much younger than me. I still didn't have faith in them to do this right. The Feds have a way of screwing these things up. They don't understand these people here.

"And we'll follow up with them after Vinson and Braden notify them and gather some information," she said. "Don't you think it'll be easier to deal with the families after they get over the shock?"

"Sometimes we can learn more while they are in shock," I countered. I felt Sam's hand on my arm. He pulled me back a step and leaned toward me.

"Let it go for now, Mitch," he said quietly. "They'll pull us completely."

I took a deep breath and closed my eyes for a second. Then I said, "So what now?"

Huff said, "You two are going to leave with Agent Dinapoli. You'll fill her in what you found out inside and your reasons for taking those two into custody."

"Parking tickets," Sam said.

Huff shook his head. "And after that—" He stopped and glanced down at his cell phone. He held a finger in the air and said, "I gotta take this."

As Huff stepped away, Dinapoli and I engaged in a stare off. The slender five-foot-six woman had a slight smile. She had us by the balls, and she knew it. She probably relished in it. Sometimes I cursed myself for not going to law school and joining in on the Federal fun. Must be nice to have that kind of power and authority.

Huff rushed back over. By the time he reached us, he was out of breath.

"What is it?" I asked.

"They found the van," he replied.

"Where?" I said.

He looked at me, then at Dinapoli. That's what it had come to? He had to get her permission to tell me something? Apparently so, because she nodded and he started talking.

"About two miles from the school, off the road. Some teenagers who were cutting class found it there and called it in." Huff then gave us the location. I knew exactly where it was.

"Where is that?" Dinapoli asked.

Sam and I started toward my car without answering her.

"Detectives?" she said.

"Hey," Huff shouted. "Bring her along."

I was fine with that. She could come along and sit in the back of the Chevy. As long as we didn't have to follow her, I could live with the arrangement.

For the time being.

We all got inside my car. I let Sam drive again. He started up the engine, pulled away from the curb and made a U-turn in the middle of the street. Huff blocked our path. He stood there in front of us, waving his arms. He must have run over to us after we got inside. The front of his shirt had grown damp with sweat.

Sam rolled down his window and shouted, "What?"

CHAPTER TWENTY-FOUR

H uff walked around the front of the Chevy to the driver's side. He stopped, leaned over and placed his hands on his knees. He looked at Sam. "After you're done with the Van, return to the precinct."

"What if a lead takes us elsewhere?" I asked.

He shook his head. "We've got the footage from the gas station. I want you to go over it with Agent Dinapoli."

Sam and I nodded. From the backseat, Dinapoli asked, "What gas station?"

Neither of us responded. Huff made a snorting kind of sound. I figured he was about to tell us to let her in on it, but needed to breathe more than talk at that moment.

"Listen to me, Detectives," she said. "The FBI is taking this case over whether you like it or not."

So much for being a team.

"If you want to be a part of the investigation," she continued, "then you better start talking now."

I shifted in my seat and looked back at her. "Ms. Dinapoli—"

"Special Agent Dinapoli," she corrected me.

"I don't care if it's God's Right Hand Woman Dinapoli," I said. "Right now you are in our car and counting on us to take you to see the getaway vehicle. You'd be wise to sit back and shut the hell up."

Anger flashed in her eyes and across her face, but she didn't say anything. She stared at me for a moment, and then looked out the side window. I felt a little bad at my outburst, but did not apologize. My cell phone started to vibrate. I pulled it from my pocket and turned away.

"Tanner," I answered.

"Mitch."

"Lana, where are you?"

"The hospital."

"Are you okay? What happened?"

"Broke my leg. I'll be fine. They say I hit my head. I don't remember that. They say that's because I have a concussion."

"What do you remember?"

"All of it, Mitch. All except hitting my head."

I needed to be in the same room with her, for one, to settle my nerves over her condition. Also, I figured she might recall a few details that would help us. Plus, she knew the kids. There had to be a reason all this happened.

"Lana, look, I'm on my way to see the van," I said. "It was ditched a few miles from school. After that I'm gonna come by and see you. Which hospital did they take you to?"

"I'm at Mercy."

"Okay, that's not far from the station. I'll drop Sam and *Special Agent* Dinapoli off, and then come check on you."

"Okay. Mitch, if that turns out to be after five—"

"It won't be."

"—well if it does, would you stop by my place and feed Envy for me?"

Envy was her cat. As far as cats go, he was all right.

"Yeah, I can do that." We said goodbye and I set my phone in the center console. I watched the trees pass through the side window, hoping that I could attach my concerns to one of them and leave it behind for a while.

"She doing okay?" Sam asked.

"Shaken up, I'm sure. Seeing the kids taken like that."

"Wait a minute," Dinapoli said from the back seat. "You have a witness and we aren't going to see her?"

I said nothing.

"Detective?"

I still said nothing. They'd get their chance with Lana soon enough.

"That looks like the spot," Sam said.

"We're not done with this," Dinapoli said. "After this, I want to know everything you can tell me about this witness."

I'd do everything in my power to prevent that. The moment they found out about my relationship with Lana, they'd kick me off the case. I looked up as Sam slowed the car down. A line of about a dozen squad cars had hopped the curb and parked along the road. Their rack lights rotated, alternating red and blue. Traffic crawled along in the middle lane. Countless faces stared in our direction. I'm sure folks passing by thought there had to be a whole host of dead bodies in the woods just beyond their view.

Sam pulled over and up onto the curb. He parked my Chevy behind the last squad car.

"Leave some room," I said. "I don't want some rookie pulling up here and blocking us in."

I stepped out and let Dinapoli out of the backseat. She stepped outside without looking at me. We walked toward the ten-foot wide clearing. Grass had grown over two gravel tracks. Turning into the clearing, I saw Sandusky's van with the white-stenciled lettering, FORENSICS. Beyond that stood the van that had been used at the scene of the crime. Primer gray and maybe sanded down in spots. Sandusky and a team of his men were busy grabbing fibers from the carpet, as well as prints from all the surfaces.

"Can you imagine being scooped up from your everyday kid life and tossed into the back of a van with a couple of madmen?" Sam asked.

Dinapoli turned to face us. "Yes. It happened to me when I was thirteen."

I hesitated, then asked, "What happened?"

She glanced at me, then over my shoulder. Her eyes took on a sheen. "Some other time, Detective." With that, she turned again and went into FBI Special Agent mode directing people here and there and yelling about the integrity of the crime scene.

"Should we pull her back?" Sam said.

"Nah," I said. "I just want to hear from Sandusky what he thinks."

"Well here's your chance." Sam pointed ahead at the approaching forensics technician.

"Any luck?" I asked Sandusky.

"Pretty clean. Got some fibers out of the carpet, some hair. Prints in the back. None up front. Little bit of blood on the front passenger seat."

I tensed at this.

"Up high, like maybe one of the kids got their fingernails into the guy's neck or the side of his face. From the accounts, the man carrying the boy was the one in the passenger seat. That right?"

I nodded, so did Sam. I wondered who had told Sandusky that. Looking around, I didn't spot any faces of those who were in the know.

"Here's something else," Sandusky said, waving at us to follow him. We walked past the van. Two men were inside dusting the ceiling. We stopped in front of the van. There were fat tire tracks on the ground and footprints in the mud next to where I estimated the passenger side doors to be. Sandusky continued, "My guess would be that they had a car parked back here as opposed to walking off somewhere else."

"Looks about right," Sam said.

"Those footprints any good?" I asked.

Sandusky shook his head. "We can get a general sense of the shoe size, but the imprints are bad. We'll get a cast of them, though."

"What size are the shoes?"

"One set is an eleven or twelve, men's. The other belongs to a kid. And there's only one print like that. So, maybe the kid pulled free and got one foot on the ground or something like that. Definitely not two."

"So no kid got away here," Sam said.

Sandusky shook his head.

"Have we sent men out into those woods?" Sam asked.

"That's not my call, of course," Sandusky said. "But, yeah, I saw some officers heading out there. Maybe they'll find something that'd been tossed from the van."

"Don't count on it," I said. My gut was telling me that this had been in the works for some time now. "Who's this van belong to?"

Kettle, a detective from robbery came forward. "It was reported missing early this morning. Some old lady out in the suburbs. Said she kept the van for her son. He's doing a stint up at SCI at Rockview for armed robbery."

Sam and I glanced at each other and nodded. Sandusky drifted back until he was no longer in view. I knew where to find him if we needed him again.

"What is it?" Kettle said.

"We got a lead on one of the men," I said.

"Possibly," Sam said.

"And?" Kettle said.

"An ex-con, maybe recently in the joint."

"Rockview?"

I hiked my shoulders in the air an inch. "Not sure. We're going to find out. In the meantime, what's this lady's name?"

By this point Dinapoli had wandered over and positioned herself between me and Sam. Kettle glanced at her, then back at me.

"Farrugio," he said.

"Okay," I said. "Do me a favor and make sure that report hits my email inbox."

"Yeah, you got it." His eyes settled on Dinapoli. He smiled at her. She turned away.

"You gonna impound the van after Sandusky's done with it?" Sam asked.

"Yeah," Kettle said. "We can hold it as long as you guys need. Like I said, it belongs to her son, so she don't have any need for it."

I watched Kettle walk away and disappear around a corner. After he was out of sight, I turned toward the tangle of bushes and trees. What was on the other side? What if the van had been a diversion? The men could have split up there. They could have split the kids up, too, each man taking one kid. Or, one could have taken the van and the other man could have left through the woods with both kids.

"Hey," Sandusky shouted, breaking my concentration. "Come take a look at this."

CHAPTER TWENTY-FIVE

When they told Debby and Beans it was okay to remove their masks, she couldn't help but feel relieved that she'd see light again. It didn't turn out that way, though. The room was dark, dry, and cool. She placed her hands in the air over her head before standing. While she assumed they were in a room, she couldn't be sure. The last thing she wanted to do was hit her head again. She scooted her legs up under her and slowly rose. When she was fully extended, her fingertips grazed what she assumed was the ceiling. She took a step forward, then back. She stepped to her left, then right. She planned on doing this until she had a general sense of where the walls were. On her next step, she felt something under her foot.

"Ouch," Beans said.

She'd stepped on his fingers. "Sorry, Beans."

"Where are we?" he asked.

She didn't know and she said as much. She also realized that if she angled her eyes to the right or left instead of straight ahead, she could sort of make out some of the features of the place.

Directly ahead was a door. Tiny slivers of light crept in from the edges. Not enough that she could see anything, though. When she looked directly at it, the light disappeared. She wondered why this happened.

Beans's wheezing had grown worse since they left the truck. Was he allergic to something in the room? She worried he might not make it much longer. Why hadn't those men given him his inhaler?

"Just relax," she said. "Breathe in and out, slow and deep." The words had come from her mother a few years ago after Debby learned of the death of her grandmother. The old woman was the only family member she got along with. All the others could have gone away and she'd have been perfectly happy to be with Grandma. Like most things in Debby's life, that wasn't to be.

"I can't breathe deep," Beans said. "That's the problem. And I can't find my inhaler."

"Do you have your bag with you? Maybe it's in there."

"They took it." He paused and took a rattled breath. "I'm scared, Debby."

"I know, Bernie." She shuffled forward until she stood over him. Then she lowered herself and cradled him in her arms. They rocked back and forth together. She hummed a tune to him, one her mother always sang to her. The combination seemed to relax Beans and his wheezing subsided.

For the moment.

She figured that sooner or later he would need his inhaler.

CHAPTER TWENTY-SIX

D inapoli stood in front of the van's opened sliding side door. The techs crouched inside, a few feet in front of her. She leaned forward, looked to the left, then the right.

"What is it?" she asked.

I'd arrived about that time. Sandusky furrowed his brow at her then glanced at me. He extended his arm over the woman's shoulder and held out something plastic.

"What is it?" I asked.

"Asthma inhaler. Last name on the prescription label says Holland."

"That's the boy," I said.

"It's a pretty strong dose from what I understand," he said.

The affliction was not one I'd ever had to deal with personally. I had been on calls as a young cop where a kid or some old lady had had a horrible attack. If I recalled correctly, one had even died from it. "That doesn't provide much of a positive outlook for this kid. One more reason for us to work every angle we can. Hopefully that boy has a backup inhaler."

"How does the weather affect asthma?" Sam asked.

"I don't know," I said. "But I know that this humidity makes it hard for me to breathe. Can't imagine what it's like for that kid."

"Let's go," Dinapoli said, turning toward the back of the van. "Nothing left for us here."

Sam and I watched as she headed back the way we entered. Neither of us had taken kindly to the idea that we had to take orders from her. This was our case, not the FBI's. I didn't care what Huff said. The guy was nothing but a kiss-up. I was certain he thought cooperating with the Feds would get him another nice shiny promotion. Enough cases like this one and he'd be running Philly P.D. within a couple years.

Dinapoli looked over her shoulder and stopped. She stared right at me. There was as much hurt as there was anger in her eyes. Despite the fact that I hated her position, I figured she personally didn't deserve this kind of grief.

"Come on," I said to Sam. "Let's get going." I looked back at Sandusky. "You find anything else, you call me. I want to know when you get confirmation on those tire tracks. I want to know what kind of vehicle." I already knew, of course. Ford F-250 Super Cab. The confirmation would cement it.

Dinapoli waited by the rear passenger door of the Chevy. I didn't argue with her requested seating position. I slipped into the seat in front of her and let Sam drive again. He always seemed to enjoy it. We left the lights and the siren off, allowing for a little reflection time.

I was lost in thought when I heard Dinapoli say, "My name's Bridget."

I looked back at her. She gave me a smile and raised her eyebrows a bit. She had invited me in, for whatever reason. I wanted to trust her, but couldn't entirely get past the fact that she was a fire breathing FBI agent.

"I'm Mitch, and my partner here is—"

"Sam," she interrupted. "I got that."

I said nothing. Sam whistled along with the radio. An Otis Redding cover by some lady named Sarah. Pretty voice. She did the song justice.

"I'm sorry for coming off like such a bitch back there." She paused. If she was waiting for one of us to tell her she's crazy, it wasn't happening. "It's just that we get so much push back from local authorities. It's... I don't care about the recognition, Mitch. The kids are the only thing that matters. We have protocols and ways of doing things because they work. You see that, right?"

"I do, Bridget," I said to her. "But we do have people that care about recognition. One person in particular that I can think of."

"You?" Sam said with a chuckle.

"Shut up," I said. "Not me. Huff. And he'd be happy to sell us out if it meant him getting his name in the paper and his arm around the Mayor. Anything to propel him up the food chain. Know what I mean?"

Sam shook his head and shot me a look. He thought I'd turned into a conspiracy nut over the last few years.

Bridget Dinapoli nodded, though. I figured she dealt with ten times as much bureaucracy than Sam and I did on a daily basis.

"I'll support you, Bridget," I said. "But only on the condition that you work with us like partners. No more hollow talk about teams. I don't want you withholding anything from me, and I promise the same from us."

"I can do that," she said.

I shifted forward in my seat and repositioned the vent so that the air conditioning hit me in the face. The cool air dried the remaining sweat on my forehead.

"Okay," she said. "You can start with telling me the link with this Farrugio person."

I stared past the windshield. We rolled to a stop at a traffic light. A man pushing a shopping cart full of cans passed in front of us while businessmen in two-thousand dollar suits strolled past along the sidewalk.

"Farrugio is the registered owner of the van. She kept it for her son. Her son is in prison. Ben McCree, the school's vice principal and the guy at that house we took into custody, has a brother named Brad. We think Brad might be involved in the kidnapping and shooting, as well as helping our murder suspect escape from the hospital." I looked back at her and waited for her to confirm she was up to speed. She nodded for me to continue. "We recently learned that Brad's an ex-con."

"Same prison?"

"We're waiting on confirmation of that. But if so, well, I still haven't made sense of all this yet. I'm sure it'll fit somewhere."

She nodded. "It usually does." She leaned forward and pointed at Gus's Italian. "Guys want to split a pie? I'm starving."

We had too much to do and not enough time to do it. At the same time, my stomach felt empty and my head light. At a certain point, it became useless to push forward. Sam could do without. Ranger training made him that way. For me, a Bear Claw at the station would do. But I agreed to stop. I had a phone call to make.

A couple minutes later Sam grabbed a table on the patio while we waited for our pizza to bake. We planned on taking it with us instead of eating at the restaurant. A warm breeze blew by, carrying with it the smell of melted cheese and fresh baked dough. I walked over to the corner of the patio and pulled out my cell phone. I had to call my mother. She'd picked up Ella from school and brought her back to her house. I figured that was the safest option in the event that the guys behind the kidnapping and murder had seen my picture on TV, or if Ben McCree really was a part of all this and his involvement not a coincidence, and somehow they knew we busted him. In any event, Roy Miller a.k.a. Michael Lipsky knew me, and I had serious questions in regards to what the guy was capable of.

Plus, there was the lingering question, how far did this reach?

"How's Ella doing?" I asked my mother after she answered.

"She's fine. A little scared. Wants to know when you'll be home."

"Can't say for sure, Momma. This case is a mess, and now we've got the FBI involved."

"They brought in the big guns, eh? What, they don't think you and Sam can handle this?"

"Technically, we aren't supposed to be working the kidnapping side of this, but those were Lana's students."

"Oh, God. How is she taking this?"

"Not well, I'd imagine. She's in the hospital."

"She wasn't shot was she?"

"No, Momma. She broke her leg, though. I'm gonna stop by and check on her before I come home."

"Okay. You want me and Ella to go over and see her?"

"No," I said, looking back at the table to see if lunch had arrived. It hadn't. "I want you to stay at your place. Got it? Don't go out, not to the hospital, and especially not to my house."

"Mitch, you're scaring me."

"You don't sound scared."

"Keeping an even voice for Ms. Ella. No point getting her worked up."

"You're right." I waited a beat, then added, "Just hang tight, and I'll be there before you know it. Any problems, you call me or nine-one-one."

She said goodbye and hung up, and I climbed back over the wrought iron fence and took a seat at the table. Sam slid an iced mug across to me.

"Everything all right?" Sam asked.

I nodded and grabbed the mug. "What kind?" I took a sip and then pulled the mug away from my mouth. "Never mind, I don't want to know. Might ruin it for me by telling me the name."

Bridget walked onto the patio carrying a cardboard box. "Drinking on the job?"

"Just a little refreshment."

She shook her head. "Finish up and let's go."

Right before we got inside the car, Sam's phone rang. He answered and nodded and said yeah a couple times. Then he hung up and looked at me.

"What?" I said.

"That was Huff," he said. "Said we need to drop whatever we're doing and get to the station at once."

"Any reason why?"

"No. He sounded serious, though."

CHAPTER TWENTY-SEVEN

The ride back to the precinct took less than five minutes. The lights and siren helped. Sam pulled the car around back and pulled into a spot near the rear entrance. We walked to the building at a pace close to a jog. I grabbed the door and waited for Sam to go in. Bridget stopped short.

"It's okay that I come in?" she asked. The wind whipped loose strands of hair across her face. She reached up and tucked them behind her right ear.

"Why wouldn't it be?" I extended my free hand and gestured for her to go in.

She nodded, smiled and stepped inside. I followed close behind while Sam led the way to Homicide. The halls were buzzing with activity. Pretty normal for the station. We entered Homicide through the door closest to Huff's glass walled office. The sight within those walls gave reason for concern.

"What's he doing here?" Sam asked.

"Who is it?" Bridget asked, craning her neck to get a better look.

"That's Chief Warren," I said.

"Mitch and Warren don't get along too well," Sam said. "No good can come from him being here."

I took a few steps back and took a seat on top of my desk, allowing me to keep an eye on Huff's office. Along with Warren, Huff was meeting with the Lieutenant in charge of Major Crimes. Townsend was his name. I had a sinking feeling that we were about to get the proverbial rug pulled out from under our feet.

"Let's go talk to McCree," I said.

"You sure?" Sam asked. "Huff sounded serious."

"When did you become the type to follow orders so easily?"

Sam shrugged and waved me off. He looked like a debutante swatting away a fly.

"He's busy. If he thinks he can keep us waiting, he can wait, too."

We left through the exit at the other end of the room. It was a short walk to interrogation. The long hallway had doors on one side and a solid cinder block wall on the other. We entered from the high end. Half of the twelve rooms were occupied. A mixture of faces stared blankly at the mirrored glass or at the cop in the room with them. I knew one thing for sure. They all proclaimed their innocence.

I spotted Laura Weaver, the student teacher, in room four. Room three was empty. Ben McCree waited inside room two. Fairchild leaned back against the glass partition, arms folded across his chest.

"What the hell is he doing in there?" I said. "We should've had first crack at this guy."

"Want to question the girl?" Sam asked.

"No," I said. "I want to talk to McCree, but that jerk snaked him from us."

Sam maneuvered in front of me. His wide frame blocked my view of the room. "Listen, Mitch. No matter what you think of those guys, we're all on the same team. You go making waves and you're going to get traded. Busted down. Is that what you want?"

I knew his words made sense, but I didn't care. "What I want is to interview our suspect, Sam. Are you with me or not?"

Sam took a deep breath, reached out and placed a hand on my shoulder. "Mitch—"

"Let's kick him out." It came from Bridget.

I looked back at her with my left eyebrow arched. Perhaps I could get away with removing Fairchild from the room if Bridget took responsibility for it. After all, she was in charge now. This was the FBI's case, not ours. I started forward. Sam slid over to block my path. Then he muttered something under his breath and stepped aside. He pulled out his phone and glanced at the screen.

"It's Huff," he said.

"Guess we should start back," I said.

Sam hung up and confirmed that Huff wanted us in his office now. We walked back the way we came. The halls still buzzed with energy. I still fumed over the fact that I hadn't gotten the chance to question McCree. I hoped the opportunity would arise after meeting with Huff. If Bridget wouldn't make the argument, I would.

We turned the final corner and nearly collided with Chief Warren.

"Chief," I said.

"Detectives," he said, stepping around us. The look on his face could be classified as disdain. He didn't stop and make small talk. Fine by me.

Huff was waiting for us outside his office. The entire room was empty otherwise. Even Old Man Flores, who typically remained perched behind a desk answering the phone all day, was out.

"Come on in, guys," he said.

Sam stepped into the office first and sat down. I took the seat next to him. The door closed behind me. I glanced back and saw Bridget standing. I rose and offered her my chair.

"No thanks," she said. "I'll stand."

I nodded and sat back down. "What is it, Huff?"

He refused to make eye contact with us. Instead, he stared at his desk calendar. He held a number two pencil in his hand and doodled in the space underneath September twenty-eighth.

"Huff?" I said.

"Warren wants Major Crimes to take over the case since it involves homicide and kidnapping."

"Shit," I said.

Sam agreed.

Huff continued, "They think that they can push back on the Feds by doing so."

"Who's they?" Bridget asked. Her movement created a breeze that blew past me carrying a lavender scent. She placed one hand on my shoulder and aimed the other one at Huff.

"Mayor Piolazzi and the Chief."

"Like hell," Bridget fumed. "You tell them they can—"

Huff held up his hands. "Not my battle, Agent Dinapoli. You'll need to take it up with your chain of command. I'm sure they can pull the right strings, if those strings exist. It's all posturing. I'm aware of that. But no matter what happens here on out, it doesn't change this next fact." He leaned back in his chair, interlaced his fingers behind his head and stared at a spot in between me and Sam.

"Which is?" I asked after a prolonged moment of silence.

He snapped forward and placed both elbows on his desk. His gaze flicked between both of us. "You two are off the case."

"Who ordered this?" I demanded.

"It comes from Warren." He sounded subdued.

"Yeah, but who told him to do this?"

Huff shrugged. "No telling. Could be the Mayor, could be that prick Townsend."

I had no reason to believe that Lieutenant Townsend was behind this. I'd never had any run-ins with him and couldn't think of any reason why he'd want me off the case. That only left two people. Either of them could have been behind it. Huff or the Mayor. For all his misgivings, Huff wasn't that bad of a guy. We disagreed at times, but things worked out. The Mayor on the other hand, let's just say words had been spoken in the past and there'd been no kiss and make up session.

"This is garbage, Huff," Sam said. "We're the two best detectives you've got. We're better than any of those jackasses in Major Crimes. We're already vested in this, too."

"You think I don't know that?" Huff rose out of his chair and slapped his desk with an open palm. His face was red and veins stuck out of his neck and on the side of his forehead. His voice had risen by a couple decibels. "Dammit, I fought them tooth and nail just now to keep you guys on." After several seconds of heavy panting, he returned to his chair. His head drifted to the right. The window there gave him a view of the rear parking lot. I noticed five pigeons sitting on top of my car.

I had a feeling he wasn't through. In as gentle a tone as I could muster, I asked, "What else, Huff?"

His head turned toward us, moving slower than before. He glanced at me, then Sam, then Bridget. He stopped on her. I would have too.

"I know there's something else," I said.

"They're keeping Horace and Fairchild on board." His gaze remained fixed on Bridget.

That must've been why Fairchild was in there with McCree. This had been determined some time ago, otherwise they would have waited until after the Chief had left. I wondered if the Chief in Huff's office had been a show for our sake. Something to make us feel a little better.

Or perhaps to redirect our anger.

I thought about raising the point, but bit my tongue. The truth would come out in time.

"I expect you guys to have a report turned in by the end of the day detailing the investigation up to this point," Huff said.

I stood and leaned over his desk, stopping when my face was mere inches from his. "You smell, Huff." With that, I turned and left the office. I heard someone come after me. The delicate touch on my shoulder told me that someone was not Sam. I didn't look back.

"Mitch," Bridget said. "I'm going to do everything I can to get you back on board."

"They might negotiate you out of this, too," I said, staring down at the floor.

"They've got no reason to do that."

I looked over my shoulder, at her, then at Huff's office. "You're giving them one right now."

She smiled and turned around. A moment later she was on the other side of the bureaucratic barrier. Sam rose and left the room as she took a seat. He walked toward me, shaking his head.

"This is ridiculous, man," he said.

"Don't have to tell me."

Escalated voices erupted from inside Huff's office. His face turned red again. He rose, sat, then rose again. Fingers pointed in all directions. Knocked down and dragged out. I hoped that I'd have both of them on my side when the time came. I sure as hell didn't plan to give this case up without a fight.

I reached inside my desk drawer for my keys. They were on top of the folder containing Dusty Anne Miller's pictures from the crime scene. It seemed like years since that happened. I remembered that the autopsy was to take place in a few hours. Perhaps I'd attend.

As I started toward the door, Sam said, "Where you going?"

"To the hospital to check on Lana. Then probably to my mother's to see how Ella's doing. I'll get in touch with you at some point."

I expected him to try to tag along. He didn't. "Okay."

I exited the room near Huff's office. I stopped in front of the window and stared at him for a moment. He glanced over at me, then looked away.

Chicken.

I'd almost made it through the building to the exit when I saw Fairchild approaching. He had a smug look on his face. Not unusual for the guy. But this time there was something more behind it. He had advanced knowledge of what went down. He got within a few feet of me and said, "Say hello to that girlfriend of yours for me, Tanner."

The look on his face and the sound of his voice and the words that he used caused me to snap. I reached over, grabbed him by the shirt and nailed him with a right cross.

CHAPTER TWENTY-EIGHT

Fairchild fell to the floor, landing on his right side. Blood trickled from the corner of his mouth. A few drops splattered on the floor, creating a tiny dark red pond. He scooted back to the wall. The heel of his shoe dragged through the pool of blood and created a zigzagged line on the tiles. He wiped his face with the back of his hand. The cuff of his shirtsleeve turned crimson. He looked down on it and muttered something, then slowly got up. He palmed his lip once more.

"Hey, you're a real asshole. You know that, Tanner?" He leaned forward, like he contemplated charging me. Instead, he let his words do the fighting. "Maybe you and that whore belong together."

I started toward him again. He took a few steps to the side, keeping me in view. I kept moving forward.

"Mitch!"

I stopped, arm cocked, and looked past Fairchild. Sam stood at the end of the hall. There were probably five or six other officers between him and me, not counting Fairchild. Horace was heading our way and had just passed Sam. By the time I readjusted my gaze, Fairchild had moved back another five feet. I unclenched my fist, dropped my arm and waved him off.

"You're not worth it," I said.

His smile had returned, despite the red trickle from the corner of his mouth to his chin and down his neck. His shirt collar had turned red on the right side. "I'll send you my dry cleaning bill along with a transcript of the interview. I'm sure you'll find it helpful."

"About as helpful as you finding a vagina."

Sam headed toward me, but I turned away and kicked the door open. By the time he made it outside, I was slipping behind the wheel of my car. I started it up and drove to where Sam was standing. He waited for me to roll down my window.

"What?"

"I was gonna tell you that Huff's going to give one last push for us."

"Think that's going to matter to me now?" I asked. "You know Fairchild's going straight to Huff to file a complaint. And Horace saw it, too. No one's going to back me on this one. No matter what Huff wants, he has to move the complaint up the ladder. He's not risking his neck for me."

Sam nodded. He opened his mouth to speak, but said nothing.

Then my phone rang. I looked down at it. "Huff," I said, tossing the phone onto the passenger seat. "I'll call you in a bit, Sam."

I pulled out of the lot and drove to the hospital. The clock on my dash said it was almost two p.m. Wouldn't be long before the traffic became too heavy to get anything done. Luckily, I didn't have that far to travel so long as nothing came up. I had a feeling it wouldn't. Not for me, at least.

My phone rang again. I pulled to a stop at the traffic light and reached across the car. Huff again. I set the phone on the center console without answering it. He could wait. I knew how the conversation would go anyway.

A young woman pushing a stroller walked in front of me. She had white cords dangling from the side of her ears. Probably didn't hear the car that honked at her.

A few minutes later I reached the hospital. The lady behind the information desk directed me to Lana's room. My heels clacked against beige linoleum tiles. The fluorescent lights gave the hallways a yellowish tint. It felt like I was coated with disinfectant by the time I reached the end of my journey through the hospital. When I reached Lana's room, the door was open, so I stepped inside. The bed was missing, though. I went back to the hall and stopped the first nurse I found.

"Where is Lana Suarez?" I asked the young woman.

She looked at me for a moment, disinterested, like she was thinking of a way to get past me. She said, "Who?"

"The patient in that room." I pointed toward Lana's room.

The nurse walked over and grabbed a clipboard hanging by the door. "Let's see," she paused to run her finger down the chart. "They are performing a CAT scan right now."

"Why? She's here for a broken leg." I recalled Lana saying something about a concussion a few seconds later.

She shrugged. "I can find out, but it will be a while before I can get back to you." She faked left and went right. I didn't try to stop her.

I shook my head. Said to no one in particular, "No, that's all right. I've got a few things to take care of, then I'll be back."

I stared at the floor as I walked back to the main entrance. It was lined with scuff marks. I figured a team of people spent all night waxing and buffing those floors. Several questions ran through my mind. The question of 'why' remained present always. Why the kids? I still had no idea. Why had Miller changed his name? Everything had moved so fast we hadn't had an opportunity to find that out. I hadn't seen Brad McCree's criminal record yet and didn't know if we could put him together with that Farrugio character. Was it a coincidence that he stole a van belonging to another criminal? Or was this thing bigger than I had originally thought?

I wondered what my punishment would be for belting Fairchild. As I exited the hospital, I pulled out my cell and took it off the silent setting. Seven more missed calls. They were all from Huff. I bit the bullet and called him back.

"Are you friggin' stupid, Tanner?" he asked.

I didn't respond. I'd learned there was little point to answering a question like that.

"You know you're going to be disciplined for this, right?"

"I'd imagine so."

"I can't back you up, Tanner. Warren is going to come down hard on you over this."

"I expect he will."

"How can you sound so calm over this?"

I wasn't sure. "I just am, Huff. What's done is done. If you can't back me up, so be it. I'll man up and take my punishment. After all, you guys already neutered me today. Now, you got anything else to tell me, or are we done here?"

He stammered for a minute, and then said, "That's all, Tanner. Keep your phone close by in case Warren wants to talk with you."

I hung up and unlocked my car. By that time, I simply wanted to get home to Ella. First I had to go take care of Lana's cat, Envy. The little guy had no idea what had happened. Hopefully I wouldn't raise any suspicion with him.

The drive to her place took me past the school again. The parking lot looked empty except for a dozen or so squad cars and a couple of forensics vans. I wondered if Sandusky was down there. The major news channels were still parked along the road, joined by some of the national news networks. I figured they all wanted in on this story. Perhaps they'd like to interview the former lead investigator on the case. The thought brought a smile to my face. How pissed would Chief Warren be then?

About two miles later I pulled into Lana's neighborhood. She lived in a small bungalow style house adorned with pale blue siding and white trim. I pulled into the driveway just in time to see a man emerge from behind her house.

CHAPTER TWENTY-NINE

I opened the door and stepped out, using the vehicle as a shield. I drew my weapon and aimed it in the guy's direction. "Who the hell are you?"

The man stopped, dropped something on the ground, lifted his arms in the air and said nothing.

Slowly, I made my way around the vehicle, keeping my pistol aimed at the guy. I cast a quick glance over my shoulder to make sure no one approached from the other side of the house. The guy was dirty, covered in dirt or soot or something similar, from head to toe.

"You don't answer me, I'll shoot," I said.

He pointed at the truck parked in front of the neighbor's house. "Replacing the chimney," he said with a heavy Hispanic accent.

"Why aren't you parked in front of her house?"

"It was blocked." His hands shook.

I got close enough to read the patch on his shirt and the ID attached to the lanyard around his neck. He'd told the truth. I holstered my weapon, keeping an eye on him while I did so.

"Can I grab my tools?" he asked.

I nodded. "I'm sorry about that. Kind of on edge today. Know what I mean?"

The guy nodded, probably out of fear. He had no idea what I was talking about.

"You see anything funny out here today?"

He shook his head. "Can I just finish my job?"

I nodded and watched him head to his truck and put his tools away. It felt like the humidity had reached its peak for the day. At least, I couldn't imagine it getting any higher. My forehead was already coated in a sheen of sweat. I decided to walk around the perimeter of the house before heading inside. Best to check things out. I hadn't been aware that Lana was making improvements. She'd said nothing about it. Or if she did, it was during a game and I'd tuned her out. It's happened on occasion.

I reached the backyard and saw that the chimney was in a few different stages of repair, or disrepair. It looked like they'd removed the exterior bricks and had already started to rebuild the bottom with new brick. The flue looked new. The sun reflected off it, creating a bright ball. I imagined the rest of the parts were being replaced as well. I continued on and saw Envy at the back door. She'd placed herself between the rear sliding door and the Venetian blinds. She walked back and forth pressed up against the glass. She stopped and looked at me. Her mouth opened and let out a meow that I never heard.

I continued around the house. Everything seemed normal. There were no broken branches on the hedges. The windows were closed and intact. The rear gate was shut and the padlock untouched. The trash cans were nestled between two shrubs at the corner of the house, like they always were. I stopped at the front door, pulled out my keys and unlocked it. Cold air rushed out as I walked in. The air conditioning must have been set at sixty. No wonder Envy paced the back door. Cat had to be freezing and the sun had warmed the glass. I wasn't sure if cats actually got cold or not, but it sounded reasonable.

I made my way through the house. The smell of potpourri was heavy. Envy's food bowl was next to the pantry door. I filled it to the top then I changed her water and kitty litter. I didn't mind going above and beyond the call of duty.

As I walked over to the fridge, I pulled out my cell and checked for missed calls. There were none. No good news, and more importantly, no bad news. Inside the fridge I found a Mich Ultra. Not my beer of choice, but I cracked it open anyway. It was cold and slid down my throat easily. I checked my forehead. The sweat had dried.

Lana's laptop was on the kitchen table. I lifted the lid and powered it on. I had my own account on the computer. I logged in and pulled up my personal email, which contained nothing but a bunch of junk mail. I then opened another tab in the web browser and went to the site for the department's web mail. The first message said that I'd been suspended for two weeks for striking Fairchild. The suspension was pending appeal, so I was to report to work as usual tomorrow. I'd be the office maid for the day was what it would amount to. Might as well stay home. Not like I was going to win the appeal if Warren oversaw it. The next message was from Kettle. He'd come through on his report on the theft of the van. Unfortunately, the report didn't contain anything new.

I did a check of the local news sites as well as a couple of the major ones. The locals all had coverage of the murder and kidnapping. They hadn't pieced together Dusty Anne Miller's murder as being related. It was then that I realized I'd missed the autopsy. I pulled out my phone and made a note to call in for the results first thing in the morning.

I checked my work email one last time before shutting down

the browser. A message from Fairchild had come in not a minute ago. I moved the mouse to the message to open it. Before I could, someone knocked on Lana's front door. Not a normal knock. They pounded on the door, ignoring the doorbell. The only ones I knew who did that were cops, and not the friendly ones.

CHAPTER THIRTY

The banging never stopped. Debby thought she'd go mad before too long. In between the pounding on the walls beyond the room, she heard Beans's wheezing. How much longer would he last? When would the men come back? She had to go to the bathroom and was sure Beans did as well. She decided to bring the subject up.

"I really have to pee," she said.

Beans made a sound like he rolled over or lifted up. It was still dark in the room. "Me, too. Go in the back corner on your side and I'll go in mine."

"What if the room is slanted and it rolls back toward us?"

"Then it does." Beans paused, took a deep breath, then laughed. The sound eased the knot in Debby's stomach. He added, "I'm going to hold it a bit longer."

"Me, too," she said after a moment of contemplation. "If only they'd come back."

"How long do you think we've been down here?" he asked.

She reached for her wrist, but her watch had been taken from her. It had a button you could push that would light up the dial. "I don't know. I've slept a couple times, I think. But I have no idea for how long. Could have been a couple minutes. Could have been all night."

"Yeah," he said.

She knew when Beans slept and when he was awake. His wheezing slowed to a rumble when he was asleep.

The banging got faster.

"What do you think they are doing?" she asked.

"I don't know. How do we know it's them? What if they just dumped us off in a shed somewhere and that's coming from something close by?"

Debby glanced up and looked to the side. She could see tiny pinholes of light coming through the floor. "We're under something, Bernie. I don't know what. But when I look to the side I can see a little light above us."

Beans started sliding along the floor. She shifted her gaze and saw his outline heading toward the front of the room. It amazed her how much better she could see in the dark now.

"What are you doing?" she asked.

"Checking this door."

"For what?"

"Maybe it's unlocked."

The thought hadn't crossed Debby's mind. "Why would they bring us out here and then leave the door unlocked?"

"I don't know," he replied. "Maybe they're dumb. Maybe it's a game to them."

She didn't doubt that. Anyone who would take two kids probably wasn't a Rhodes Scholar. Not that she knew what that was either. It had been an insult her brother had tossed at her once. In front of her, she heard Beans pound on the door.

"What are you doing?" she asked.

"I can't find a latch or knob," he replied. "I'm seeing if anyone's out there."

"What if *they're* out there?"

"Then they can come open this door."

"But what if they hit you for banging on it?"

"Then let them. They can kill me if they want to, but they'd better open this door!"

She'd never heard Beans curse before. She'd only ever heard him raise his voice once as long as she'd known him.

And then, the door opened. The light that flooded the room was bright. Brighter than Debby had ever seen before. It was like the sun had come in through the opening. Beans screamed. A moment later he landed on the floor in front of her. He cried and clutched his right arm. Debby shielded her eyes with her hands, blocking the source of the light. She saw a man crouching just inside the doorway. It was the guy who'd watched her in the school building, and later stole Beans from the recess yard.

"I told ya to shut up," he said. "Keep at it and I'll do the same to your other arm."

Debby glanced down and saw that Bean's wrist bent unnaturally.

"Please," she said as her eyes flooded with tears, "he needs his inhaler. His asthma is really bad and he'll die if he doesn't get it."

"Which one is he?"

"What?"

"His name, girl."

"Bernard Holland," she said.

The guy scooted back through the opening then slammed the door. It bounced open a few inches, allowing enough light into the room that she could see everything in it, which wasn't much more than her and Beans. There was a bucket in the back corner. She tried not to think of what it contained. She heard the sound of the door slam shut and the light disappeared.

"Are you okay?" she asked Beans.

"My arm hurts really bad."

She reached over and stroked his hair. She heard the sound of something scraping against the door and then it was pulled open again. The man crawled inside. A wave of putrid body odor washed over Debby. She resisted the urge to throw up. The guy placed a bag on the floor. From the bag he pulled out a sling and tossed it to Debbie.

"Put that around his neck and his arm through it. It'll keep it from becoming any more damaged."

Debby started to wrap the sling around Bean's neck when something hit her side.

"There's his inhaler. If he dies, it's on you now."

She choked back her tears and focused on placing Beans's arm inside the sling. The man started to retreat through the doorway and closed the door. Debby glanced down, located the inhaler and scooped it up before the room went dark.

"Here's your inhaler," she said, searching for Beans's good hand.

He took it from her. She heard the compressed medicine being shot into his mouth in a puff of air a few seconds later. The wheezing and crackling sound that had accompanied his every breath faded at once. He exhaled with a sound of relief.

She waited a beat, then said, "Beans?"

"Yeah."

"Did you have anything that could help us in your backpack?"

"Maybe. Why?"

"Because he left it by the door."

CHAPTER THIRTY-ONE

I'd fussed at Lana at least a dozen times about the fact that her door didn't have a peephole. With everything I'd seen, it didn't make sense. She never saw my point. There's windows there, she'd say. Yeah, there were windows on either side of the door, but she had to slide the curtains over to look through. And it's not like the glass was tinted. Anyone standing outside could see her. So I had little choice but to take my chances and open the door. I held my pistol in my right hand and cracked the door with my left.

Special Agents Vinson and Braden stood on the porch, side by side. Their Ray-Ban knockoffs shielded their eyes. They'd removed their jackets, exposing holstered weapons. Couldn't blame them for doing so, either. The heat and humidity demanded it.

Braden robotically said, "FBI. We need to speak with..."

I guessed they didn't recognize me. I said, "What's up, guys?"

"What the hell are you doing here?" Vinson said, lifting his sunglasses and pushing them on top of his close-cropped dark hair.

"Who were you expecting?"

"We're here to question a Lana Suarez? Is she here? You're not questioning her are you?" Vinson eyed me. "We were told that you were not only off the case, but also suspended. If you're in here—"

"Who's side are you guys on?" I asked.

"How do you mean?" Braden said. He looked more relaxed than his partner. Guess every duo needed some balance.

"Mine or theirs?"

"We're not on any side," Braden said. "We report to Special Agent Dinapoli. We do what she tells us."

I tucked my pistol behind my back in my waistband and pulled the door open. The humidity went to war against the frigid air conditioning. I stood in the middle of the battleground. Frozen sweat began to form on my body.

"Is she here?" Vinson said.

"Dinapoli?"

"Lana Suarez." Vinson maintained that stone-faced look. Couldn't even get the guy to crack a smile.

"No, she's not. She's at the hospital. She was injured when the kids were taken." I pointed to my leg then head. "Broke her leg and sustained a concussion."

Vinson said, "How do you know all this? Did you go to interview a witness when protocol forbade you?"

Forbade? Fancy lingo for the FBI guys.

"No, I did nothing I was forbade to do." I contemplated how much to tell these guys. Since my relationship with Lana wasn't a secret to Huff and the other detectives, I figured I could mention it to these two. "Lana and I have a relationship. My visit was for personal reasons."

"Is she still at the hospital?"

I thought about giving the guys the run around and sending them to the other side of the city to Nazareth Hospital. I figured I could convince them she had to be transported there because of the head trauma.

"She's not here," I said.

"Where is she?"

I shrugged. "If I'm suspended, I probably shouldn't help out with the investigation. Don't want to violate protocol, you know."

Vinson took a step inside. I squared up to block his path. He didn't back down. We stood inches from one another.

"We just want to take a look around," Braden said.

I didn't move.

"Please, Detective, move," Vinson said.

I waited a minute. Tension built between us. Two versus one. The odds were probably not in my favor in the confined entryway. Out in the open, that'd be a different story. More room to maneuver.

So after a few more seconds I stepped aside and followed the men around the house. They went into her room. I could have stopped them, but knew they'd find nothing in there. All they were doing was wasting their time. They opened and closed a few drawers, and then checked out the closet. After that, they went to the kitchen. Vinson noted my open beer bottle and shook his head.

"Suspended," I said. "Remember?"

I presumed they were satisfied when they made their way to the front door. Vinson stopped and turned toward me. "What's your read on this woman, Tanner? Think she's involved?"

I said nothing. What the hell kind of question was that to ask her boyfriend? My smile masked my anger over the accusation.

"Seems fishy, you know? Teacher watches and does nothing as two kids are abducted."

Now, I'd already struck one cop that day. It wouldn't bother me to hit another. Vinson got this look on his face, like he realized he'd gotten to me. He smiled and gave a quick nod, then he and Braden left. I hooked my finger, behind the curtain and pulled it wide. The two agents got inside their government issued black sedan, pulled into the driveway and then backed out. I noted that the chimney repairman's truck had also left.

I decided to take another look around the place. They'd touched some of her personal effects. The conspiracy nut in me wanted to ensure that they hadn't planted any evidence. Of course, that could be what they expected me to do, only to have them show up and catch me red handed. For that reason, I slid the dead bolt to the locked position.

Turned out nothing of the sort had occurred, nothing out of the ordinary. No reason to rouse the ghost of J. Edgar.

I went back to the kitchen, finished my beer and said goodbye to Envy the cat. He brushed against my leg, then went back to the rear sliding glass door for a little more time in the sun. Before I left, I adjusted the thermostat to seventy-two. Might as well save Lana a few bucks on her power bill while she was in the hospital.

I'd left my car windows cracked to allow airflow. Instead of being one-ten inside, it was a balmy ninety-five. The air conditioning always blew hot the first few minutes. I waited outside while it kicked in. At least there was a breeze out here. I leaned back against a shade tree and stared out at nothing. The cool breeze was welcomed, and I hoped it meant that a cold front was on the way. After a long hot summer, we needed it.

My cell phone rang, dragging me away from my thoughts concerning the weather. I glanced at the screen. Sam.

"What's going on, partner?" I said.

"Just checking in to see how you're holding up," he said.

"Doing okay, I suppose. Went by to see Lana, but they took her down for a CT scan. So I came by her house to feed Envy the cat. Those two knucklehead Special Agents showed up. Wanted to take a look around. I presume that was on orders of Dinapoli."

"Not that I'm aware of, Mitch. I've been with her since you left. She hasn't spoken to them."

"Interesting. They even made a point to say that they took orders from her. Whose back pocket are they in?"

"I'll bring it up to Bridget when I see her again."

"You're not with her now?" I asked

"Nah, she had to leave."

"Well, don't trust anyone, Sam. Make sure you keep an eye on all of them."

"Like I have a choice," Sam said. "We are one hundred percent done with this case."

"You sure about that?"

"Ninety-five percent sure."

I smiled and let out a half laugh. It sounded defeated, much like I felt. I'd tell everyone up to the Mayor to kiss my ass, I'm working on this case. But Sam followed orders better than I did. Guess the Army taught him that, too. "Hey, you didn't happen to get over to Miller's autopsy did you?"

"Is that still our case?"

"I don't know. Not mine for sure. Maybe still yours."

"I'll call on it in a few and see if I can get the report faxed or emailed over."

"Sounds good. Try and stop by the house tonight."

"You got it, Mitch."

I hung up and walked over to my car. I opened the door and slipped inside. The cold air found its way through my clothes. An icy wave washed over me. Quite enjoyable.

I figured I'd stop by my mother's and check on her and Ella. The girl had put on her brave face today. By now, she'd be in need of another dose of daddy reinforcement to help her get through the night after the terrifying day at school.

I did twenty through the neighborhood, then turned right onto Marshall. A couple minutes later I noticed the black sedan following five or six car lengths behind. I made a random right turn. So did the other car. I made a left. So did the other car. Finally, I made a u-turn and went back to the main road. The black vehicle followed along every step of the way.

CHAPTER THIRTY-TWO

Turns out the Feds hadn't gone that far, after all. They gave the impression they had left, and then they'd waited for me to leave. Probably parked across the only entrance and exit to the neighborhood. In a supermarket parking lot, it would have been impossible for most anyone to notice them. They saw me, and then pulled out after I did. Why, though? What did they want from me? Sam had all the information I did. Was this the work of Bridget Dinapoli? If not her, then who? Couldn't be the Chief or the Mayor. They spent their time fighting involvement from the Feds.

I pulled the zoom back to get a better look at the big picture. There were a few possible angles. I assumed that they were aware of my relationship with Lana. It was common knowledge around the station, after all. Perhaps Sam mentioned it in passing to Bridget and she decided to follow up on it. If someone wanted to start connecting dots, it wasn't all that far to travel from Roy Miller, a.k.a. Michael Lipsky, to me. Of course, this all depended on them throwing logic out of the window.

I thought it also might be possible that there was someone who wanted to meet with me in an off-the-record kind of way. To do that, they had to involve people who could operate beyond the department's legal scope. Then it would make sense to send a couple of FBI Special Agents to tail me until they found me in a compromising position, at which time they could take me into custody. Now, who would want that to happen? The Mayor was a strong candidate. The Chief, too. But why? Hadn't I already determined that there was no way those two groups could co-exist?

Except in an effort to take me down.

There's that conspiracy nut again.

I hadn't left Marshall since my series of turns to determine whether or not I was being followed. The car remained seven or eight lengths behind. I led them away from the city. At this time of day, traffic started to pick up. The closer one got to the city, the thicker the congestion. The last thing I wanted was to get stuck in gridlock and provide those two an opportunity to trap me.

I continued another couple of miles, past the land of suburbs, to an area where traffic was light. At that point, I'd had enough. Time to see what these guys really wanted.

Though the traffic light said go, I pulled to a stop just shy of the intersection. I opened my door to a chorus of honks and windows rolling down so drivers and passengers could shout at me or extend a warm greeting with a single finger. Ignoring them, I walked around to the back of the Chevy and climbed up on the trunk lid, then onto the roof.

The Feds came to a stop about forty feet away, behind three other cars. As those vehicles veered to the left or the right to get by me, the FBI agents pulled up another twenty feet, and then stopped.

"Come on," I shouted. "This is what you wanted, right? Now you got it. Come and get me. I'm sure this is a crime somewhere."

The sun glared off their front windshield. Through the bright burst of light, I saw the men look at each other, then at me. They spoke, perhaps trying to figure out what to do. Braden was behind the wheel. His hands animated his side of the conversation. He eased the vehicle forward a few more feet. Vinson had his cell phone pressed up to the side of his head. I'd have paid twenty thousand dollars to find out who was on the other end of that call.

Their lights started flashing, small and blue at the corners of the windshield. I figured they were about to come and place me under arrest. Why? No reason other than I was acting like a belligerent jackass. They didn't need a reason, though.

Instead of coming for me, the car lurched forward then whipped around in a half-circle and took off in the other direction, headed toward the city. Their lights continued to flash and they went right through five red lights before they disappeared from sight.

"Get off your car asshole," some punk kid said. He'd stuck his head out the window and had a big smile plastered on his freckled face. I pulled my jacket to the side, revealing my pistol. I patted the handle. The kid quickly ducked back inside the cab of the small pickup and rolled up his window. No matter how hard I stared, he didn't look back at me again.

I waited until the little pickup drove off, then I hopped off my car. I pulled my cell from my pocket and placed a call as I slipped behind the steering wheel. The phone rang five times before she answered.

"Where are you?" my mother asked.

"I'm not going to make it over," I said.

"Ella is going to be disappointed. Are you sure you can't come by?"

"It's not that I can't. I shouldn't."

"What do you mean?"

"I really can't get into it, Momma. A lot's happened today, most of which I can't tell you. I'm suspended, pending appeal."

"What did you do?"

"Don't worry about it."

"Hope it was worth it."

"He had it coming."

She made a disapproving noise, but said nothing.

"I just spent fifteen minutes with a couple of Feds following me. Don't know what it means, but I don't feel safe leading them to you and Ella."

"What if they already know about us?"

"I'm working on that. You can expect Sam to come by at some point. Worst case, I'll send Jerry over to get Ella and bring her to his place. They won't bother him."

"And you'd leave me here by myself?"

"Any man crazy enough to mess with you will get what he deserves."

She laughed and said, "Damn right."

"The language," I said.

She said nothing.

"Okay, look, I'm going to give Sam a call now. Make sure all the doors and windows are locked, and don't leave the house. Not even for a carton of milk. You got it?"

"I know, I know."

We said our goodbyes and I hung up. The light turned green. I hit the accelerator and placed a call to Sam after I'd leveled out my speed.

"What's going on, Mitch?"

"Crazy day," I said.

"Tell me about it."

"Vinson and Braden were following me."

"Say what?"

"After I left Lana's place. I'd say it was maybe ten minutes after they left. Should have been in the city by then, but apparently they

THE DEPTH OF DARKNESS   175

waited across from the neighborhood in the shopping center parking lot."

"Sure it was them?"

"Yeah, I'm sure. I made a couple crazy turns and they stuck with me the whole time. Kept a good distance back. Pros, you know. They followed me for another fifteen minutes or so until I stopped and got out of the car. Made like the roof of the Chevy was a stage on Broadway."

"Intriguing," Sam said. "I'll have to check online for video footage."

"Isn't it?" I paused a beat, wondering if anyone had filmed the encounter. "Anyone there give any indication that they wanted to have a word with me?"

"Lots of people, but nothing that demanded immediate attention. You sure it was them?"

"They got close enough I could see the razor burn on their necks."

"I'll feel some people out and call in some favors."

"That's why I'm calling, Sam. I need a favor from you."

"Anything."

"Go by Momma's and either stay there or bring Ella and maybe even Momma over to your place. Those Feds got me spooked. I don't know what they know about me, and I don't want either of the girls to be placed in danger. Maybe it's my paranoid side working overtime, but I think that they, someone, thinks that I'm involved in this mess. Now, if they want to show up at my place at two in the morning, so be it. As long as Ella isn't there."

"Okay, Mitch," Sam said. "I agree, it's probably a bit paranoid, but better to not take chances. I'll take care of Ella and let you know."

"Just let me know when, not where. Probably best that I don't know in case this heads in the wrong direction."

After I hung up with Sam, I pulled off onto a side road and

took quite possibly the longest way home I could think of. Lots of turns and back roads. Less traffic back there. It made it easier to see if someone tailed me. And since I didn't have Lana or Ella to get home to, an hour-and-a-half drive didn't bother me.

The temperature readout on the dash said it had dropped below eighty degrees outside. Some fresh air would be nice. I rolled down all four windows and turned the radio up. The baseball game was on. I didn't pay attention. I let it act as background noise to drown out my thoughts.

By the time I reached my neighborhood, the sun was deep in the west, behind the trees. The sky faded from deep red, to a light pink, to dark blue to the east. I pulled up to the curb and stopped a few houses down from mine. I waited there for fifteen minutes while watching the shadows.

What a day, I thought as I opened the door and stood. I crossed the street to the sidewalk, cut across my front yard and then opened the door to the screened porch. A nice breeze blew through. Mosquitoes hummed from the other side of the protective netting. Best investment I ever made, screening in this porch. Before sticking my key into the doorknob, I made sure it was still locked. It was. I righted that situation and stepped inside. After a quick search, I heated up some leftover pizza and finished off the five stray beers that had once been part of a twelve pack.

Dinner was good. The beer dessert had been better. During my meal, Sam called to let me know he'd picked up Ella and my mother and had them safely at his house. Confident they were okay for the night, I settled in on the couch for a little TV time.

I'm not sure what time I fell asleep. I hadn't made it to Letterman. Hadn't even seen the late news. Probably better. That stuff can be depressing. I knew it was two in the morning when the doorbell rang, though. The cable box said so.

CHAPTER THIRTY-THREE

It felt like hours had passed since Debby had last heard the banging. In the time since, she'd dozed off a few times. How long? She had no way of knowing. Of all the things that were in Beans's backpack, there was no watch. They found some snacks, which were welcomed to say the least. A bottle of water, which they split equally, as best they could tell. His books were in there, and two small flashlights. Debby took one, Beans the other. Neither had been brave enough to use them, not even to make sure they worked.

As she lie there wondering what had hit her in the face, she fought against the temptation of pulling the flashlight from her pocket and turning it on. What if the men were out there? They'd see the light and come in and take it from her. At the very least, that was all they'd do. They might beat her for it. The ceiling creaked. Footsteps followed, a pattern of three steps, then a pause. The steps resumed as the walker went from one side of the room to the other.

Debby reached over and shook Beans's leg. He kicked back in

response. She needed for him to wake up, so she shook him again. Not too hard, though. She didn't want to make his arm move and cause him any more pain.

"Get up," she whispered.

"What?" he asked, sounding groggy.

"Quiet down." After a pause, she added, "Did you hear that?'

"Hear what?" he whispered.

"Those footsteps."

She felt a slight breeze as he shifted forward, followed by the smell of his lotion. A few moments passed. His hand wrapped around hers when the footsteps started again.

"I thought whoever was up there had left," he said.

She nodded, and then realized that he couldn't see her. "Me, too."

The sound of the steps went around the perimeter of the room once, then twice. After that, they crossed to the middle and stopped right above them. Debby dug her nails into Beans's left hand.

"I've already got one broken arm," he said. "You squeeze any tighter, I'll have two."

She let go and said, "Sorry."

He laughed softly. She wondered how he could do that through the pain of a broken forearm. She'd broken her leg in the past and could still remember how bad it hurt, and they'd given her pain medication. She didn't get to take all of the pills, of course, thanks to her mother.

The sound of a door opening and then shutting echoed through the small room. A second set of shoes walked on the floor above. The door opened again. A third person entered the room. The steps became a hodgepodge of *clicks* and *clacks* that reverberated inside Debby's head like an unmatched drum set.

"Who do you think it is?" she asked.

"Has to be them," he said. The fear had left his voice. It was as if locking Beans in this room with Debby and having a broken arm had made a man out of him. He had to protect her. She was impressed by his resolve. Maybe she'd never have to protect him from the other kids again. Beans the Recess Yard Conqueror would make them pay for years of previous torment.

It sounded like two distinct sets of feet passed overhead. A snare and a bass. They traveled in the direction of the door. At least where Debby figured the door was located. A couple minutes passed. Debby hoped that the ruckus was nothing more than a changing of the guard. The overnight shift taking over for the late shift. Please, let it be that, she thought.

The scraping sound against the door that held them inside the room told her otherwise.

She attributed the sound to a piece of wood or metal that they used to secure the door. A lock could be picked. Maybe not by kids, but why take chances, right? But barricading the door would prevent any chance of Debby and Beans escaping the dirty dungeon.

The scraping stopped. A thump and a click followed. Maybe another lock, she guessed. For a second she felt hopeful that they were being rescued.

"Get behind me, Debby," Beans said.

She didn't. Beans would not take the fall. She stayed right beside him, clutching his hand in hers.

The door opened, grating across the floor. The doorway remained dark for a moment, then it erupted into light. The bright artificial sun had returned. Pain shot through Debby's eyes all the way to the back of her brain. The hope that she held for a rescue attempt disappeared with the darkness.

"Opposite sides," the guy said.

Debby held onto Beans's hand, and he hers. Neither of them moved. She covered her eyes with her free hand, using it to block out the bright bulb. She made out the shape of the man who'd taken Beans from the recess yard. Behind him was another man. Maybe the guy who drove the van.

Who remained upstairs?

The guy duck-walked his way through the doorway. He looked at her, then Beans. "Opposite sides!" he shouted.

Beans clutched her hand tight, refusing to let her go.

"You little bastards," the guy said. "You want another broken arm?" He pointed at Beans.

"Go ahead, break it," Beans snapped back. Beans the Brave. His story would be told from the highest slide at every playground across the country.

The guy smiled. "Oh I will. And then I'll break hers."

Beans let go of Debby's hand and then scooted along the floor to the other side.

"Beans," she said.

"Just do what he says, Debby," Beans said.

"Yeah, Debby," the guy said. "Do what I say." The smile on his face broadened. He'd cut his hair down to his scalp since she'd last seen him. She thought he looked like some kind of sick dog, hunched over and ready to pounce. She bet that if she looked closer, there would be drool hanging from his mouth. "Move!"

Debby jerked to the side. She crawled to the wall and leaned back against it. Inspiration filled her at that moment. "What do you want with us?"

The guy stared at her and said nothing. She looked past him and noticed that the other man had left. Where had he gone? Why had he been there if he was only going to leave again?

Her questions were answered a moment later.

The guy reappeared. He ducked down and stuck his head into the room. Once again, he looked familiar to her, but she couldn't quite place him.

"Get the girl," the man outside the room told the other guy.

"And leave the boy for now. He's the important one. She's just...trash."

Debby had been called many things during her short life. Nerd, geek, loser, dork, pain in the ass, dumb little kid, and a few others that she'd blocked from her memory because they'd come from her mother. But she'd never been called trash. She never wanted to be called that, because there were only two things you did with trash.

Throw it away, or burn it.

"Come on girl," the buzzed head guy said.

She balled up and began to cry. The man wrapped his hands around her upper arms and dragged her along the floor.

"Let her go," Beans said.

"Don't you move," the other man said. It sounded like a gun was cocked immediately afterward. Debby didn't open her eyes to check.

"Debby," Beans said.

She wanted to call out to him. So many things to say, so few feet left to say them in. *I love you, Beans. Be careful, Beans. Cooperate, Beans. Tell my mom I love her.* She wasn't sure if the last one was true or not, but at least it would make her mom feel better. Not a single word escaped her mouth, though. She felt herself hoisted into the air and heard the door slammed shut. She opened her eyes and saw a thick board being placed across the door. Then her world went black. They'd slipped a hood over her head. The footsteps returned moments after. Close, this time. Underneath her. *Thump, thump, thump.* Up the stairs they went.

Inside? Outside? It was all the same to Debby, who remained in the dark.

CHAPTER THIRTY-FOUR

I rolled over on the couch and felt around the floor for my pistol. Cold steel brushed against my fingertips. The gun had somehow ended up underneath the ottoman. I grabbed it, rose and walked to the door. Unlike Lana's front door, mine had a peephole. I peered through to the dark porch. The light was off. I expected to find Vinson and Braden on my porch. The figure I saw standing there belonged to a female. I couldn't tell who, though. Definitely not Lana.

"Open up, Mitch," the woman said.

I took a moment to place the voice. The distinct southern accent was not one you heard around these parts that often. It belonged to Bridget Dinapoli.

"Come on, I know you're there." She tapped against the door lightly. "You blocked the light in the peephole."

"Shit," I muttered. "All right, give me a moment." I looked to my right. A full-length mirror hung on the wall. I stood there in my boxers and nothing else. What would the neighbors say? Who cares, I thought. I unlocked the door and pulled it open.

Bridget stood on the porch, about two feet from the open doorway. She had on blue jeans and a white t-shirt with a logo I couldn't make out in the dark. Her hair splashed across her forehead and cheeks, and hung over her shoulders. It framed her face. Made it seem softer. She smiled at me and stuck her thumbs in her front pockets.

"What are you doing here?" I asked.

"I'm sorry," she said. "I know it's late. I couldn't sleep. Kept thinking I should apologize."

"For sending your guys after me?"

"What?" she leaned back. "Sam told me about that. I had nothing to do with that, Mitch. I still don't know who did, but I'm trying to find out."

I studied her for a minute. She looked sincere, but that's what made the best liars successful. Came with the territory. "Well, what are you apologizing for then?"

"I feel like this mess you're in is my fault."

"You didn't make me hit another man."

"But I might have contributed to extra stress that in the end sent you over the edge."

I laughed at this. "A murdered woman contributed to this. A murdered principal, gunned down in front of his school, contributed to this. A girlfriend with a broken leg and concussion, two kids taken, that's what contributed to this. Believe me, Bridget, you had nothing to do with this. I'm used to dealing with adversity on the job. I leave it at work. Besides, you already eased up. This morning is water under the bridge." I paused and shook my head. "Then that asshole goes and makes a comment about Lana. It set me off."

She nodded. "I'm sure that's a touchy subject." She reached out, placed her hand high on the door frame and leaned forward. "I'm sorry about that, too."

"About what?"

"I..." She straightened and hiked her thumb over her shoulder while looking to the side. Her hair whipped around. I caught a whiff of the scented shampoo or conditioner she used. Lavender, I thought. "I should probably leave. I think I've overstepped my boundaries and said too much."

I took a step back to unblock the doorway. "Come on inside."

"I shouldn't." She retreated a couple steps back.

"You came all this way. I think I've got a few beers in the fridge in the garage. Might as well come in for one. We're both up."

Bridget chewed on her bottom lip while looking toward my feet. After a moment, she agreed to come in. I waited for her to pass, then shut and locked the door.

"What's this about?" I asked.

"Beer first," she said without looking back. She stopped at the end of the hall and waited for me to lead her to the garage. I opened the door and flipped on the light. "Nice Mustang." She walked over to the Boss and traced her fingers along the hood. "This a seventy?"

"Sixty-nine. All original."

"How long have you had it?"

I opened the fridge, pulled out two beers and opened them with the bottle opener mounted to the freezer handle. "A little while."

"Gift to yourself when you became single?"

I shrugged and looked away. "Let's get back to Lana. What's there to be sorry about?"

"Fairchild said he sent you the transcripts of his interview with Ben McCree."

I recalled seeing the message right before Vinson and Braden knocked on Lana's door. I'd forgotten about it until that moment.

"Did you read it?" she asked.

"I haven't."

"Maybe you should."

"I can right now."

"You might want to be alone."

My curiosity was beyond piqued. "That's okay. Come on."

We walked back into the house. My garage wasn't very well insulated, so the air was hot and damp out there. The kitchen felt like Canada in comparison. My laptop idled on the kitchen island. I ran my finger along the track pad to wake up the screen. A few moments later I had the email open and scanned the transcript. When I saw Lana's name, I stopped. I glanced over at Bridget. She tried to hide the concerned look on her face. I returned my gaze to the screen.

Fairchild said, "Tell me about Lana Suarez." He noted in the transcript that McCree smiled.

McCree said, "She's a special one, all right. She's been with us since she was a student teacher. We got along real well. Real, real well, if you know what I mean." I imagined the guy lifting one of his eyebrows high into his forehead or winking. McCree continued, "I couldn't let her leave, so I had to clear a position. This old bat, I can't even remember her name now, well she chose to retire early and Lana Suarez took her position."

"Chose to retire early?" Fairchild asked.

It was noted that McCree nodded.

"Continue."

"Well, every year, hell every semester, brings in a new crop. I usually have nothing to do with the women afterward. They go back to school and then onto their new jobs at schools elsewhere. But Lana and I kept seeing each other on and off. I guess seeing is the wrong word. It's just sex."

"When's the last time you saw her outside of school?"

"A couple weeks ago. At my place." It was again noted that Ben McCree smiled.

I'd read enough. Betrayed wasn't a strong enough word to

describe my feelings. I closed the lid to my laptop and finished off my beer.

"I'm sorry," Bridget said.

I glanced over at her. "Want another?" I asked, tipping my empty bottle in her direction.

She shrugged, pouted her lips and said, "Sure."

A minute later I returned from the garage with a six-pack of beer. Stuck four in the fridge and opened two.

"You okay?"

I sat down across from her. "I'd say I can't believe it, but, after nearly twenty years in this job, nothing surprises me anymore."

Bridget nodded, took a sip from her bottle and said nothing.

"The thought that it wasn't going to last, or that it was going nowhere, was there. Ella, my daughter, enjoyed her company. Lana had started spending more time with her recently, watching her at night for me when I got stuck on a case. I guess I thought something could grow from it. It had only been four months, after all. But this, man, I didn't expect this."

"We never do."

My gaze shifted from the ceiling toward Bridget. I dipped my chin halfway to my chest. "You speak from experience?"

She nodded.

"Recently?"

She nodded again.

I glanced down at her left hand and saw the tell-tale sign of a recent divorce. A thin pale line below the second knuckle of her left ring finger. She moved her hand below the countertop.

"Sorry," I said.

"It's okay, Mitch. These things happen."

"I suppose they do." I took a deep breath and exhaled, letting my lips flap. "Want to talk about it?"

A few tense minutes passed where we did not speak. Our gazes crossed paths a few times. Uncomfortable stares between two strangers who knew too much about one another.

"Was there anything useful from the McCree interview?" I asked, re-breaking the ice.

She shook her head. "He answered everything perfectly. Saw nothing. Knows nothing. Hates his brother, but feels compelled to help him out in hopes that the guy would change his ways. Hadn't seen Lipsky in years. Said he'll take responsibility for the hire."

"Responsibility?" My voice rose in anger and my chest and arm muscles tightened. "Then he can carry his ass to jail since he's responsible for getting those two children kidnapped."

She reached over and placed her hand on mine. "I know, Mitch. Trust me, they are going to go after him once this is all over."

"They?" I asked.

She stared at me for a moment before answering. "I don't know if I'm on this case anymore. All those changes, Major Crimes and the Mayor, just posturing to get us removed."

"I see," I said, nodding.

"My guys did find out that the little girl, her name's Debby Walker, her family is pretty poor. No real reason for a motive there. Mother's a piece of work. Said she seemed distraught enough, but something was missing."

I felt my heart break a little. Would the girl truly be missed by anyone if she were never found? "The motive, well, they said it looked like she attacked the guy that took the boy."

Bridget nodded, placed her forearms on the counter and leaned over the island. "Bernard Holland. They call him Beans. His parents recently started calling him Bernie, at the kid's request. The poor thing, he's got a ton of health issues, asthma, as we learned earlier, being the least of them."

"What else?"

She waved her hand in front of her face while taking a pull

from the beer bottle. "I'll get to that in a minute. First, I wanted to tell you what Vinson found out."

I waited while she took another sip of beer. She wiped her mouth with the back of her hand, leaving a small drop behind. It slid past the corner of her mouth and dripped off her jaw.

"Mitch, his parents are loaded."

CHAPTER THIRTY-FIVE

"Loaded?" I repeated.

"Rich," she said. "His father is some kind of engineer. They couldn't give us all the details because it's classified. They," she paused, "really him, because the wife doesn't even know."

"Is that right? So, something he sold to the government, then?"

She nodded. "Exactly. We're working on getting someone with the appropriate clearance and seeing if there is anything that can be declassified if it pertains to the case in any way."

"Who else might know of this? I mean, depending on what this is, we could be dealing with a situation that none of us envisioned. What if someone wants what he invented and won't give the kids back until they have it?"

"Vinson thought of that and asked if it would be anything along those lines. Mr. Holland really couldn't say, but he downplayed the notion."

"When did all this happen?" I asked.

"It's very, very recent from what the father said. They only recently received the money, and hardly anyone knows about it.

Just some family. They wanted to get the funds spread out, investments and so on, before moving away."

"Did Beans know they were planning on moving?"

She chewed on her lip a moment. "I don't know. Vinson didn't say. We should follow up on that."

"Yeah," I said, wondering about her use of *we*. I went to the fridge, grabbed a couple more beers and pulled out the last two slices of pizza. I offered her a piece.

"Cold is fine," she said.

I grabbed a couple paper towels and handed her one along with the slice.

"So if not espionage, then you're thinking that someone got wind of the Holland's recent influx of money and they've taken the boy for that reason?" I asked.

She nodded while taking a bite of pizza.

"Why haven't they called yet?"

"Ransom?"

I nodded.

"Maybe the girl threw a kink into their plans. They have to get rid of her first."

My hand stopped with the pizza inches shy of my mouth. Call me optimistic, but I'd held out hope that we'd find both kids alive. This sounded more and more like the girl was useless to the kidnappers. What would they do with her? My mind flashed images of a child found half-buried in the woods, or floating in a lake.

Bridget seemed to feel the effect of her words as well. She looked down at the granite countertop. "We're going to do everything we can to get both of them home safe, Mitch. They'll call. We know they'll call. This went down as it was planned, not some random pervert taking a kid for some sick reason. The FBI has people experienced in negotiating these things to a safe resolution."

I stepped back until I reached the wall. I leaned my head back. A spider crawled along the ceiling. A quick shiver ran through my body and I moved out of the spider's path. Every few seconds I glanced up at it.

"Want me to kill it?" Bridget said.

I glanced over and saw her smiling at me. Sure, mock my pain, Special Agent. "No, he has as much right to live as we do. Don't do anything to piss him off, and I think we'll be all right." Despite my words, I still couldn't stop focusing on the arachnid.

"Want to go in the other room then, Mr. Pacifist?" she asked.

"Yeah, let's do that."

I followed her into the living room and set my beer and pizza down on the coffee table. Lana smiled at me from within a picture frame. I set it face down on the table. Bridget noticed this, but didn't say anything. She leaned back into the cushion and pulled one leg up under the other, angling her body so she faced me.

"I was thirteen," she said. "On my way home from school. It was only a mile, so I walked there and back. It's warm most every day in Florida, so that was never a big deal. Rain every once in a while. Again, no big deal. We lived in a quiet community, for the most part. It had its bad part of town, just like everywhere else." Bridget paused to take a drink. "One day, this beat up pickup truck pulls up next to me. The thing was all rusted over. Big hole in it above the rear tire. Two guys were in the truck. I recognized them as friends of my mom's boyfriend, Gary. I forget what they said to me at first. I ignored them, you know, trying to act like I didn't hear them. I was maybe three blocks from home and I figured that if they kept it up, I'd run. Anyway, they didn't like that I wouldn't acknowledge them very much. One of them called me a whore and said something like, we're gonna teach you a lesson for Gary."

"Gary, your mom's boyfriend?"

She nodded and continued. "We didn't get along. I refused to listen to him, and he hated me for it. So, anyway, they kept it up, so

I started to run. The truck stayed right behind me until I hurdled a fence into someone's yard. Big mistake. They had some kind of dog who came tearing after me. I was forced to climb right back over, and the guys waited for me. I tried to run, but couldn't get away. The short one pulled a gun and forced me into the truck. I sat in the middle on this torn up, duct taped vinyl seat. The inside of the cab was covered in dirt. The ashtray was full of cigarette butts. The wind whipped the ashes around. I remember how they burned my nose. The whole ride, he kept sliding the barrel of the gun along my leg, down to my knee, up to my crotch. They passed a bottle back and forth, taking turns drinking from it. It wasn't long before the barrel was replaced by his hand on my leg."

I tensed, knowing where this likely led.

"They drove me deep into the woods. We got out and they led me down a worn out path. Eventually the path became overgrown. We kept walking. If I stopped, they jammed the barrel of a rifle into my back." She stopped and looked toward the back door, holding her finger in the air. Eventually, she shook her head and started up with her story. "They had a deer blind out there. You know what that is, right?"

I nodded.

"So, this place was all boarded up, and there were some old weathered two-by-fours scattered on the ground. They forced me inside the blind. One of them followed me in there. He kept coming toward me. I backed up into the wall, then slid along to the corner. I ended up with this huge splinter in the back of my leg. It got infected and they had to cut it out at the hospital. Anyway, I had nowhere to go. I remember my heart beating so fast and I wished it would just explode." Her eyes glossed over, but she didn't stop. "He grabs me by my neck. His fingers were calloused, and the skin jagged. It scratched me pretty good. He leans in to my left, and licks the side of my face. He pulls back and smiles, and even in the dimness of the room, I could see the stains on his teeth. The putrid smell of his saliva stayed with me for a week, even after I'd scrubbed my face so hard that the skin broke."

"What happened next?"

"He backed out of the blind. They used the two by fours to board up the door and the windows. Little cracks let the light in. I heard a swooshing or a splashing sound. Next thing, I smelled gasoline vapors. I went hysterical at that point because I thought they were going to burn me. I remember screaming, please help me, I'll do whatever you want."

I looked her over, wondering if she wore jeans to cover up the burns.

She must have noticed my gaze. "They didn't light it. It was all to scare me. That bastard Gary put them up to it. Worst part is, Mitch, my mother knew about it and didn't do a single thing about it. They kept me out there for a week. Every day or two, they brought me some bread to eat and water to drink. There was a bucket in there for me use as a toilet. A whole horrifying week I stayed in there with spiders and mosquitoes biting me. Snakes came in and out, slithering over my legs. Some lesson, right?"

"How'd you get out?"

"They let me out. They rode in on four-wheelers, pulled off the boards and then drove off. The sun was setting at the time. No way in hell was I waiting there. What if they came back the next morning? I had to find my way out of the woods and then home. And I did it. It took me all night, but I did it. I waited outside of the house until both my mother and Gary were gone, then I went in, got a shower, packed, stole some money and got on a bus to Charlotte. My grandmother met me there. She took me in and raised me. My mom didn't put up a fight, even after Gary went to jail for attempted murder."

"He tried to kill her?"

Bridget nodded slowly, looking toward the ceiling. "I haven't seen her since I graduated high school. Even then, she didn't come up to see me. She sat in the back and then walked out. Didn't show up for my college or law school graduation, or when I graduated from the Academy."

"I'm sorry, Bridget. I really am."

She shrugged and then stretched. "It's all in the past. It made me who I am. I can't complain about that."

We both walked to the kitchen to grab a fresh beer. The clock on the microwave said it was three in the morning. I opened the fridge, reached in and pulled out two more bottles. Lavender rode a breeze that blew in my direction. When I turned around, Bridget was standing in front of me. I leaned in and so did she. Our lips met. I didn't stop kissing her until well after our clothes were off.

CHAPTER THIRTY-SIX

I woke up on the floor between the couch and the TV, on top of a comforter I had pulled out of the linen closet. Though it covered most of the floor, Bridget and I only took up a small section of it. I'd fallen asleep with her in my arms. I woke up alone. Rising, I glanced toward the kitchen. An open pizza box stood between a half-dozen or so beer bottles. I reached my arms in the air and twisted the kinks out of my back.

"Bridget?" I called out.

There was no response. I assumed she'd gone home. Had she tried to wake me before she left? Perhaps she felt too embarrassed. No reason to dwell on it. Not yet, at least. We were both professionals, and could act accordingly the next time we were in each other's presence in a professional setting.

Alone, though? Time would tell. I hoped.

My phone beeped from somewhere in the kitchen. I found it on the counter, silenced it and started a fresh pot of coffee. While waiting for my morning java to brew, I checked my missed calls. There were sixteen. Guess that's what I got for silencing the ringer.

I counted five calls from Sam, eight from Huff, two from my mother, and one from Bridget. Had she called to apologize? And if so, for what? Coming over, or running out?

The final drips of fresh brew fell from the filter into the pot. I filled a mug and topped it off with some cream. Anticipation built as I lifted the hot liquid to my mouth. Like a junkie and a needle, I tell you. The first few sips went down hot. Instantly I felt awake. My finger hovered over Bridget's number for a few seconds. Instead, I called Sam.

"I just heard the news, Mitch."

"What news?" It could have been anything. *I heard about the ransom demand. I heard about Lana banging McCree. I heard about you banging Bridget.*

He hadn't heard any of those things. "A month without pay, man. That's harsh."

Ah, my suspension. "Christ, is that what I got?"

"You don't know yet?"

"I just got up."

"Say what?"

I said nothing.

"You didn't go in to defend yourself?"

"They had at least eight witnesses. It was a lost cause."

"You might have only got two weeks, though. And with pay."

"Perhaps."

"Yeah, perhaps. That's all you got to say?"

I said, "Whatever. I can use the time off."

"You're crazy."

"I know." I took a sip from my mug. "What's new with the kids?"

"No one's telling me anything."

"I heard that the boy's parents are loaded. Something about the dad selling something to the government."

"I heard something like that myself."

"Wonder if it's from the same source?" I asked, trying to be as smooth as possible while gathering information on Bridget.

"Is that source the reason why you woke up so late?"

I didn't reply.

"So what are you going to do?"

I hadn't thought about it. Figured then was as good a time as any. "I'm going to go pick up Ella and head out of town for a couple of days. Go camping or something. Spend some time just me and her and hope that clears my head."

"I heard about Lana," he said. "Sorry."

"Yeah, well, it was bound to happen sooner or later."

"Like I said from the beginning, Mitch, she was too hot for you."

"Screw you," I said and then I hung up the phone to the sounds of Sam's laughter.

I fixed a couple eggs, scrambled, then called Huff to receive the official word that I'd been suspended. The call was much shorter than my conversation with Sam.

Huff said, "One month, no pay. Don't even think about coming around the station, not even to use the toilet."

I didn't bother to reply. After I hung up, I checked my email. My personal account was full of new junk mail. Apparently, someone in Africa wanted to send me eight million dollars if I helped them open a bank account. Maybe I could look into that if this cop thing didn't work out. Perhaps not. When I tried to access my work email account, a message popped up that told me it had been suspended as well.

One month, no pay, no email.

Bummer.

Not for Ella, though. Not at first, at least. After a few weeks, she'd grow tired of daddy telling her what to do and when to do it all day long, every day. Then again, maybe not. Kids that young have a way of bouncing back relatively quickly. It'd be a good thing, overall. A chance for the two of us to reconnect. I'd worked so hard to shield her from the realities of life without her mother and brother that I worried I'd begun shielding her from the rest of the world around her. A month could help us both rediscover our place in this crazy world.

After I finished my second mug of coffee, I powered off the laptop and headed upstairs. Folded clothes covered my bed. I'd forgotten to put them away. It made it easy to pack. I tossed a pair of shorts, jeans, some t-shirts and boxers into a duffel bag. Should be plenty assuming there was access to a washing machine. I showered, skipped shaving, and put on some fresh clothes. Jeans and a polo. Casual Tuesday's, you know. I left the rest of the clothes on the bed and headed downstairs. I emptied the contents of the coffee pot into a travel mug and headed out the front door. Only problem was, the Chevy was gone. The department had reclaimed it already. They didn't waste any time. It'd be thirty days or so before I saw it again. Maybe they'd make Sam drive it around from now on.

The cold front had come through last night. It made driving the Boss a little more bearable since the car didn't have working air conditioning. I backed the beast out of the garage and let it idle in the driveway while I got out to shut the garage door. Mine was the only house in the neighborhood without an automatic opener. Wasn't the only way I stood out from the rest of my neighbors.

With the windows down and the radio turned up too loud, I drove to the hospital to pay a visit to Lana. I still hadn't decided whether or not I'd confront her over the revelation made in the transcripts of McCree's interview. It could have been that McCree was aware of our relationship and said that stuff just to get a rise out of me. Or it could have been the truth.

I parked at the back of the visitor's lot. The sun beat down from directly overhead, absorbed by the blacktop. The tall buildings blocked the breeze, leaving the air hot and stagnant. I crossed the lot quickly and made my way through the main entrance. Double glass sliding doors slid open, freeing a burst of disinfected chilled air that quickly cooled me off. I walked past the information desk. The old woman seated behind it smiled. I nodded back. No directions today, ma'am. After five minutes of walking through plain hospital hallways, I stood outside of Lana's room. I took a deep breath and knocked on the door, and then I stepped inside the room.

She looked up, surprised. A weak smile formed on her lips. "Mitch." Her smile faded as quickly as it appeared, and her eyes glossed over.

Part of me wanted to go over and comfort her. The woman had been through a lot. Seeing those kids taken while under her care could not have been easy and probably hurt worse than her physical pain. Of course, there was a lot she'd been through that she hadn't told me. Things that she didn't want me to know. And now I knew. The two sides warred within me. The side that won kept me rooted where I stood.

"They say I should be out in a couple days," she said.

I nodded. "That's nice. I'm sure they're going to want to question you," I paused and watched her. "About the kids and what happened."

"Of course. I'm ready. You can send them now or I can give you a statement."

"No questions from me. I'm off the case. In fact, I'm so off the case that I'm suspended without pay for the next month."

"Mitch, what happened?"

I stared at her with dead eyes and no expression. "Just Mitch Tanner being Mitch Tanner. You know how I get when I'm worked up. The case got to me, as it did everyone else. Only I exploded and hit another detective."

"Oh, honey," she said.

I wanted to tell her don't honey me. But I'd decided to wait until she was out of the hospital before confronting her over McCree's statement.

"Anyway," I said, "I'm taking Ella out of town for a few days."

"Where to?" she asked. "I'll come meet you there. I could stand to get away for a few days."

I shook my head. "Just her and me for a few days. We both need it."

She nodded and said, "Is everything okay, Mitch? You seem, I don't know, distant."

I walked toward her, leaned over and kissed her cheek. "I'll see you in a week or so, Lana." She called after me as I exited the room. I didn't bother to turn around. At that moment, I didn't care if I ever spoke with her again.

A half-hour later I pulled up to my mother's house. The door opened before I stepped out of the car. Ella ran toward me, arms outstretched. I lifted her into the air and hugged her like I hadn't seen her in a year.

"You got the cool car out, Daddy," she said.

"That's right," I said. "The cool car for the cool chick."

"That's me," she said, smiling ear to ear.

I kissed her cheeks a dozen times before setting her down. She ran around the front of the Boss and pulled open the passenger door. Her smile didn't fade. I wasn't sure if it was due to me being there, or the car.

Momma came up and said, "Where you headed?"

"Out of town," I said. "You might want to do the same. Go visit your sister down in D.C. for a week while I'm gone."

"You think I should?"

I nodded and said, "I do."

"Then I will." She turned and walked up to her house. At the front door, she looked back and said, "You two have a safe trip."

That's my mother. No need to waste words when they weren't needed. She'd been that way since I was a kid. I could have a mountain of a problem and her advice wouldn't stack up higher than an ant hill. But it always worked. It was always right.

So I got Ella settled in the car, gassed up, grabbed some sodas and snacks, and we headed west for the mountains. I called on the way to reserve a cabin for two, hopefully on the lake.

I never could have guessed the surprise that waited for us there.

CHAPTER THIRTY-SEVEN

I'd been going to this campground since the age of eight or nine. It was our family vacation spot. Momma couldn't afford to take us anywhere else. The cabins were cheap, so we got up there a few times every year. I guessed we spent a cumulative month there every year until I graduated high school. The owner of the place had a son named Terrence. The two of us were about the same age and we hit it off right away. From the moment I'd arrive till the time when my mother had to pull me out of a canoe, or off a bike, or out of a tree, Terrence and I were together. And we were trouble.

The memories flooded me as I pulled the Boss up to the wooden building that served as the check-in office and convenience store. The sign out front had been replaced and the shutters had been repainted. Otherwise it looked the same as it did twenty years ago. I reached over and gently shook Ella to wake her up.

"Are we there?" she asked, yawning and stretching her slender arms above her head.

I nodded and pointed toward the building. She smiled and hopped out of the car. I climbed up a set of creaking stairs and met her at the front door. She pulled it open and went inside. The place smelled like mothballs and beef jerky.

"Son of a bitch," the guy behind the counter said.

Ella giggled. I smiled. "Terrence," I said. "How've you been?"

Terrence came around the counter and shook my hand. "What's it been? Four years now?" He reached down and placed his hand on Ella's head. "This one was still in diapers back then."

I nodded. "It's been a while."

"The rest of the crew outside?"

I took Ella's hands in mine. "Just the two of us this time."

His eyes grew wide like he remembered something. I nodded at him, letting him know it was okay.

Terrence went back behind the counter and opened up his reservation book. "A little daddy and daughter adventure, eh? I see you spoke with my wife. That's why I didn't know you were coming." He tossed a set of keys to me. The fob attached said cabin thirteen. "Right on the water, in front of the dock."

"Excellent."

"We rebuilt it a few years ago. Perfect condition."

I stood there, smiling, holding Ella's hand.

"Ah, right, well you two go get settled in. Come on back up and I'll have some bait and poles waiting for you so you can get some fishing in. Then tonight, we'll grill whatever you catch."

"I don't like fish," Ella said.

"Then I'll make you some hot dogs," Terrence said. "Fair?"

Ella said, "Sure."

I thanked him, and Ella and I went back outside, got in the car and drove until we found cabin thirteen. The gravel driveway beside the cabin was already occupied by a black Acura. I parked behind the vehicle and told Ella to lock the car doors and remain in there until I returned. I left my cell phone with her in case anything happened to me. I hadn't been by the station, so I still had my pistol. Even if I had turned it in, I would have brought my personal piece. I drew my gun and crept around the side of the cabin, stopping just short of the front corner. I heard a squeaking sound from the porch. I eased around the edge and saw the back of a woman, seated on the porch swing that hung by chains from the ceiling.

"Bridget?"

She put her foot down and stopped the swing's momentum. Her head turned toward me. She smiled. "I wondered when you'd show up."

"What are you doing here?" I continued around and climbed the three stairs that led to the front porch. A fish splashed in the water behind me.

"Turns out you're not the only one who got suspended."

"What? Why?"

"Fraternizing."

"Was someone outside my house?" I felt the anger rise in my throat like bile.

She shook her head. "I'm under investigation. They've got no real proof. My boss said I should be back on the job in a couple days. Anyway, I figured I could use a few days away and Sam mentioned you'd be out here."

"Why would Sam care?"

She smiled and then shrugged. "I guess he has some suspicions about us."

"You shouldn't have come out here," I said.

She leaned forward and placed her hands on her knees. "I can leave, if you want."

"I don't want that," I said. "But I've got my daughter out here and I don't want to confuse her."

Bridget reached into her pocket and pulled out a key fob identical to mine. "That's why I've got my own cabin. Number fourteen. Right there." She aimed her finger across the porch at an identical cabin positioned twenty feet away. "Now, where is that daughter of yours?"

"Christ almighty. I'll be right back." I jumped off the porch and ran around the cabin. Ella smiled when she saw me. I waved for her to get out. She opened the door, raced up to me and handed me my phone. Then she ran past me toward the lake.

"Oh, that's so pretty, Daddy. Can we go swimming?"

"I suppose we could," I said. "But there's snakes out there."

"I don't care."

Bridget met us in front of the cabin. "I can take her out, Mitch."

"Who's this, Daddy?"

"This is Special Agent Bridget Dinapoli, Ella. She and Daddy were working on the same case. Turns out she needed a vacation as well, and she ended up with the cabin next to ours. Is it okay if she spends some time fishing and hanging out with us?"

"Cool," Ella said. Kids had it so easy. A new friend. Cool. Let's go chill.

And chill we did.

Terrence didn't wait for me to come back to the office. He pulled up next to the cabin in a golf cart and honked three times. Sounded like a Tercel that had swallowed a balloon full of helium.

"Give me a hand, Mitch," he said.

I noticed that he had trouble moving his left arm. There were no visible injuries. I gestured toward it and asked, "What happened?"

He waved me off. "Come on, help with this cooler."

We unloaded the cooler and set it on the porch. He opened the lid and pulled out two cans of Budweiser. Good enough for me on this warm September afternoon. Then Terrence went back to the golf cart and grabbed a tackle box, three rods and reels, and a couple Styrofoam cups that I presumed contained worms for bait. He dropped all the gear next to the steps and took a seat next to me on the swing. I stared out past the rustic railing, watching Bridget and Ella.

"Who's the girl?" Terrence asked.

"Some FBI agent."

"That's all? You co-workers or something like that?"

I turned toward him, smiled, said, "Something like that."

He wiggled his eyebrows. Looked like two caterpillars dancing. "I saw you on the TV, Mitch."

"You're kidding, right?"

"Nah," he said, looking out over the water. "Shame about those kids."

I nodded and said nothing. What could be said?

"Hope you find them."

"Won't be me, old friend."

"Why's that?"

"Bureaucratic BS."

Terrence smiled and said, "If all bureaucracy is bullshit, does that make all bullshit bureaucracy?"

"What the hell are you talking about?" I said, turning to face him. The ridiculous look on his face along with the dancing caterpillars on his forehead caused me to laugh. Terrence joined in. It turned into one of those moments where everything reaches that tipping point and you can't control yourself. Funny how two grown men could turn into eleven-year-old boys when paired up again.

The sound of Ella screaming "Daddy" put an end to that.

CHAPTER THIRTY-EIGHT

The dark never let up, it seemed, to Debby. When they put her inside the trunk of the car, she began counting the seconds. She'd almost reached one-thousand before she fell asleep. She'd awaked a couple times, maybe the car had hit a bump or come to a stop, causing her small body to roll.

When the trunk had finally opened, she could tell it was no longer dark outside. Though the hood over her head prevented her from seeing anything, stray rays of sunlight penetrated the dark fabric.

Hands wrapped around her upper arm and her thigh. She stifled a pained scream, fearing that if she yelled out it would result in a hand across her face. Those hands pulled her from the vehicle and lifted her into the air. She felt a breeze against her exposed skin, for a moment at least. A door opened, squeaking on rusted hinges. The light and the cool air faded. The door closed with a high pitched squeal.

An odor pervaded the hood that covered her head. What was

it? Mold? Mildew? Was that what a musty smell actually smelled like?

Debby resisted the urge to ask where she was. It didn't matter if she knew. Someone else needed to know. Someone who would risk their life to save hers.

Was there such a person? And if so, where?

It was easy for Debby to give up hope. She meant nothing to anyone.

"Don't you friggin move," the guy said to her, setting her down on the ground. His words echoed a few times, softer and softer with each renewed call, leaving Debby to wonder about the structure they were in.

The floor was cold, hard and damp. She pulled her legs to her chest so that the only bare skin touching the ground were the soles of her feet. She heard the guy grunting and the sound of something being moved, maybe slid, to the side across the floor. A cool draft slid past her. The musty mildew-mold smell intensified. She wanted to gag or sneeze, but stifled the urge for fear of retribution.

Slow deliberate footsteps approached. The guy's ragged breath came with them. She felt him hovering over her. He sniffled. Fabric grated against an unshaven face. She thought of her brother sanding down a birdhouse he'd made a year ago for shop class. He'd hung it from a tree branch outside her window. She recalled watching as the first bird circled, then landed, eating the food that she'd placed inside. She stared in horror as her brother shot that bird with his pellet gun. It stiffened and then fell out of sight.

Like that bird, would this be Debby's final house?

"Get up," the guy said.

She placed her palms on the floor and pushed herself up. His sweaty hand wrapped around the back of her neck. If she walked too slowly, he pushed her. Too fast, he squeezed and pulled back.

She let him guide her across the room.

"Duck your head," he said.

She lowered her head and took another step forward. His hand released from her neck. She reached her arms out in front, then to the side. Her left hand grazed something solid. It was cool and dry. She took a small step to the left.

"Don't turn around," the guy said, tugging the hood off her head. "I'll kill you if you do."

She heeded his words. She didn't want to look back anyway. At first glance, the room had no light source. She had to take in every inch of it before he closed whatever barrier would stand between her and freedom. There was shuffling behind her. Was he entering the room? Now she wanted to look, but didn't.

"I'm leaving you with some food and water, girl," he said. "Should be enough to keep you going for a week, maybe two if you ration. Someone should be along to collect you by then. If we don't forget about you, that is."

Debby began to cry.

"Don't worry, girl. If you don't want to prolong it, don't eat. Or eat it all at once. Nature will take its course. Simple, really."

Panic set in. Debby began to hyperventilate. The guy's footsteps traveled away from her. He grunted as something slid along the ground. The light began to fade. The grinding sound stopped. The room turned dark.

Debby found herself in the dark, again. Would she ever see the light?

Yes, she thought. She reached inside her front pocket and pulled out the little flashlight from Beans's backpack. Turning it on, she spun around in a half-circle and saw the rations she'd been left with. A six pack of large water bottles and a loaf of bread. Ration that over two weeks? Yeah, right. Maybe the guy was on to something. Maybe she should just give up.

She couldn't, though. Not yet. She still had hope. The room

was fairly large, to a nine year old. She walked to the back wall. The room rose toward the middle and then sloped downward. She hadn't been able to see the floor until she got close to the rear of the room. There she found a shovel. The blade was orange with rust, and long splinters dangled from the handle. She picked it up, and using it like a spear, attacked the back wall. To her surprise a small chunk of the wall fell to the floor. There might be a chance, she thought. She could get out alive, maybe, if she broke through the wall.

From the other side of the room she heard someone banging against the door. She extinguished her light, placed the shovel flat on the ground and returned to the opposite side of the room.

The banging continued for five to ten minutes. The longest five or ten minutes of Debby's life. And there'd been plenty of minutes that had stretched to eternity lately. Too many, in fact. She waited in anticipation for the door to open and for the guy to discover her plans. But it never did. He never came back. The banging stopped and Debby found herself alone in the dark room with an instrument that could lead her to freedom.

CHAPTER THIRTY-NINE

E lla's scream jarred me back to reality. I launched myself from the bench. Ignoring the stairs, I placed my hand on the railing and vaulted over it. The drop was further than I anticipated and the ground uneven. I let my legs buckle and I rolled forward. A second later I found my footing and was up racing toward Ella and Bridget. They'd walked along the lakefront, disappearing behind a thick row of trees.

A thousand thoughts went through my mind. First and foremost, I feared that Roy Miller-Michael Lipsky had found us. I pictured the guy stalking through the woods, waiting for the right moment to snatch my little girl. I decided then and there I would act as judge, jury, and executioner if I saw him.

With my pistol in my right hand, I sprinted as hard and as fast as I could, pushing beyond the limits my lungs tried to place upon me. As I rounded the trees, I heard Terrence's golf cart whining behind me. He shouted my name a couple times. I didn't bother to look back. Not with only a few feet remaining between me and whatever had frightened my daughter.

When I had them in view, I came to an immediate stop.

"What the hell is going on?" I said between heavy breaths.

Bridget lifted her arm. Ella stood a few feet away, smiling and pointing at the snake dangling from Bridget's hand.

"Ella, get away from there!" I shouted.

Bridget smiled and said, "Relax, Mitch. It's only a water snake."

My hands shook from the heavy shot of adrenaline I'd taken. I said, "Then why is it on land?"

Both of them laughed at me. Terrence, who'd joined me on foot and now stood beside me, joined them.

"I'm glad you all think this is funny." I patted my chest. "About gave me a heart attack." Another deep breath, with a loud exhale. "Why'd you scream like that, Ella?"

Ella bent forward, placed her hands on her knees and laughed harder.

"She almost stepped on him," Bridget said. "She was scared. I reached down and scooped this little guy up."

"Better get rid of him before I blow his head off." I aimed my pistol at the sky for emphasis.

"Oh, he's not going to hurt anyone. I used to find them everywhere when I was a kid in Florida. Used to bring them home and keep them as pets until my mom found them and made me bring them back to the lake."

Ella looked at me with wide eyes. "Oh, can I keep him, Daddy? Please?"

"Not only no," I said. "Hell no. Now put that thing back in the water where it belongs."

"Come on, Ella," Bridget said, taking her by the hand. "Let's release him."

Ella whined a bit, but she had no choice in the matter. I'd denied her request to get a dog. What made her think I'd let her keep a snake?

Terrence placed a hand on my shoulder. "Come on. Let's get those poles in the water."

I gladly hitched a ride on the golf cart back to the cabin. We grabbed a few beers, the rods and some bait. Bridget and Ella met us at the dock. It was a good eight feet wide and extended fifty feet out over the lake right to the channel, Terrence had said. Where the big catfish lurked.

"I can run back and get you a pole, miss," Terrence said to Bridget.

She placed a hand on Ella's shoulder. "That's okay. I'm happy to help Miss Ella out for a bit."

Ella grabbed Bridget's hand and started to pull her down the dock. Terrence pointed out a spot filled with blue gill. Not much for eating, but they'd keep her busy. In all, we spent about two hours fishing, landing a decent sized channel catfish and a couple five-pound largemouth bass. A feat not as easy as it was when I was a kid.

We beer-battered the fish fillets and cooked them in a fryer that Terrence's wife had brought over. The kids played while the adults talked. After the sun set behind the lake, Terrence and his family left in the golf cart. His wife had to drive. Terrence had had a few too many. So had I if I was being honest. Ella tried to stay awake, but didn't last five minutes. I brought her inside and placed her in bed.

"It's a beautiful night," Bridget said as I stepped onto the porch.

I walked up to her and wrapped my arm around her waist. Kissed her neck. She turned around and our lips met.

I pulled back and said, "Maybe when this is all over, we can pursue this, see where it goes?"

She looked away. Her hands wrapped around mine and pulled them apart.

I took a step back from her. "What is it? Is there someone else? Something to do with your ex-husband?"

"Almost my ex," she said. "And no, that's not it. There's no one else." She looked me in the eyes. "I think there could be something here, but, Mitch, they're reassigning me in October."

I knew I should let it go right then and there. I'd just found out Lana had been cheating on me, yet here I was, trying to find a way to jump start a new relationship.

"To where?" I asked.

"It's between Denver and D.C."

"Well, D.C. isn't that far."

"But Denver's across the country."

"But if it's D.C. we can make it work."

"And if it's Denver, we've both wasted a month of our lives."

I nodded and said nothing.

"You're just getting out of a relationship and I'm going through a messy divorce. And we've only just met, Mitch."

I reached for her hand. "So why'd you come out here?"

She bit her lip and shook her head. "I don't know. I..."

"You...?"

"I just wanted to see. Away from the madness, you know?"

I nodded. "And did you see what you wanted?"

"I saw that you're every bit the great guy I thought. And if things were different, then maybe..."

"I know," I said. "I know."

Bridget leaned forward to kiss me. I pulled back. "Maybe you should go to your cabin."

"Is that what you want?" The way she looked at me, leveled me.

"No. But I think that would be for the best. For tonight, at least. Let's sleep on this and talk tomorrow."

She kissed my cheek and then slipped off the porch and into the darkness. I waited until I heard the sound of her cabin door close, then I went inside. After the combination of sun, fresh air, fishing and beer, it didn't take me long to fall asleep. Normally I'd lay there for a half-hour. Not tonight.

I woke up at five-thirty in the morning. The cabin had a small four-cup coffee maker and sealed packages of Folgers. I took a fresh brewed cup onto the porch. The sun had started to rise over the east end of the lake, painting the sky red and pink. High wispy clouds looked like strokes from a paintbrush.

I stepped off the porch and walked toward Bridget's cabin. The shades were up and her car was gone. I peered through the front window and saw that the bed was made. There was no luggage visible. I wondered if she stayed through the night or left after I went inside. In a way, I was glad she'd taken off. Too many questions there. And if she did get the transfer to Denver, what was the point? Neither of us was in a position for a long distance relationship built on one month, post-betrayal.

I finished my coffee and went inside my cabin for a refill. My cell indicated there was an unread text message from Bridget. It said, "Sorry. I've been reinstated. I... Sorry." I nodded and tucked the phone in my pocket without responding. It wouldn't do any good.

Ella came out of her room at that time. We dressed and then got in the car and found a place down the street open for breakfast. They had all you can eat pancakes for five dollars. Neither of us could resist. Ella could put away some pancakes. I had to tell the waitress not to let her size fool the woman.

Halfway through the meal, my cell rang. I didn't bother to look at it. At least, not until the third call. I pulled it out a second too late. All three calls had come from Bridget. I figured I'd hear from her sooner or later, calling to offer an explanation. Part of me didn't buy the whole reinstated excuse. But this was what you might call overboard.

It rang again. I looked from the phone to Ella, smiled, and said, "I need to take this sweetie."

She wiped orange juice off her upper lip with the back of her hand. "Okay, Daddy."

I rose and walked through the front door, stopping where I had a clear view of the booth Ella and I sat at. I had expected to hear a soft hello, followed by an apology and maybe even a request to give this another try when I got home.

I got nothing of the sort.

CHAPTER FORTY

Bridget's voice was higher than normal. She spoke at breakneck speed. "Get back here now, Mitch. We need you here. If you could be here five minutes ago, that would be best. Something's happened with the case."

"Hold on a minute," I said, confused about what was going on. "What are you talking about? I'm suspended. A month without pay. Remember? I'm not going anywhere." In truth, I was ready to hop in the Boss and do one-ten all the way back to Philly if necessary.

"Mitch, there's no time for that bureaucratic nonsense. Get back here now."

"Am I reinstated?"

"No clue. And I don't care. This is my call and I'll take the fall for it if need be."

"Bridget, you're not making much sense. Let me rephrase that. You're not making any sense."

"I know. Neither did they when they called me last night after you went to bed. But they told me pretty much what I just told you."

Ella watched me from inside the restaurant. She grinned and waved while stuffing a forkful of pancakes in her mouth. I waved back, forcing myself to smile at her. "I need some information, Bridget."

"There's no time."

"Does Huff know about this? The Chief? Hell, the Mayor?"

Bridget said, "Let me put it this way. Everyone who needs to know, knows."

"Everyone except me, yet you're on the phone freaking out and saying I need to be there now. Why?"

"Dammit, Mitch. We're wasting time."

"And we'll continue to waste it until you give me some idea of what is going on."

"We received the ransom demand."

I knocked on the window loud enough that everyone inside the restaurant turned and looked up at me. I didn't care about them. I waved and gestured for Ella to come outside. She got up. I headed toward the door, fishing in my pocket for my wallet. I pulled out a fifty and handed it to the hostess. Ella grabbed my hand.

"What's wrong, Daddy?"

I didn't answer her. I ushered her toward the car.

Bridget said, "There's more, Mitch."

"What is it?" I said, settling in behind the wheel.

"They want you to make the drop."

"Me? Why?"

"They didn't say."

"Where?"

"We don't know. They're calling back in ninety minutes. They said you better be here, or they'll kill the Walker girl."

They'd taken two kids in broad daylight, and then murdered

the school principal. I had no reason to doubt that they'd carry out their end of the ultimatum.

"Okay, listen to me, Bridget. You get a state trooper or two, or some county cops, I don't care which. You get them to meet me at the campground entrance to give me an escort back to the city. We can make it, but we'll have to tear up the road."

She agreed and we hung up. I pulled out of the lot and raced back to the campground. The Boss slid in the gravel, coming to a stop a foot from Terrence's store. He came running outside. When he saw the look on my face, he said, "What's wrong, Mitch?"

"Terrence, I need for you to watch over Ella for me for a day or two."

"I don't want to stay here, Daddy," Ella said. "I want to go with you."

"Baby," I said, "Daddy needs to go back to Philly and take care of something. Grandma's away visiting her sister and Lana is in the hospital." I had to force Lana's name out of my mouth. "My friend Terrence can take care of you. I'll be back in a couple days. I promise."

I knelt down and she wrapped her arms around my neck. I rose and carried her inside. Terrence waited in the doorway.

"Is she in danger?" he asked.

"I hope not, Terrence. But I know you can take care of her. Keep her out of sight. If anyone shows up, you call me right away. I'll try to get someone out here to help out."

"I got all the help I need behind that counter." He gestured toward the rifle on the wall. "And there's more underneath. You don't have to worry about her safety."

I nodded, squeezed his shoulder, and then left. At the campground entrance, two state troopers waited for me. We hit the highway, lights and sirens blaring, and did close to one-twenty for most of the ride.

They passed me off to a couple squad cars when we entered

city limits. I expected them to lead me to the station. They didn't. Fifteen minutes later we pulled into an upscale residential neighborhood. Not the kind of place millionaires would live, but then again, the boy's family had new money and they hadn't decided what to do with it yet. I picked out their house right away. Three dark sedans and four unmarked police cars were parked out front. I figured the case wrangling hadn't resolved itself yet. Inside, I'd face the Feds, Major Crimes, maybe even the Chief himself.

I got out of the Boss and glanced down at my watch. Made it with ten minutes to spare. The front door opened and Bridget Dinapoli stepped out. Her hair was pulled back. Sunglasses perched atop her head. She had on dark pants and a blue shirt with the FBI shield on front. She walked over, stopping a few feet away.

"Detective."

"Special Agent."

We stared at each other for a moment.

"It's a good thing you were able to make it in time."

I nodded. "What are their demands?"

"We don't know yet. Only thing they said was you had to be here for this call."

I nodded toward the house. "What's the scene like in there?"

"They reinstated me, and we pulled rank. This case belongs to the FBI now. Townsend and his guys are being pricks. Cooperative pricks, I suppose. He tried to get the Chief involved, but it did them no good. For now, at least, I'm running the show."

"Vinson and Braden in there?"

"They are."

"Sam?"

She shook her head. I made a mental note to try to get him involved after we spoke to the kidnappers.

"How are the parents holding up?" I asked.

"As well as you would expect. Wife's a mess. Husband blames himself."

"Why?"

She shrugged. "Wouldn't you?"

"Probably." I glanced around at the other houses. Folks lined up on their porches and huddled together in a couple of driveways, studying the scene. "Am I reinstated?"

"It doesn't matter, Mitch. If these guys say you have to be around, then you have to be around. If your Chief wants to take on my boss, let him. He'll get his ass handed to him on a plate."

We both looked toward the front door as it opened. Vinson stepped outside and pointed to his watch.

Bridget lifted an eyebrow and said, "Let's go, Mitch. We're expecting a call."

CHAPTER FORTY-ONE

The Hollands's home smelled heavily of vanilla cream. It seemed every room had a candle burning. Maybe they had intended it as a vigil. Keep 'em burning until our boy comes home. It made me want to sneeze, but I managed to stifle the urge out of respect.

Mr. and Mrs. Holland huddled close together on the far side of a round kitchen table. A large uncovered bay window gave me a view of the backyard. The grass was neatly manicured. There were no trees. I noticed a dog run at the far right. Across from it stood a wooden play set.

A phone had been placed in the middle of the granite tabletop. The mother had tears in her eyes. So did the father. I couldn't imagine the mixture of dread and anticipation they felt at that moment.

Bridget walked into the kitchen and took a seat at the table. I followed her through and stopped while she introduced me. I nodded and said nothing to the Hollands. Until that call came in, there was nothing to say. I didn't know my place in the unfolding events.

Apparently, neither did Townsend. He leaned in to me and whispered, "For the record, I'm one hundred percent against this. If it turns out you botch this, I'm going to recommend they kick you off the force."

"For the record, Townsend, I don't give a fuck."

When I looked back at the table, all eyes were on me. Mrs. Holland's mouth hung open. Her husband shook his head. So did Bridget.

"Sorry, folks," I said.

The phone rang. All eyes stared at the center of the table. Everyone forgot about my outburst. Bridget nodded toward Mr. Holland, then she answered the phone by pressing the speaker button.

"Hello," a voice said. It sounded like Roy Miller-Michael Lipsky, but more confident than I'd ever heard him. It lent a bit more credence to the argument that he'd played Sam and me.

"What do you want from us?" Mr. Holland asked. "Whatever you want, we'll do it. Just give us back our boy."

Mrs. Holland sobbed heavily. Her husband wrapped his arm around her. His thick jaw muscles clenched tight. He was a large man, well built. His wife looked tall as well. The pictures I'd seen of Bernard indicated that he was what you might call a runt. Due to all the health issues, I supposed.

"Ten million dollars," the man on the phone said.

"T-t-ten million?" Mr. Holland said.

"We both know you have it," the man said.

"By when?" Bridget said.

"Who is this?"

"Special Agent Dinapoli."

"Hello Special Agent. Is Detective Tanner there?"

She looked up at me and nodded.

"I'm here, Roy" I said.

"Ten million dollars, noon, Lincoln Memorial. And Detective Tanner, don't you ever call me Roy again. Got it?"

"That's only two hours from now," Bridget said, not allowing time for me to respond.

"I know," the man said.

"I can't get that kind of money together in two hours," Mr. Holland said.

"You can, and you will. Because if Detective Tanner isn't at the Lincoln Memorial by noon with a bag filled with ten million dollars, I'll start chopping digits off of this little boy. One finger per hour. Don't comply within ten hours, then he loses a hand. Then the other. Then we begin with the toes. In twenty-four hours he'll have no hands or feet. I guess I could be nice and bypass cutting the fingers and toes off, but what fun would that be?"

Mr. Holland shouted, "If I get my hands on you I'll rip your head off your shoulders."

The guy didn't hear it, though. He'd already hung up. Dial tone filled the air. Bridget ended the call. The phone rang again a few seconds later.

"Does everyone there understand?" the guy said.

"We've got it," Bridget said.

"Good. Now, Detective, I'll see you at noon. You had better be unarmed and alone, or you and the boy will pay."

The line went dead again. The room remained silent for a few seconds. I glanced down at my watch.

"We'd better get going if we're going to make it in time."

Bridget rose. "Travel by car is too risky. I-95 is a mess all times of the day. We might not make it in two hours."

"What do you suggest?"

She pulled out her phone. "Helicopter."

The Feds went into action, the three of them focusing on separate tasks. Bridget arranged for the helicopter and transportation for me once we landed. Vinson arranged for the ten million to be made available and waiting for us when the chopper landed. Braden got on the phone with the D.C. branch and set up a secure perimeter. The Hollands didn't want this last thing. They felt that the FBI was taking a risk with their son's life. In between calls, Bridget assured them it was only to make sure everything went smoothly. They'd only move in if something were to happen to me. When she told them that Bernard would be safer with them around, they relented.

I hated helicopters. Took a ride in one on my honeymoon and hadn't been near one since. It wasn't flying. Planes I could handle. Helicopters just gave me the shakes. I placed them right up there with snakes and spiders.

"You okay, Mitch?" Bridget said.

I nodded. "Yeah, I'll be all right."

"Remember, you're doing this for the kid."

"It's not that."

"What is it?"

She'd think I was a coward if I told her. I shook my head. "Nothing."

"All right, then. The chopper will be here in a couple minutes."

"Here?"

"Yup. Going to land right down the street. We'll be in D.C. in forty-five minutes."

"We?"

"I'm going with you. At least until we land. You'll be on your own after that."

"Unarmed and alone."

She gave me a thin smile. I wanted to lean in and kiss her. The look she gave me told me that she wanted the same. We stood there for a moment, forgetting the reality of the situation.

"I don't know if we'll have the money in time," Vinson said.

Bridget's eyes flicked back and forth, then she turned around.

"Then we do whatever it takes to get it. I don't care if the FBI has to break open the vault. The Hollands have the money. It's their money. Securing it should not be a problem. Get someone on the phone and let me talk to them."

I left the kitchen and walked through the house to the front door. Townsend and his guys stood in the driveway. They glanced my way when I stepped outside.

"How's it feel?" I asked.

"How's what feel?"

"Having your case pulled out from underneath you?"

"Eat me, Tanner," Townsend said. "You might as well extend this little ride as long as you can, 'cause as soon as this is over, so's your career. The Chief is gonna bust your ass down to the Philadelphia Parking Authority. Hell, that might be too good for you. You ought to be mopping up the floors in a triple-X theater."

"I don't need to see any more footage of your wife, Townsend."

The guy smiled at me, then took a swing. I started boxing at the age of ten. To this day I still sparred monthly. Now, Townsend was fast for an old guy, but not fast enough. I dodged his wide right hook and drove my fist into his solar plexus. He bowed over and fell to his knees.

"Anyone else want some of this?" I said.

His guys shook their heads, then moved to Townsend's side to help him to his feet.

"What happened here?"

I looked back and saw Bridget approaching. "I think he had a bad sausage or something."

She nodded while looking at me out of the corner of her eye. Then she turned her head and pointed. "There's our ride."

The helicopter approached, growing larger by the second. It landed down the street in the middle of a wide oval court. I followed Bridget to her car. She started it, threw it into drive and pressed the accelerator to the floor. We covered the short distance in a couple seconds. The tires squealed as she slammed on the brakes. Bridget threw open her door and jumped out of the car a second after she put it in park. She'd left it running in the middle of the street. I didn't bother to pull the keys out.

I caught up to her and shouted, "Who else is coming?"

She shook her head. "Just us."

"His parents aren't going?"

"Another chopper's coming for them."

CHAPTER FORTY-TWO

It was too loud to talk inside the helicopter, so I spent most of my time staring out the window at the expanse of forest below. Occasionally, Bridget and I would look at each other at the same time. While our voices couldn't be heard, our eyes said plenty to one another. If things went well today, perhaps we'd have the chance to explore each other the remainder of the month. Maybe with some persuading, she'd agree. At the same time, I had a feeling today might be the last time we ever saw each other.

Forty-two minutes after we left the Hollands's neighborhood, we entered D.C. airspace. Three minutes after that, we set down at the Pentagon on a helicopter landing pad just north of the main building. I wanted to check a news site on my cell phone to find out if hell had actually froze over.

Once we were far enough away from the helicopter that I didn't have to yell to be heard, I asked her, "Why not the FBI building? Wouldn't that have been closer?"

She looked over at me and nodded, never breaking stride.

"And if they're watching it, they would have seen us. Chances of them watching the Pentagon are slimmer."

"Where are we going now?"

She pointed across Washington Blvd. toward Arlington National Cemetery. "Come on, we need to hurry."

I glanced at my watch. We had over an hour for me to get the money and then get to the Lincoln Memorial. If memory served me right, that was only a half-mile away.

We waited a moment for traffic to pass. Bridget's hand grazed past mine. My head turned toward her. She was already looking at me.

"Promise you'll buy me a drink after all this is over, Mitch."

I nodded. "Promise."

She grabbed my hand and stepped into the street. We jogged across, left the road behind and hopped a fence. To the left were a couple maintenance or facility buildings. A dark sedan was parked there. A man I didn't recognize leaned against the back of it.

"You got it?" Bridget asked the guy. She didn't introduce us.

The man nodded, turned and opened the trunk. He pulled out a dark bag and unzipped it.

"So that's what ten million in cash looks like," I said.

The guy said nothing. He handed the bag to Bridget, then left us.

"Why'd we have to come over here for this?" I asked.

"For the family," she said. "Felt it best that you not have to see them before this goes down."

"Why?"

"Heroics." She glanced over at the rows of white tombstones. Her eyes watered over. At first, I thought it might be the wind, but it blew against the backs of our heads.

"What is it?" I asked.

"I like to think that my dad's out there."

"Was he military?"

"My grandmother said he was a Navy SEAL. Killed in action."

"You ever meet him?"

She shook her head. "Never."

"Perhaps he is out there," I said. "He'd sure be proud of you today."

She looked up and smiled. "Thanks, Mitch." She stared at me for a long minute until the engine of the sedan behind her started. "Okay, let's get you on your way."

We walked back the way we came, crossing the street together. There, we split up. She headed toward the Pentagon entrance. I headed north toward the Arlington Memorial Bridge. All in all, it wasn't a bad day to be out for a walk. If you forgot about the whole kidnapping and ransom thing, it'd be a good way to clear your head. Only problem with that was I couldn't easily forget.

After crossing the bridge, I stood behind the Lincoln Memorial. I checked my watch. Still had about thirty minutes until it was time to make the exchange. So I walked around the circle, then up and down the length of the reflecting pool. The crowd wasn't too thick, but I expected that to change over the next half hour as lunchtime drew near. Worked out better for the bad guys this way. Maybe me, too, depending on how they planned to work the release of the boy.

I stood at the edge of the reflecting pool with the water behind me, watching old Abe. The President loomed large, sitting in his chair, watching over his small section of D.C. I wondered what he'd think of this situation. What would he do? Could he exercise the restraint that I'd be forced to use in the very near future? Standing face to face with a killer and a child abductor, could Lincoln hand over ten million dollars in exchange for a life, knowing that he might never catch the men responsible?

It didn't matter what Lincoln would do. I was the one who had to shovel that crow.

My trained eyes scanned the faces in the crowd. There were at least four classes of kids on a field trip milling about in addition to the regular tourists making their pilgrimage to the nation's capital.

My cell phone buzzed in my pocket. I glanced around to make sure no one watched me. Then I looked at the message from Bridget.

Don't forget, you owe me a drink.

I figured that was her not so subtle way of telling me to keep my cool. Don't do anything stupid. Don't play hero. Hand over the money, collect the kid.

I glanced at my watch. Five minutes to go. I cut through the thickening crowd and started up the stairs to the memorial. I reached the top and stopped in front of giant Abe.

"Tanner," a voice called out.

I looked to my right. Roy Miller-Michael Lipsky stood at the end of the platform, leaning against the last column. I glanced over my shoulder, then down the stairs. No one caught my eye. I didn't expect anyone to. These guys hadn't gone through all this trouble only to blow it by all showing up at the same place. But I didn't see the kid, either. And that was a problem.

I held the bag tight in both hands as I approached. The guy pushed off the column and took a few steps toward me.

"That the money?" he asked.

I nodded. "Where's the kid?"

"Hand over the money."

"Not until I see the kid."

"You don't hand that money over, both kids die."

CHAPTER FORTY-THREE

I was faced with a terrible decision that only had three options as I saw it. One, back away with the money and potentially seal Bernard's and the girl's fate. Two, step forward and attack Roy Miller-Michael Lipsky. I liked this option. A lot. I wished I had done it a few days earlier. The problem with it now was that it would also seal young Bernard and the girl's fate. The last option involved me handing over ten million dollars and depending on a kidnapping murderer to honor his end of the deal.

"I see you're having trouble with this," he said, reaching into his pocket. "Let me help."

My first instinct was to reach for my pistol, only I had left it behind with Bridget. It turned out he wasn't reaching for a weapon. Instead, he pulled out a cell phone and placed a call, putting the phone on speaker, for my benefit I presumed.

"Yeah, you got the money?" I figured the guy talking on the other end of the line was Brad McCree.

"I'm here with the good detective right now," Roy-Michael said.

"Detective, can you hear me?" McCree asked.

"I hear you," I said.

"Hand over the money, if you haven't already, and allow Mr. Lipsky to leave untouched and unharmed. He's going to remain on the phone with me, updating me with his every movement and every single thing he sees and hears. If at any time he shouts out in pain, or if the line should go dead, the child dies. Then the other child dies. Then maybe your child dies. Do you understand?"

"You leave my child out of this!"

"Do you understand, Detective?" McCree's voice rose in anger.

I understood lots of things. How someone could do such a thing, that was beyond me. But I had to play my part. The time to put these guys away wasn't now. This was the time to rescue the kids. Forcing myself to cast my anger aside, I said, "I understand." Then I dropped the bag next to my feet and took a few steps back.

Roy Miller-Michael Lipsky squatted down, keeping his gaze fixed on me, and grabbed the bag. He rose and said, "Got it," while taking it off speaker. He winked at me as he passed. "Nice working with you detective."

"What about the kid?" I said, taking a step back and blocking his path.

He leaned to the side, his smile widening. He held out the phone for me. I reached for it and he pulled back, shaking his head. "Put your ear to the speaker."

"Detective," the other man said. "In one hour we will call the Hollands's house phone with the location of their son. I want to speak only with Mr. or Mrs. Holland. Understand? If anyone else answers, the boy will never be found. You can take that any way you want. Goodbye, Detective."

My brain dumped every other thought as it processed what McCree had just told me. It must've shown on my face, because Roy-Michael laughed at me as he backed away.

The Hollands weren't at their home. They'd left in a helicopter right after Bridget and me. They were here, at the Pentagon, unless the FBI had moved them to the J. Edgar Hoover Building. I had to find out and warn Bridget. I pulled out my phone and called her.

"Get them back to Philly," I said after she answered.

"What? Mitch, did you make the exchange?"

"I thought you guys were watching?"

"We have agents watching, but no one has reported in yet."

"The money's been handed over, but the boy is elsewhere."

"You gave them the money without the kid?"

"They threatened to kill him, and the girl, and Ella."

"Okay, okay, we can make this work." Bridget paused for a few seconds, during which time I glanced around and noticed what looked like an FBI agent approaching me. "What else did they say?"

"Guy on the phone said he'd call the Holland's house in one hour with the location of Bernard. Said if he didn't speak with either of them, we'll never find the kid."

"This isn't good, Mitch."

I started walking east. "What isn't?"

"They just left in a car."

"The Hollands?"

"Yes."

"Well, get them back."

"I have to get off the phone with you to do that."

"Okay." I pulled the phone away from my head. "Wait, where are you?"

"Hoover Building."

"What's the fastest way there?"

"Down the lawn, cut across the Ellipse between the White House and Washington Memorial, then east on Pennsylvania Avenue."

I hung up, pushed my way through the crowd and began to run. I estimated I had a mile to go, give or take. I figured that by the time I reached the Hoover Building, the Hollands would be in the air and the next helicopter would be ready to go. I hoped they'd be, at least.

I ran straight down the middle of Pennsylvania Avenue, ignoring the stares, gestures and honking cars. A man in a dark suit stood on the corner of 10th and Pennsylvania. When he saw me, he started waving his arms.

"This way, Detective."

He led me inside the Hoover Building. We bypassed security, and then took an express elevator to the roof. I heard the thumping of a helicopter's rotors and the whine of its turbine before I saw the contraption. As I rounded the small elevator room, I saw Bridget standing between me and the chopper.

"Did they get off yet?" I asked after jogging to her position.

"They left five minutes ago."

I glanced at my watch. We were cutting it close. No chance Bridget and I would make it on time. I had serious doubts the Hollands would, either.

"Can we forward their phone to a cell?" I asked.

Bridget nodded, then shook her head. "They'll know, Mitch. You were just inside a helicopter. Can't hardly think, let alone talk."

She was right. We were screwed. The kids were in immediate danger.

"Come on, Mitch." She grabbed my hand and pulled me toward the helicopter. We sat down, placing the headgear over our ears. Bridget instructed the pilot to get us there as fast as possible, emphasizing that this was a life or death situation.

Now, off the top of my head, I had no idea how to estimate the speed at which the helicopter traveled. When I glanced at my watch, I saw the return trip took seven minutes less than our flight to D.C. Presumably, that meant we flew pretty fast. We'd made it back before the call was due to come in, which meant the Hollands had as well. Bridget's car still idled in the middle of the street. I half-expected to see a parking ticket plastered to the wind-shield. There wasn't one. We both got inside as the helicopter lifted into the air. Bridget circled around in the space the chopper had occupied. A few seconds and four squealing tires later we were in front of the Hollands's house.

"Bridget," I said moments after we exited the car.

She glanced over her shoulder. "Yeah?"

"I had no choice. I couldn't risk the lives of those children. These men are killers. They'd stop at nothing to—"

"I know, Mitch."

"I mean it. They threatened the boy, and the girl, and then Ella. I can't lose her, Bridget. She's all I got left."

Bridget turned and stepped closer to me. She placed a hand on my chest. Our eyes, our lips were inches apart. Her hot breath washed over my skin. "You did nothing wrong, Mitch. This doesn't end until we find these guys. Regardless of what happens, today was just one more piece in the puzzle. And none of it is your fault. Okay?"

"Okay," I said.

We entered the house. It was silent except for the ticking of an antique grandfather clock. I followed Bridget to the kitchen where Mr. and Mrs. Holland had resumed their positions at the kitchen table. Her eyes were wet. He smiled at me and then looked away. The anticipation in the room was thick enough that you had to wade through it. No matter what happened in the next few minutes, their ordeal wouldn't be over. Whether they found their son or not, this nightmare would be relived for years to come.

The phone rang and nearly everyone in the room jumped.

"It's 'go' time," Bridget said, reaching for the speaker button.

Mr. Holland leaned forward and said, "Where's our son?"

"What? No hello or how you doing? You're not even going to ask how I plan on spending your money?" Brad McCree said.

"Hello, how are you, would you like for me to pay for you to go to a ballgame? Take 'em all, sir. Now tell me where my son is!" Mr. Holland hovered over the phone and had to be restrained by Bridget.

The man on the other end laughed. "Is Detective Tanner there?"

"I'm here," I said.

"Detective, you had a chance to prevent all this. Did you know that?"

I took a step forward, placed both hands on the table and leaned over. "Not sure what you mean."

"My partner had cold feet. See, an unfortunate incident occurred in his home last week. His darling Dusty Anne discovered our plans. She threatened to go to the police. Michael said she wouldn't, but I had my doubts. Frankly, I had them about her from the beginning. She didn't know Michael, not the way I did. She knew Roy Miller and the lies that surrounded him. Anyway, he kept her from leaving while I raced over. Together, we shut that whore up." McCree paused. No one spoke up to fill the void. "That was your case, right, Detective?"

I glanced around the table. My stare met Mrs. Holland's and remained there. "I was assigned to the investigation of the death of Dusty Anne Miller. That is correct."

"And what happened on Friday night, Detective?" McCree asked.

"I went back to ask Roy Miller, or Michael Lipsky as we know him now, a few more questions. On the way out, I noticed some blood on the hedges that wrapped around the porch. He'd followed me out, stood in front of the door. I guess he knew what I saw. When I turned, he'd bolted. I followed him through the house, the backyard, a few more yards. He ran inside an old abandoned water tower. I chased him up to the top."

"And he threatened to kill himself, didn't he, Detective?"

I felt Mr. Holland's stare burning a hole through me. Tears

dripped off his wife's chin, their tracks staining her cheeks. "He climbed over the railing, but I had no idea if the intent was to jump or to get me to back off. I had no intentions of allowing him the easy way out, not after he murdered his wife."

"He was scared, Detective. And angry and depressed. He'd just lost his wife. I'm sure you can relate."

I didn't reply. McCree had done his homework on me and was trying to get me to bite.

"And he had cold feet about what we were going to do," McCree said. "I firmly believe that he left the evidence out there for his wife to find."

"What's this got to do with the boy, McCree?" I asked, tiring of the game he was playing.

"You can find the boy in the same place you found Michael that night, Detective. You'd better hurry, though. A child as weak as him, and with a broken arm nonetheless, no telling how much longer he can hold on."

CHAPTER FORTY-FOUR

I had the image of Bernard Holland, struggling to maintain his balance at the top of the water tower, burned into my brain. McCree's heavy breathing through the speaker was the only sound in the room. I grabbed Bridget by her wrist and dragged her out of the house. Behind us, I heard McCree start to laugh. He sounded exactly like his brother.

We exited the house with the Hollands right behind us. They bombarded me with questions. I tuned them out.

"Give me your keys," I said to Bridget.

"Where are we going?" she asked

"Just give me your keys," I said.

She pulled them from her pocket and tossed them to me. "Now will you tell me?"

"Get in the car." I stood outside the driver's side and pointed at the Hollands, who'd stopped halfway down the driveway. "You two coming with us?"

They didn't need to be asked twice. Mr. Holland opened the

rear passenger door and ushered his wife into the backseat. The car dipped to the right as he sat down behind Bridget.

"Where's the lights and sirens?" I asked, dropping the shifter from Park to Drive.

Bridget leaned over, reached across me and turned them on. "How far is this place?"

"About ten minutes or so. I'm going to get us there in less than five."

"What was all that about? On the phone?"

"Miller led me up that water tower and out onto this rickety walkway. I mean, it was decrepit. Every step I took, I thought it was one more step closer to my death. And not to mention, I hate heights."

"Hard to believe," she said.

"Right, anyway. The guy climbed over the railing, like he was about to jump. I pulled him back over. He landed on his head. That's how he ended up in the hospital."

"So this guy," Mr. Holland said, "could have taken his own life. Instead, you save him and he takes my son?"

"Sir, with all due respect, that was going down one way or another. Miller is nothing but a patsy. You heard the way the guy on the phone talked about him. I wouldn't be surprised if he turns on Miller and gives us his location after the money hits his hands."

Holland glared at me through the rear-view mirror. I ignored it and focused on the road. I was there to help them, dammit. At the same time, I understood their anger and frustration. How many times do we lament a lenient sentence handed out to a repeat offender and then have to watch as he returns to the street and kills? This situation had plenty of similarities. A few minutes later I slammed on the brakes and jerked the car into the water tower parking lot.

"Where is he?" Bridget said, getting out of the car.

"I don't see him," I said.

"He said he might not be able to hang on much longer." She started to run. "Please don't let him be on the ground."

I started after her when I heard a small voice. I shielded my eyes with my hands and looked up. "He's up there," I shouted. "Clutching to the rails."

Bridget met me at the door that led inside. "It's locked."

I kicked the door three times before the deadbolt snapped. Then I plowed into it with my shoulder, breaking the door from the frame. I took the stairs two at a time, full speed, until I reached the top. "Dammit," I shouted.

Bridget was a few paces behind me. "What is it?"

"Chain and padlock," I called back.

She appeared a few moments later with her gun drawn. "Stand back, Mitch."

Shooting a metal lock inside a building with corrugated steel walls wouldn't be considered the best idea. We didn't have the luxury of choice or time though. General fatigue could set in and cause the boy to lose his grip. A solid gust of wind could blow by and knock Bernard off the platform, sending him sailing to his death.

Bridget fired four rounds before declaring victory over the lock. She unhooked it from the chain and let it fall. A few seconds later it banged against the ground floor. The chain slithered through the door handle and an eye bolt on the wall. She pulled the door open. A heavy gust of wind blew inside. Bernard's cries for help rode the gust and echoed throughout the hollow building.

I stepped out ahead of Bridget, proceeding along the weathered planks with caution. "Don't move, Bernard."

He only glanced in my direction to acknowledge me. His skin looked ashen, his right arm grossly disfigured and dangling by his side. He wrapped his good one around the railing. If he slipped, it was sure to snap as well.

"Hurry, Mitch," Bridget said from behind me.

I glanced over my shoulder at her. Her face was drawn and pale. She nodded at me. I turned and pushed forward. Every fiber in my body told me to turn around and get off that deathtrap of a platform. I railed against it, repeating a simple mantra of *I will not allow myself to fail this child.* I kept going, and soon I stood behind Bernard. I reached out and placed my hands under his armpits. He didn't weigh much, and I easily lifted him and pulled him over the railing. Shifting Bernard in my arms, I pulled him close to my chest. He draped his broken arm across his stomach. I stepped back cautiously, until my shoulder blades touched the side of the building. He started to cry, and his teeth chattered uncontrollably. I could only imagine the harrowing situation he'd been through. And even then, I'm sure I hadn't scratched the surface.

I took one step after another, making sure I had secured my footing before moving on. Those fifteen feet might as well have been fifteen miles. The wind blew into me, threatening to knock me back and send both of us tumbling over the railing. Bridget stood at the door, holding it open and urging me forward.

I stopped moments after passing through the doorway. Bridget closed the door behind me. The wind rush faded, and the interior of the tower fell silent.

Bernard's cries quieted. Halfway down the stairs, he asked, "Have you found Debby?"

I didn't say anything.

"They took her away a couple days ago," he said.

Bridget glanced back at me. I wondered if she shared my fear that we'd never find Debby Walker. Deep inside, I had a feeling that the girl might already be dead.

"We're working on that, Bernard," I said.

"Bernie," he said.

"Okay, Bernie. We'll do everything we can for Debby."

When we reached the bottom, Bernard's parents were waiting for us. Behind them were two paramedics.

"He's got a broken arm," I said. "Mr. and Mrs. Holland, I know you want to wrap your son up in your arms, but he needs to be seen by those paramedics right there."

"That's fine," Mr. Holland said, ignoring what I said and taking his son from my arms. Who was I to stop him? He looked me in the eye and said, "Thank you, Detective. I mean that."

I shook my head. "Not me, sir."

They headed through the door. I watched them long enough to see the paramedics take over and then I collapsed on one of the bottom steps. My hands shook, and my stomach ached, and my chest tightened. I forced air in and out, inhaling deeply and exhaling loudly.

Bridget came over, stopping a few feet in front of me. "You okay?"

I glanced up, forcing a smile. "I'm fine."

"You sure?" Concern spread across her face as she knelt down.

"It's still not over," I said.

She nodded. "I know. We've got to find that girl." She rose, turned and took a few steps away. Then she returned, standing over me. "They'll slip up, you know. Sooner or later they'll spend a large chunk of that money, brag to someone, and then we'll find them."

"It was marked?"

"Of course."

I looked around the barren room. The place looked different with daylight filling it up. "A little risky, don't you think?"

"Maybe."

"This place looks different when it's dark."

She shrugged. She hadn't seen the inside of it before. Probably not the outside, either. "It's abandoned right?"

I nodded. "Yeah. Why?"

"All the rattling sounds. That's all."

"Old pipes, old steel," I said. "Trapped water and sludge. Humidity and temperature changes cause expanding and contracting. Same kind of thing you hear in old houses."

She nodded and said nothing as she stared up toward the top of the building. A tiny pinprick of light shone through at the top.

"What if the girl can't wait long enough for the guys to slip up?" I asked.

She looked away, shaking her head. "What other choice do we have, Mitch? We notify everyone we can and hope they show up somewhere."

I rose and reached for her hands. "What do you think about taking a trip to Savannah, Georgia with me?"

CHAPTER FORTY-FIVE

B ridget's eyes flicked back and forth, and she shook her head slightly. She must've thought I'd lost my mind asking her to go to Savannah.

"Before you answer," I said, "hear me out."

"Mitch, no," she said, turning toward the open doorway. "We've got to catch these guys and find the girl. I can't run off with you right now."

"Bridget, listen to me." I reached for her elbow. She stopped and turned. "There's a woman who lives down there we should go see."

"What woman? Why?"

"A few years back she helped Sam and me on a case we'd made little traction on. She... I don't know how else to put this other than saying she talks to the dead."

"What? Are you kidding me, Mitch?" She lifted her hands about shoulder height, palms out, and backed away from me.

I followed her through the doorway, pulling my sunglasses over my eyes to shield them from the sun. "I know it sounds crazy, but dammit, she led us right to the killer. Call it whatever you want, and believe me, I've wrestled with this over and over. But I was there. I saw it with my own two eyes, Bridget."

"How'd you find about this woman?"

"She came to me."

"She could have had advanced knowledge of the murder, Mitch. She could have known and acted only because her conscience got the best of her."

I shook my head. "I had her checked out. Talked to some of the detectives down in the Savannah PD. She'd helped on over a dozen cases."

Bridget looked toward the paramedics loading Bernard into the back of the ambulance. One jumped out and helped Mrs. Holland into the back. Vinson and Braden escorted Mr. Holland to their car. I presumed they'd take him to the hospital.

"Look, it can't hurt Bridget. Worst case, we lose six hours." I reached out and touched her elbow again. She pulled away. I added, "If we leave for the airport now, we'll be in the air maybe by two o'clock. That'll put us in Savannah no later than four."

"This is crazy. Six hours is a lot of time, Mitch."

"I know, but we're running on nothing right now. Not a single lead."

She glanced at me, then away. Her eyes rolled up like she was thinking. Finally, she said, "I can get us on a jet."

"No," I said forcefully. "Don't invite the Feds. I don't want them harassing this poor woman. She told me once she felt like a victim trapped inside a hell she can't escape. You let them know about her, and they'll be busting down her door looking for help."

"Not likely."

"Yes, likely. Once she produces results they can't deny, they'll be all over her."

Bridget stood there, staring past me and biting her bottom lip. I knew it sounded crazy. If she were the one telling me that we should do this, I'd have called her nuts and told her we'd be wasting time. The fact of the matter was that time was running out and we didn't have a single lead on the whereabouts of Debby Walker. If we didn't find the men, we'd never find her. While everyone else worked to track them down, maybe my Savannah contact could help us find Debby.

"Okay, Mitch. How can we do this without letting anyone know?"

I pulled out my cell and called Sam. He picked up after the second ring. "I need you to do me a favor."

"Anything. What do you need?"

"Cover for Bridget and me."

"Where are you going?"

I cleared my throat. Bridget watched closely. I turned away from her. "Savannah."

"Mitch, no."

"Sam, yes."

"Come on, that woman is crazy, man." Sam grunted a couple times and I heard a slapping sound, like he hit his steering wheel or the dash with an open hand. "She's certifiable."

"She led us right to that man, Sam. You can't deny that."

"No, I can't. But you can't tell me with one hundred percent certainty that she didn't have some kind of previous knowledge. She could have met a guy in a bar who confessed the whole thing to her and then she used it to her advantage. I mean, they give shows out to people like this now. Not fictional shows, that reality TV crap."

"He thinks you're crazy, too. Doesn't he?" Bridget said.

I waved her off. "Sam, we're doing this. Anyone asks, we're with you, but can't talk." I hung up and turned toward Bridget. "Let's go."

It took twenty minutes to reach Philadelphia International and another ten to park and get inside. Our badges got us to the front of the ticketing counter, and then through the security checkpoint. We had fifteen minutes from the time our boarding passes were printed to get to the gate. We made it in fourteen. The plane was only half-full. Bridget and I bypassed our seats and sat in the middle of a section of empty rows toward the rear of the craft. We spoke infrequently, usually after I tried to initiate conversation. I figured she thought I was a crazy person now. I didn't blame her. But the fact was, I considered myself one of the most sane people I knew. I didn't believe anything most would consider hokey.

Except for the woman in Savannah. I'd seen the results.

Eventually, I gave up trying to talk to Bridget and fell asleep. I awoke an hour later, during our final descent.

Before the plane had stopped, Bridget was up flashing her credentials to the stewardess. It worked and we departed before anyone else on the plane.

"I'm going to get us a car," I said. "See if you can scrounge up some coffee."

"Where from?"

Savannah Hilton Head International was a smaller airport with only fifteen gates. It looked like it had been recently upgraded. It had a southern feel to it. Almost like you'd stepped into a small town rather than an airport. "I figure in a small place like this, there might be a coffee pot sitting out for anyone to use."

Bridget disappeared on her quest for coffee, and I found a car rental counter. When the guy asked what kind of car I preferred, I told him one then ran. Made it easy on the guy. By the time I'd finished signing papers, Bridget returned with two cups of coffee.

The sweltering September air hit us with full force when we stepped outside. The humidity levels matched the temperature, which hovered in the low nineties. We walked to the rental car lot, where a compact Ford awaited.

"You know where we're going?" she asked.

I nodded.

"Been there before?"

"Once."

"And you still remember how to get there?" She looked at me out of the corner of her eye without turning her head all that much.

"Won't ever forget it."

She got in the car on the passenger side. When I opened the door and took a seat, she said, "Care to elaborate?"

"Nope."

And that ended the questioning. She didn't say another word until I slowed down and pulled to the curb in front of the house. We waited there for a minute, both staring at the small bungalow style home. The gray exterior was lined with red trim. There wasn't much of a front lawn, but the grass that did exist was deep green. Small Mediterranean style shrubs wrapped around the house.

"Huh. I figured a psychic would live in a creepy old house with boarded up windows and cobwebs on the front porch. Surely they have plenty of those down here."

Bridget opened her door, stepped out and walked toward the gate that crossed over the perfectly lined pavers leading to the front door. I joined her a moment later.

"She's not a psychic," I said. "She's a medium."

"Like there's a difference?"

"Apparently there is."

"Enlighten me."

"Google it."

Bridget jumped when the front door opened. I almost walked right into her. I glanced down and saw her hand hovering over her weapon.

"Detective Tanner," the woman said, stepping onto the porch. "What are you doing down here?"

"Hello, Cassie," I said to the woman. "This is Special Agent

Bridget Dinapoli of the FBI. We're working together trying to find a kidnapped child. Do you mind if we speak with you for a few minutes?"

Cassie stepped out of the shadows, crossing the porch and stopping in front of the top step. Her auburn hair reflected the sun. Her blue eyes looked pale. So did her skin, which poked out of her shorts and tank top, causing me to think she didn't get out much this summer. She studied Bridget for a few moments, then said, "Come on inside."

Bridget looked back at me. She seemed a little uneasy. I placed my hand on her shoulder and nodded for her to move forward.

Once inside the house, Cassie led us to the living room.

"Please excuse the mess. I haven't felt like cleaning much lately." She looked sad, distant.

I glanced around the room. There were a couple cat toys on the floor, and a magazine or two on the sofa. Other than that, the place was spotless aside from a fine layer of dust on the side tables and mantelpiece.

"You have a lovely home," Bridget said.

"Thank you."

I shot a look at Bridget. People in our profession didn't enter a house and say things like that. Cassie must have thrown her off her game.

"What about the child?" Cassie asked.

"Nine years old," I started. "Abducted along with another child from the school playground. Two men, one had remained in the car. They escaped and dropped out of sight for a few days. The reason for the abduction was—"

Cassie held up her hands. "No, don't tell me that."

"Okay," I said, trying to figure out where to go next. "We've got the boy back. The girl is still missing."

Bridget said, "Her name is—"

Cassie again threw up her hand. "No, not yet."

"Why not?" Bridget asked. "Don't you need it to contact her or whatever you do? We should have stopped by her house and brought a shirt or her favorite doll or something. Right?"

Cassie smiled at Bridget and then me. She leaned forward, placed her elbows on her knees, resting her chin on her hands. Her gaze traveled back to Bridget and remained there for two or three minutes. Bridget shifted around a few times. I could tell it made her uncomfortable. Cassie smiled, looked away, and let her eyes close slowly.

Bridget glanced over at me. I shrugged. I had no idea what Cassie was doing.

Finally, Cassie opened her eyes and straightened up. "It doesn't work that way, Bridget. I don't call in to anybody or have some spirit guide that follows me around. At least, not that I know of. I can't hold something of the child's, a doll or favorite piece of clothing, and see where she is. Honestly, I don't control this."

"Then how does this work?" Bridget looked intrigued, like she had started to believe that the woman could help us.

"They come to me." Cassie's gaze remained focused on Bridget, unblinking.

Bridget's tone and chin both dropped. "Who does?"

"The deceased. I give them a voice."

"So, you can only help us if she's dead? She'll come and tell you where her body is?"

"Sometimes."

"But I thought you said that they had to come to you?"

"Sometimes it is the victim. Other times it is a friend or family member. Once, it was a total stranger who had witnessed the events but had been too scared to speak up. At least, while alive."

"Right." Bridget slapped her hands on her knees and rose. "I'm sorry we wasted your," she glanced at me, "and our, time." She started toward the door.

"Please, don't go," Cassie said. "I know this makes no sense.

Trust me when I say I used to be the biggest skeptic there was. Even growing up in a place like Savannah, where there is no shortage of ghost stories, I never believed in any of that. I wasn't born like this, Bridget. I didn't ask for it. It just...happened." She glanced at me. The look in her eyes told me that she did not want to recount the story of how she received this gift. She'd told me once that it drained her to relive it. So I shook my head and gestured for her continue. "I understand what you're thinking. Even Detective Tanner has doubts I can really do this. He's only here because he's superstitious. You guys came here, and if anyone out there was watching, they might have followed. And if they did, they might approach me. And then I might be able to tell you something."

"Lots of mights in there, Cassie," Bridget said.

Cassie's lips parted, but she said nothing. I imagined that she was used to this level of skepticism.

"All right then," Bridget said, sitting down on the sofa next to Cassie. "Can you tell us where she is?"

CHAPTER FORTY-SIX

Debby's hands hurt. The muscles of her fingers were frozen in a death grip. The skin between her thumb and forefinger on each hand was split open and raw from broken blisters. Wooden splinters of every size stuck out of her palm and fingers. She pulled them out by pinching them between her fingernails or her teeth. Some splinters were buried so deep she couldn't get them out at all. She wondered if turning off the light would make the pain go away. Maybe the darkness would wash away her misery. It didn't. She flicked the flashlight back on and moved forward to inspect her progress.

A smile crossed her face as she realized that she'd broken through the wall. No light passed through the small hole. She stood within a few inches of it and shone her light. It appeared to be wide enough for her to maneuver around in there. All she had to do now was break through enough of the wall to allow her to slip through. She considered this for a moment. If she made the hole too big, then the man could get through it as well. His body looked frail. The trick would be creating a hole big enough for her, but too small for a less than normal sized man.

So long as they didn't have a dog with them, she figured she'd be safe back there even if the room behind the wall turned out to be nothing more than a few feet of space. It'd devastate her of course, but at least she'd go out on her own terms. And while Debby wasn't quite sure what that meant, it sounded better than being murdered.

Not knowing the time had been the worst part of the ordeal. She could handle being hungry and thirsty. But how could she expect to manage her food and water without knowing the time, let alone how many days she'd been trapped in the room? For this reason, she limited herself to half a slice of bread when the hunger grew too intense. Likewise, she'd only take two or three sips of water at a time. The first bottle neared being empty. She felt tempted to use the water to clean her wounds. She didn't, though. Wounds would heal. Once you died, that was it.

As she swished the water around the bottle, her thoughts turned to Beans. What had they done with him? Did they move her because they planned on killing him? She spent most of her time awake thinking about him. A few times she shut her eyes tight and did nothing but call out to him mentally. There hadn't been any response. Not yet, at least. She refused to give up hope.

Debby lifted the bottle to her lips and drained the remaining liquid. It went down warm and did little to squash her thirst. However, the water did dull the ache in her throat and helped get rid of that cotton feeling in her mouth. She set the empty bottle on the floor in the middle of the room. The thought of urinating into it had crossed her mind. Once, she'd stayed up and watched a show about a survivalist who'd done just that and later drank it to stay alive.

"Gross," she whispered, looking away from the empty plastic bottle. She held the little flashlight between her teeth and attempted to remove the remaining splinters from her hand. They gave her varying levels of pain as she pulled them free and tossed them on the floor. There were a few that remained buried, joining the other splinters she had been unable to remove. She hoped they would not fester and cause her skin to rot.

Debby rose, picked up the shovel and headed toward the back of the room. She went to work creating her freedom hole, as she'd dubbed it. The metal blade made a tiny clanking sound with every thrust into the wall. She aimed for a spot a couple inches below the hole she'd made. If she could create enough small holes, it'd be easier to break apart the remaining wall between them. She got the idea when she recalled the one time her brother had let her use his pellet gun. He taped a target to a large oak tree in their backyard. She stood a few feet away and fired off ten or so rounds. The ten shots had all hit pretty close to the center. He let her keep the target. When she pressed her finger against the area, the paper tore. Punching a hole through the wall would be as simple as tearing paper, she told herself.

It never crossed Debby's mind that she might be deluding herself. She didn't think that far ahead. Her focus remained on the next jab with the shovel and creating the next hole in the wall. And it happened, eventually. It might have been ten minutes, or maybe a hundred and ten. She had no way of knowing.

CHAPTER FORTY-SEVEN

Cassie remained silent for several seconds while her unfocused eyes gazed at a spot somewhere above my head. I wondered what went through her mind at that time. Did she try to force the image of the child? Could she do that? Did she plead for someone to appear before her and show her the way?

Did I really believe all that?

No, not really. I had a tendency to think things were simpler than that.

"I'm sorry," Cassie said. "There's nothing."

Bridget shot me an *I-told-you-so* look, turned her head and smiled at Cassie, and pushed off of the couch. "Thanks for your time, Cassie. Detective Tanner and I will be on our way now. Sorry to have bugged you."

Cassie didn't move, seemingly still caught between reality and wherever she had gone a few minutes ago. I caught her glance as I rose, but she looked away.

"Cassie," I said. "You call me if something pops up. Even if you don't think it means anything. I mean it. Okay?"

She nodded. "Yes, Detective Tanner. I have your number."

Bridget had rushed out of the house, brushing me with a stiff shoulder as she passed. By the time I reached the front door, she had slammed her car door shut. I knew coming to Savannah was a long shot, but we had little else to go on. Perhaps I should have left Bridget behind and come by myself. After all, her presence wasn't necessary here. I'd brought her along for selfish reasons, and it had the opposite of the intended effect. On top of that, I wondered if having her inside the house had left Cassie feeling uneasy and unable to perform.

I turned back toward Cassie. "Is there anything else I can do or tell you, Cassie?"

She rose from her seat and walked toward me, stopping a few feet away. A hint of lavender passed by me a moment later. She leaned against the wall, resting her head to the side. Her hair spilled down across her chest. She stared at me with intense burning eyes. "You can pray, Mitch. Pray for that little girl to get home safely."

I nodded, turned and stepped outside, glancing back a few times. I reached the car and took one last look back. She stood behind the front window, staring out at the street. I waved to her and she didn't respond in kind.

The inside of the car had to be over a hundred degrees. Bridget had been in there with the doors shut and the engine and air conditioning off. She refused to look at me as I slipped in behind the wheel. Her cheeks were flushed red. From the heat, or anger?

I started the engine. The air conditioning was set to max and blew on high. It took two or three minutes for the air that escaped the vents to cool to a bearable temperature. I used my thumb to wipe a sheen of sweat off my forehead.

"I'd just like to say that—"

"What, Mitch? That you wasted our time? That you risked my job by bringing me down here for some supposed psychic who told us absolutely nothing? God, what was I thinking agreeing to this? We're not getting these hours back. Every minute we're not out looking for that girl, or searching for those men, they get further away, and our chances of finding Debby Walker alive drop closer to zero."

"Medium," I said under my breath.

"What?" Her head whipped toward me. I didn't have to look at her to see the anger in her eyes.

"Cassie's not a psychic," I said in a hushed voice. "She's a medium."

Bridget groaned and rolled her eyes. I wasn't sure which was colder by that point, her or the air conditioning.

We didn't talk the rest of the way to the airport. I dropped her at the curb and then I continued on to the car rental check-in. I found Bridget inside. We stood side by side in line, but we might as well have been on opposite ends of the country. I purchased two tickets back to Philly. She requested a seat at least ten rows away from mine. I didn't protest. As far as I was concerned, our job was to do everything in our power to find that girl and bring her home alive. If Cassie had given us a viable lead, this trip would have paid itself back a million times over and Bridget would be proclaiming my status as a hero.

Before boarding, I called Sam and asked him to pick me up. I had the feeling that Bridget would want to be alone in her government-issued sedan. Once seated on the plane, I closed my eyes and dozed off, waking up every ten or fifteen minutes it seemed. It helped pass the time at least. Coming to the end of a particularly heavy sleep, I felt a presence and looked up. Bridget stood in the aisle. She gave me a thin smile and then plopped down next to me.

"I'm sorry," she said.

"No," I said, "I'm the one who should be apologizing. I could have made this trip alone."

She nodded while looking past me. "You were only trying to

help. To be honest, I don't discount the method. I've read case reports where those types of people were fairly accurate. If she would have given us just one thing we could go on, it would have been worthwhile." She paused and I said nothing. Bridget continued, "Chances are I would have been chasing my tail in circles back in Philly. I just wish..."

"I know, Bridget. Me, too." I reached out and grabbed her wrist as she rose. "You don't have to leave."

She freed herself from my grasp. Looking down at me from the aisle, she said, "Yes, I do."

She walked away, and I turned my attention to the view out the window. In between thick white clouds, I caught glimpses of thin blacktop roads and neighborhoods full of dot sized houses. I wondered if I'd ever run into Bridget again. It wasn't as if we had a long history together, no real relationship to speak of. We shared a connection, though, and I couldn't discount that.

The plane landed and the few passengers on board lined up to depart. Five people separated Bridget and me. Might as well have been five miles. She never once turned to look at me. As a group, we shuffled to the front of the plane, and then picked up the pace through the stifling hot jetway. Bridget practically jogged to the gate and through the terminal. I kept up with her for the first few minutes, weaving through the bi-directional foot traffic. Then, I stopped. I decided if she wanted to be alone, I'd let her. Nothing good would come out of me chasing after her and forcing the issue.

Sam met me outside. The sun hung deep in the west. It was hot, but the humidity had relented. That made it a little easier to breathe in the exhaust that plagued the area. Sam had my Chevy and had taken full liberties with it, double parking and blocking one of the traffic lanes. Every car that had to merge into the other lane had a driver or passenger who shot a scornful look in our direction.

I got in on the passenger side and adjusted the air vents so that the cold air blew toward my face. "Thanks for coming out, Sam."

"Did the trip result in anything positive?"

"Cassie couldn't help and Bridget hates me now."

"Zero for two."

"Feels more like zero for twenty."

"We got the boy back."

"But the girl is still missing, and the assholes that did this are still out there."

Sam nodded. We remained silent for a few minutes while he navigated toward the highway. As I watched the sun drop lower in the sky, I wondered about the fate of Debby Walker. Was the girl still alive? Would we ever see her? Why hadn't the kidnappers made demands for her return? Did they deem the risk of collecting a few thousand dollars in exchange for a poor white girl too high?

"Want to get a drink?" Sam asked.

"Yeah, but first I'd like to pick up my car. Is it still outside the Hollands's?"

CHAPTER FORTY-EIGHT

How long was long enough? Bridget asked herself that question every thirty seconds. She'd been inside the airport restroom for close to twenty minutes. Surely, Mitch would have left by then. Even if he hadn't, he'd be outside the building waiting for his ride, not hanging around the check-in counters. She couldn't wait too much longer. The flight she'd booked from her cell phone took off in a half-hour. If she missed that, there weren't any more flights to Savannah that day.

She pulled her hair back into a bun. He was less likely to notice her that way in a crowded space. She exited the bathroom, her chin tucked to her chest, and headed directly toward a self-check-in kiosk. Five minutes later a TSA agent scanned the boarding pass on her cell phone. Fifteen minutes after that, she was seated comfortably on the plane.

The drag of the day, and the week for that matter, caught up to Bridget, and she fell asleep shortly after takeoff. A patch of turbulence woke her, but only momentarily. She rose from her nap as they approached the runway. After departing the plane, she found her way to the rental car counter and secured a Taurus. At this point in the day it mattered little to her what she drove.

Bridget drove to Cassie's house, navigating from memory. She took a wrong turn along the way, but quickly recovered.

She pulled up to the curb and shifted the car into park. *What am I doing here?* It was a curious decision, made in a matter of seconds, to return to see Cassie. She couldn't think of a concrete reason why she returned. It was a feeling that gnawed at her throughout the flight back to Philadelphia.

Bridget waited until the sun sank below the horizon, then she opened her car door and stepped out. Her stomach and chest tightened as she stepped onto the walkway that led to the front door. She stopped and took a few deep breaths to steady herself. "Calm, calm, calm," she whispered after each exhale. Feeling in control, she continued on.

The door opened before she reached the first step. Cassie stood in the open doorway and smiled. "Bridget, please, come in."

Bridget climbed the steps and turned sideways to pass through the opening. The two women were eye to eye for a second. The way Cassie looked at her reminded her of the visit earlier that day, and she knew then that was the reason she had returned.

"I'm surprised to see you again," Cassie said from behind her.

"I was just—"

"In the area?"

Bridget stopped, turned and smiled. "Yeah, something like that."

"I was just sitting down to eat. Care to join me?"

"No, I'm okay." Bridget paused. Her stomach knotted at the mention of food. "On second thought, I'll have some."

"Right this way, then." Cassie led her away from the living room and into the kitchen. The table looked like something out of the 'fifties. The chairs were sparkling red vinyl, and the legs of the table were chrome.

"This original?"

Cassie nodded. "Belonged to my grandmother." She turned away, grabbed two plates from a cabinet and placed two slices of pizza on each. She set one plate down in front of Bridget and grabbed them each a bottle of water. "It's homemade, organic."

Bridget took a bite. The cheese burned her tongue and roof of her mouth. Despite that, she savored the taste. "Delicious."

They next five minutes was filled with awkward silence and even more awkward stares between the two women. They didn't speak until Bridget was halfway through her second slice.

"So what's this about?" Cassie said.

Bridget shrugged, unsure how to phrase it.

"If it's about me and Mitch, I can assure you there is nothing between us."

Bridget straightened up. "Why would I care about that?"

Cassie glanced up at the ceiling and then back at Bridget. "The tension was, shall we say, thick."

"Yeah, well, it wasn't the kind of tension you've got in mind."

"But it was at one point, right?" Cassie asked.

Bridget nodded. "Short lived. That's all."

"He's only trying to help the girl, Bridget. That's why he came down here."

Bridget said nothing. She bit into her crust and tore like a lioness shredding the meat of a wildebeest.

Cassie's eyes narrowed. "Touchy subject, I see. Look, you may not believe in me and what I do, but I can assure you I'm legit. This may or may not work out, I readily admit that. Regardless, I'll do everything I can, in the event that I am able to."

"Sounds like a politician's speech."

Cassie jerked back as if Bridget had just shot her.

"I'm sorry," Bridget said. She dropped the last bite of crust on her plate and wiped her hands and mouth with a paper towel.

"Look, I'm here because I can't get the image of you staring at me earlier today out of my head."

Cassie crossed her arms in front of her chest and shrugged.

Bridget leaned forward, placing her elbows on the table. "Why? Why were you staring at me like that? It wasn't like it was a brief look, Cassie. You just honed in on me and stayed that way for a few minutes."

Cassie took a deep breath, looked away, and said, "It was an old lady." She shifted her gaze toward Bridget. "Your grandmother. She said, 'tell her to stop trying to do everything.'" She looked away again. Her cheeks reddened.

"And you didn't tell me. Why?"

Cassie said nothing.

"You were jealous, weren't you? You have a thing for Mitch."

"That's absurd," Cassie said. "Not only that, it's completely unethical."

"Isn't not delivering a message to me unethical?"

"It wasn't what you were there for. Besides, the read I had on you at that time told me you wouldn't be able to handle it, or you'd accuse me of lying."

Bridget did not respond. She raised her eyebrows as she leaned back in her chair. She'd upset the woman, and while she felt justified, she also felt guilty for having done so.

"I'm sorry," Cassie said. "That was unprofessional."

Bridget shook her head. "It's okay. We all have our moments."

"Wine?" Cassie rose and walked to the counter.

"Sure."

Cassie uncorked a bottle of merlot and poured a glass for each of them. She set one in front of Bridget and then returned to her seat.

"I was twenty-four," she said.

"Pardon?" Bridget said.

"When I received this...*gift*."

Bridget nodded. "Go on."

"It was stupid, really. We had no business being there."

Bridget could tell this story would require a lot of assistance from her. "Being where? Cassie, just spit it all out. I'm used to people confessing."

"It's not a confession." Cassie leaned back, eyes narrow and arms across her chest.

"I didn't mean to offend you."

Cassie took a drink. "It's okay. This is uncomfortable for both of us. All right, I'll continue. A friend of a friend had an idea to break into a cemetery. You know ghosts and all that."

"*Midnight in the Garden of Good and Evil*," Bridget said. "I saw the movie."

"Book was better. Anyway, so, yeah, we didn't go to Bonaventure, but to Greenwich, which is an annex of Bonaventure and still open for public burials." She paused to take a sip from her wine glass. "So there's a group of five people and I'm tagging along. The only one I know is my friend Cara, and she's real into this guy who was leading the expedition. I started to feel a bit shunned and I kind of wandered off on my own with a flashlight, reading the different tombstones."

"Always a good time," Bridget said, forcing a smile.

"Right," Cassie said. "So, I come upon the grave of a woman who had died a few years earlier at exactly the same age I was then, twenty-four. I'm standing there, wondering how she died, was it an accident, cancer, when I recognize the name." She bit her bottom lip for a second. "Lucille Whitehurst. That ring any bells?"

Bridget shrugged and shook her head.

"She'd been brutally murdered, stabbed to death, then dismembered. Her body was left in pieces along the riverbank, not far from where her remains were eventually buried in the cemetery."

"Jesus," Bridget said softly.

"Right? That's what I'm thinking at the time. I get a hold of myself and turn to find my friend, but before I can take a step, someone has me in their grasp."

Bridget felt her pulse quicken. She had a feeling she knew where the story was going.

"It was a man. He whispered something in my ear. To this day, I'm not sure exactly what, but I think it was something along the lines of, 'What are you doing out of bed, Dear?' I tried to scream, but it was like my vocal chords were paralyzed. A second later he had one hand over my mouth and the other across my chest. I remember feeling terrified that he was going to rape me. Relief washed over me when he pulled his hand away from my chest. That was short lived, though."

Cassie's eyes drifted away and she went silent. Bridget watched as the woman focused on nothing.

"What happened next?" Bridget asked.

"It's funny, you know. To this day, I only remember the first time he stabbed me. They say he did it ten times, and I guess the scars corroborate that. At some point, I managed to scream. I guess that's why I wasn't stabbed forty times like Lucille was. After I yelled out, he dropped me on the ground. The flashlight had fallen and been kicked around. It shone at the headstone. The diffused light bounced back toward us. He hovered over me, blood on his hands and smeared across his face. His tangled, matted hair hung down. And he said to me, 'Now go back to sleep.' He took off and my friend and her friends showed up a few seconds later. I lost consciousness right after that. They say I died."

"Did you?"

"I never saw bright light at the end of a tunnel or heard harps playing or anything like that, but I did see a woman who appeared to be about my age. I say appeared, but it wasn't really like that. Hard to explain. She, I guess shimmered is the right word. Beams of light protruded from behind her. So maybe the light was beyond where she was, and she was blocking me from going to it? I don't know, and honestly, I try not to dwell on it."

"So they revived you, obviously. What happened next?"

"I woke up in the hospital a week later. They tell me it is a miracle I'm alive, and my recovery will take a few months, and I should seek counseling. I'm questioned and grilled. One of the cops had the audacity to ask what we were doing in the cemetery. Guess that's his job, but, whatever. I get out of the hospital and the first thing I want to do is go visit the grave. They had put police tape around it. I ducked under it and knelt in front of the spot where I'd been left to die. The ground was still dark with my blood. I pulled out a handful of the stained grass and put it in a plastic bag I had in my purse."

"You shouldn't have done that, Cassie. The police might need that for evidence."

Cassie held up a hand and smiled. "I'm aware of that now. I wasn't thinking in such terms then. Anyway, let me finish. I'm kneeling in front of this woman's grave, and I start to look around. I see this little boy. He's maybe six or seven years old. He's got on a green shirt and jean shorts. It's fifty degrees out, so that seems odd to me. I smile at him. He doesn't smile back. I get up and walked toward him. The closer I get, I can tell his face is dirty, and so are his clothes. I hear something off to my right. I turned to look, thinking maybe his parents were over there visiting a loved one buried in the cemetery. There's no one there, though. When I looked back, the boy was gone."

Bridget felt her pulse quicken again, and her chest started to tighten.

"I go home, tell my boyfriend at the time all about it. He's freaked out, but I laugh it off. We go to sleep. Remember, this is the first time I'd been home. I wake up in the middle of the night. I can feel the breeze coming in through the window, so I roll over toward it to cool off my face. And it hits me here," she pointed to her forehead, "and here," she pointed to her chest, "but not here. The middle of my face, nothing. I opened my eyes and saw the little boy, kneeling next to my bed, green shirt, jean shorts, and his dirty face inches away from mine."

Bridget thought about telling the woman she was crazy and storming out. She didn't, though.

"Turns out the little guy needed my help. I met Mitch for the first time a week later. He can tell you the rest of the story if he wants."

"Wow," Bridget said. "The guy who stabbed you, did they ever find him?"

Cassie nodded.

"And he killed the woman in the grave, right?"

"Very perceptive, Special Agent Dinapoli. He was deranged, obviously. I looked a lot like Lucille. He stated that every few months he went to her grave to check up on her. I just happened to be there at the wrong time."

Bridget glanced down at her watch. "Cassie, I'm sorry, I need to get going."

"I have an extra room. You can stay here."

"No offense, but I don't think I'd sleep all that well if I did." She rose and headed toward the front door.

Cassie got up and escorted her out. "I'm not going to give up on that little girl, Bridget. I promise."

Bridget looked back and nodded. "Neither am I."

"And don't give up on Mitch," Cassie added.

"I won't if you don't." With that, Bridget got inside the rental and drove two blocks away. She pulled up next to the curb and grabbed her cell phone. There were no flights back to Philadelphia that night. Best she could do was a flight plan with three layovers. It would get her home by eight the next morning. She decided to skip the flight and drive back. It would take less time. So she picked up I-95 and headed north.

CHAPTER FORTY-NINE

S am altered our course and drove to the Hollands's neighborhood. Media trucks clogged the entrance while a couple of uniformed officers kept them at bay. They were faces I didn't recognize, from another precinct I supposed. Sam pulled up to the checkpoint and we showed them our badges. They waved us through.

The neighborhood was eerily quiet. No kids out in their front yards taking advantage of the final minutes of daylight. The effects of a tragedy hitting so close to home, I thought.

We turned onto the Hollands's street. Two more officers were positioned on opposite sides of the intersection. The Boss remained where I'd parked it earlier that day. Sam stopped the Chevy behind it.

"Since the Chevy is officially your car, I guess I ought to take the Boss for you," Sam said.

I chuckled at the thought. "I'm suspended. Only authorized personnel can drive a city issued vehicle."

He cut the engine and we waited in silence for a few minutes. I figured the same thoughts I was having also raced through his mind. For us, this case wouldn't end until Debby was found and the men were brought to justice. The outlook, however, looked bleak. I feared that the case, and the little girl, would haunt me for the rest of my days.

"I'm going to go up to the house," I said.

"I'll join you," Sam said.

We exited the vehicle and trekked up the driveway. At the halfway point, the door opened. Mr. Holland's large frame blocked the opening. The lingering sunlight washed over him, giving his overall appearance a reddish tint.

"Detectives," he said with a nod, crossing his arms. He didn't appear threatening or intimidating. The man looked tired. Worn out by the whole ordeal. Who could blame him?

We stopped in front of the bottom step. "How's Bernard?" I asked.

"Physically, he's going to be okay. They set his arm and gave him a painkiller. Mentally, though? I don't know. He's pretty distraught, as are my wife and myself."

"I can imagine," I said. "We feel the same way."

"Do you?"

The emotional impact of the words felt like an uppercut to my chin. "Yes, sir, we do. I'm not going to rest until we have that girl safe and sound."

Mr. Holland straightened up and let his hands drop to his side. From the top of the stairs, he towered over us. "Then why'd you run off the other day? And then again today?"

Sam took a step up. "He was kicked off the case and his daughter was threatened. He took her away to get her out of harm's way. Would you have preferred another child be harmed?"

"Seems to me the best thing Detective Tanner could have done was stay around and offer to help."

"It doesn't work like that," Sam said. "And today, you know what he did? He went down to Savannah to look up another lead."

"Savannah?" Mr. Holland asked, unleashing his scowl toward me.

"And he did it on his own time," Sam added.

Mr. Holland shifted, turning sideways, and I caught a glimpse of Debby Walker's mother inside the house. She stood just outside of the kitchen with her gaze fixed in our direction. I wanted to push past the large man in front of me to speak to the woman. Her tears glinted in the light as they streamed down her cheeks. I deemed our presence as counterproductive.

"Sam," I said.

"He could have bailed on that little girl after getting your son home, but he didn't."

"Sam," I repeated.

"What?"

"We should go."

"Yes," Mr. Holland said. "You should."

I understood the anger, as misguided as it was. That didn't lessen the impact any further. While I didn't expect the Hollands to drop to their knees and bow before Sam and me, I didn't expect the mistreatment, either.

Sam stepped down and we both turned toward the street.

"Officers." The small voice came from behind Mr. Holland.

I spun around and saw Bernard peeking through the doorway.

"Yes, Bernard," I said.

"Have you found Debby?"

I glanced at Sam. His face grew grim. "Not yet, son."

"Please don't give up on her," he said. Such powerful words for a small child.

"We're going to do everything we can to bring her home," I said.

Mr. Holland reached down and placed his hand on top of his

son's head. The hardened look on his face faded and his eyes watered over. He felt his son's pain. I did, too.

Thirty minutes later Sam and I occupied a booth at Schmitty's. We'd dropped the Boss off at my place, after which I'd called to check on Ella. She'd already gone to bed, worn out from a day of boating and fishing, Terrence had said. He'd also told me that no one had been by. A relief to me. I figured I'd leave her there a few more days and pick her up once things seemed to have settled down. Now that the men had their ten million dollars, they had little use for me.

Sam raised his drink, took a sip and set the glass down. "What's next for you?"

"I figure I'll hang around for a couple days and see if Bridget calls with any leads."

"Think she will?"

"Find a lead? Yes. Call? No."

"Things didn't go so well down in Savannah I take it."

"You could say that."

"I did say that."

I nodded and said nothing.

"I'm going to do what I can to get involved with the case, Mitch. With you out, I don't have a partner, so I don't think they'll assign anything to me. Figure I can latch onto the investigation. Maybe I'll turn something up. If I do, you'll be the first person I'll call."

"Appreciate it. Now, Sam, do me a favor."

"What?"

"Stop talking about it."

We talked about sports and our hopes for the upcoming football season. I figured I'd get to catch a lot of games, being recently single and suspended. Although Lana and I hadn't talked, the breakup would occur soon.

Midnight rolled around and I decided to head home. A few

detectives we knew had joined us and one who remained sober promised to get Sam home safely. With the temperature in the sixties and the humidity about the same, I walked. The temperature had cooled enough and the humidity had dropped enough so that the mile and a half trek didn't result in me covered with sweat.

I stopped on the sidewalk across the street from my house. There was a car in the driveway. A woman on my porch.

Only it wasn't the woman I wanted to see.

CHAPTER FIFTY

I crossed the street and cut across the lawn toward the screened in porch, well aware that Lana watched my every step. She waited on the sofa next to the front door with her hands on her knees and her back straight. As I neared, the light caught her face and her eyes sparkled with tears. I pulled the door open. She wore a plain t-shirt and cutoff jean shorts, frayed white at the bottom. A cast extended from just below her left knee and covered her foot. Her bare toes poked out. Someone had painted her toenails pink or red. The light was too dim to tell.

"What are you doing here, Lana?"

"I hadn't heard from you. I wanted to see you."

I felt cold and distant. Was I really here with her on the porch? We'd shared many embraces in front of the door, sat up late into the night on that couch, talking about our pasts and the possible future. A future that had no chance of happening now.

"Mitch, what's wrong?"

I walked past her. She reached out. I avoided her hand.

"I'm going inside."

"Help me up?"

I glanced over my shoulder. Our gazes met. Her eyes were wide and wet. Her right arm extended toward me. I stepped inside and let the screen door slam shut behind me. I'd hoped she'd take the hint that I didn't want her around. She didn't, though, and a moment later the front door closed and she navigated down the hall, on crutches, toward me.

"You know, don't you?" she asked.

I stood in front of the refrigerator with both doors wide open. The cold air washed over me. I inhaled it deep. My damp shirt clung to my chest and felt as though it had iced over. I thought I'd be the one to resort to point blank questioning, not her. I grabbed a beer and then let go of the French doors. They swung shut, cutting off the cool air.

"Mitch?"

"Yeah, I know, Lana."

"Did he tell you?"

"McCree mentioned it when they interviewed him. I wasn't there, but one of the detectives sent me the transcripts."

"What did he say?"

I turned around and walked over to the kitchen island where she stood on the opposite side. I twisted the cap off my beer and placed it in my pocket as I set the bottle on the counter. The escaping carbonated gas looked like steam slipping through a street grate.

The tears that had been gathering in Lana's eyes now fell down her cheeks. She didn't bother to wipe them away. The tracks crossed and intermingled and her shirt absorbed her tears. Despite the sorrow she exhibited, I did not find it difficult to be angry with her.

"He said that he had a thing for student teachers. He meant twenty-something women, I suppose. A few he kept around. Some longer than others." I dipped my head so our eyes were level. She glanced away. "And he said that you kept coming back for more. Week after week, even while we were together. And here I thought you didn't show up on Sundays because you were a church going woman."

"It's not like that, Mitch."

"No? Then what's it like? Please, Lana, enlighten me, because I'd sure the fuck like to know what you've been doing."

Her hands gripped the counter top like she expected it to float away, and she'd been tasked with keeping it in place. "He threatened my job, Mitch. My career was in jeopardy. Nobody would have believed me. He's a man, an administrator, they'd have taken his word for it and I'd have been out on the street made to be the evil seductress. I wouldn't have been able to teach anywhere, ever again."

"This is how you justify it? I'm the law. You could have told me this early on and I could have fixed it."

Her head shook, but she said nothing. The tears continued to fall. We were more like strangers now than we'd ever been.

"Mitch, please, I want to fix this."

"Then show yourself to the door."

"Mitch," she said as I turned my back on her. "Don't go."

I headed toward the garage. Her tears had given way to heavy sobs. Without turning, I said, "Lana, if you're still here when I return from the garage, I'll have you arrested." I let the door fall shut behind me and leaned back against it. My head started to ache. A combination of too much beer, stress, and dealing with her. It had to be done though, and I began to feel relieved that I'd never have to face her again.

I spent the following two days murdering my lawn with industrial strength weed killer, working on the Boss, and wasting time on the computer. Sam called three times a day. His updates were brief and lacking substance. Bridget didn't call at all. I wondered if she'd taken early leave for her new position. Which would be the city lucky enough to have her, Denver or D.C.? I kept up hope that she'd stop by if for no other reason than to allow me to apologize to her. Of course, I could have asked Sam to look up her address for me. But I didn't. It didn't feel right. It had to be her choice, not mine.

On that second night, as I drifted in and out of sleep, wondering about Debby Walker and whether or not she was alive, my phone rang. I ignored it. Nothing good happens when you answer a call at two in the morning. It rang again. Being forced awake moments before, I picked it up to answer it. The call came from a number in the 912 area code. I nearly sent it to voice mail, but then I remembered that the 912 area code was used in southeastern Georgia.

It was the only area code used in Savannah.

CHAPTER FIFTY-ONE

As quick as I could clear my throat, I answered the call. "Cassie?"

"Mitch, have you found the girl yet?"

I righted myself on the sofa and took a drink from the glass of water I had on the end table. "I haven't done anything since I left. I'm suspended and that FBI agent is pissed off at me, so she shut me out."

"Personally or professionally?"

"You sure you're not psychic?"

Cassie did not respond to my failed attempt at humor.

"Both," I said. "Sam is trying to latch himself onto the investigation, but not having much luck. It's a dead end up here, both on the girl and the murderer-kidnappers."

"Bent," she said.

She threw off my train of thought. I paused for a few seconds. "What are you talking about?"

"Bent," she said again.

"What is bent? What's this have to do with the girl?"

Cassie breathed heavily into the phone, like she was hiding it from someone, or something, while talking.

"Cassie? Talk to me."

"That's what he says his name is. Does Bent mean anything to you, Mitch?"

"Bent? Do you mean Ben?" I glanced at the portable hanging on the wall. I thought about calling Sam to find out if something had happened. "We've got a person of interest named Ben McCree."

She remained silent for a few moments, then said, "No, that's not it. Think, please. Bent? What's it mean?"

"Bent." I repeated the word verbally and mentally several times over. "Bennett? Cassie, Principal Bennett is the man who was murdered."

"Bennett," she said, followed by several words spoken too low for me to decipher. "Yes!"

"Is Principal Bennett there with you now?" I asked.

"In a way," she said. "It's not like that all the time."

"Well, what's he saying?"

Cassie took a moment to respond. Then, she whispered, "Bricks, bricks, bricks."

"What?" By this point, I'd risen and now stood in the kitchen, waiting for a pot of coffee to brew. I decided after this I'd buy one of those single serving machines with the little plastic cups. As often as my nights were interrupted and called for a heavy dose of caffeine, it'd save me a lot of time.

"Bricks," she whispered again. She kept repeating the word. I'd only watched Cassie in action once before, and this fell in line with what I saw then.

"Cassie," I said loudly. "I need you to talk to me."

She coughed, then groaned. "Mitch?"

"What's going on? What is it about bricks?"

"That's what he kept saying, Mitch. That, and he told me time is running out. Soon to be gone. Bricks secured the wall between the past and the future."

"What the hell? We've got a riddling ghost?"

Cassie groaned, deeply. I had a feeling it wasn't her and that I'd upset a ghost. I said, "Bricks, time running out, soon to be gone."

"Yes, Detective," she said. "Does any of that make sense?"

"No," I said. "Can you ask him to elaborate?"

"He's gone."

"Gone?"

"Yes, he left."

"Was it something I said?"

She started to speak, then hesitated. "It's not like that. He's just...gone."

"When these beings come to you, do you get any kind of imagery?"

"Sometimes, yes."

"Did you tonight? Like maybe an image of where the girl is or of these bricks?"

"No. There was nothing, Mitch. Blackness and his words, that's all."

"How's that..." I cut myself off. No point in asking how the man sounded. It did little to advance our case. "Okay, listen, Cassie. I've got your number on my phone, and you've got mine. You hear anything, get any more visitors, whatever, you call me. Got it?"

"Okay, Detective."

"And I'll do the same." Although, I didn't expect to receive any spectral guests anytime soon.

We hung up and I ran upstairs and showered, skipped shaving, and got dressed. By the time I returned to the kitchen, the coffee had brewed. I poured some into a mug while thumbing Sam's number. The phone rang several times, then the call went to voice mail. I called twice more before he answered.

"Sam, you up?"

"What do you think?"

"Probably not."

He groaned into the phone. I imagined him sitting up and grabbing his head. He'd had a lot to drink, and I guessed he'd drank plenty more after I'd left. The clock on the microwave said it was two-thirty in the morning. He might have only been asleep for half an hour.

"Cassie called me," I said.

Sam drew in a sharp breath of air, then exhaled loudly. "What'd she say?"

"She said that Principal Bennett was with her." I wanted his reaction to that before I gave him the rest.

"Okay," he said, drawing the word out.

"He had a message for us."

"What was it?"

"He said bricks and that we'd better hurry the hell up."

"Hold on." After a few moments of silence, followed by the sound of running water, Sam returned to the phone. "What's the context of this ghost message?"

"Cassie kept saying bricks over and over again. And then, I guess his final message, was time was running out and something about a wall and the past and the future. I figure he meant the girl. But bricks, I mean, what else do kidnappers do with bricks other than tie them around someone's neck or ankles when they toss them overboard into the water? And if that were the case, time would have run out long ago."

"Unless they built something with the bricks."

"Or closed something." I reached into the cabinet and pulled down a travel mug.

"Mitch, didn't you say something after we left McCree's house about bricks."

I searched my memory, but could not recall. "It's not registering at the moment."

"Horace or Fairchild, one of them mocking you."

"About the bricks in the corner of the yard." It came back to me. I pinched the phone between my neck and shoulder while dumping the contents of my mug into the travel mug. "Sam, get dressed. I'll be there in ten minutes."

CHAPTER FIFTY-TWO

My headlights washed over Sam's front lawn as I turned into his driveway. He stood on the porch, coffee mug in hand, and with his shoulder holster hanging open. His shirt was unbuttoned and his slacks looked wrinkled. I was dressed in jeans and a t-shirt. Sam was dressed for work.

He jogged over, opened the door and plopped onto the passenger's seat. "Damn car's gonna wake the neighborhood."

I revved the engine. It sounded like two dozen lions roaring. "Let's go, man." I backed out of the driveway, shifted into first and pressed the gas. The Boss's tires screeched along the asphalt. I could care less who it woke up. We had a lead.

"Did you call Bridget?" Sam asked.

"No, why?" I hoped he hadn't.

"Just curious how much we were sharing, that's all."

"Nothing," I said. "You and me right now. That's it. We figure out for sure where the girl is, we can make some calls. To hell with everyone else for right now."

"Okay. Just wanted to know where we stand."

I raced past an unmarked going at least thirty over the speed limit. Had to have been a cop I knew. He didn't come after me. I wouldn't have stopped even if he had.

The lights inside McCree's house, like most in the neighborhood, were off. The empty driveway offered no clues as to whether someone was home or not. We drove past and stopped two houses down. Sam and I approached McCree's from the front. The garage door had eight square tinted windows cut into it about head high. We each shined a flashlight through the window next to us and peered inside. Our beams bounced off the bare floor. It looked the same as a few days before.

"Think he fled?" Sam asked.

"I'm wondering," I replied.

"He came off as an arrogant prick in that interview, but nothing that he said gave any indication he might have been involved. It really sounded like he hated his brother and only loaned his truck to appease their mother."

I nodded and said nothing.

"Try the door?"

"Nah, let's go around back."

We walked around the side of the house. Ten feet of grass separated McCree's house from his neighbor's. A six-foot privacy fence ringed the backyard. The gate was padlocked, so we climbed over.

"He didn't have a dog, did he?" I asked as I threw my right leg over the top of the fence.

Sam forced a laugh, grabbed the top of the fence, and pulled himself up. "Better hope not."

I dropped to the ground and pulled my pistol. I swept my flashlight across the yard in wide arcs, the barrel of my gun following along. The shin-high grass could stand to be mowed. Dew reflected off the tall bending blades.

"Where was it?" Sam asked.

"Other end," I said, starting toward the opposite side of the yard. I passed by the sliding glass door and raised porch. I recalled those two yokels Horace and Fairchild standing there, mocking me. I swore right then and there that if they did anything to screw this case up, I'd nail their asses to the wall. As it turned out, I might have to thank them if this bricks revelation helped the case. I shined my light through the uncovered back door. Nothing stood out in the illuminated portion of the home.

Sam's light shot ahead of me and fell upon the stack of bricks. "There you go."

We continued forward and stopped a few feet shy of the pile.

"So, you think that's what the message was about?" The tone of Sam's voice told me he still didn't believe in Cassie.

I leaned forward to inspect them. "They look old, worn. Keep that light on them for a minute." I backed up a step or two before heading toward the deck. The wooden stairs bent slightly with each step. I reached the top, turned, and located the bricks again. "The pile's maybe half as tall as it had been a few days ago."

"These bricks are the ones then."

"Presumably, yes. But, for what?" I shone my lights on McCree's house. The sides and back were siding, but the front was brick. I grabbed a brick from the pile in each hand and told Sam to do the same. We kicked at the gate until the latch broke and then jogged around to the front of the house. I placed one brick on the ground while holding the other in my hand. It felt weathered and gritty. I took a step back and aimed my light toward the bricks, and then on the house.

"They don't match," Sam said. "The house is newer. That brick is old, faded."

I nodded. They weren't even close.

"Where do you think they're from?" Sam asked.

I thought for a moment. It turned out that was all it took for me to realize where they'd come from.

"Let's go," I said. "Bring those with you."

Sam scooped them up and raced toward me. I stood at the rear of the Boss with the trunk open. He dropped the bricks inside. I closed the trunk and we both got in the car. I created as much noise as I had when I picked him up. He didn't complain this time.

Five minutes into the ride, Sam asked, "You going to tell me where we're going?"

I glanced at him and shook my head.

"Mitch," he said.

I still said nothing. I knew if I did, he'd try to talk me out of it.

"Dammit, Mitch!"

I responded by taking a turn at forty miles per hour. I leaned to my right. Sam slapped against the door. He cursed. I yelled. Two minutes later I turned into Lana's neighborhood. I pulled up to the curb in front of her house and cut the engine. The sound of our breathing filled the car. The windows started to fog. I reached for my door handle.

"What's going on, Mitch?" Sam asked.

"Come with me," I replied.

Sam grunted his disapproval at having to enter a situation without any idea why we were there. But he followed along. This wasn't the first time, and I knew it wouldn't be the last. So long as we both survived the night, that is.

Accessing Lana's backyard proved to be easier than McCree's. We walked around back without any fence or gate to block us. I stopped in front of the still-in-progress chimney. The new brick stood stacked off to the side with the old brick next to it, half as high as its newer counterpart.

"Let's see how that matches up," I said, circling the pile with my flashlight.

Sam walked over and set one of the bricks from McCree's onto the pile of the old stuff. We turned them over, stood them on end, even compared the leftover mortar.

"We can get forensics to verify," Sam said, "but I'm pretty sure this is a match."

I nodded, said nothing, and looked toward the far end of the house where Lana's bedroom was located.

"You think this implicates her?" Sam asked.

"I don't know. I think you ought to call it in and have a couple of guys come out and babysit her until we find out what McCree's up to."

"We can go in now."

I shook my head. "If we go in there, the whole thing will fall apart. I can't be anywhere near this case. Legally, at least."

Sam pulled out his cell. "I'll make a call."

I heard the sound of water rushing through pipes, then saw Lana's bedroom window light up momentarily. The water trickled to a stop. So did my mind. One single thought spun out of control and I realized how stupid I'd been.

"Hang up, Sam," I said.

"What?"

"I know where she is." I pulled out my cell, found Bridget's number in my recently called list, highlighted it and hit send. A moment later she answered breathlessly. I could tell I'd roused her from a deep sleep. "Bridget, it's Mitch. Before you say anything, you need to hear me out. We've got a lead and I think I know where Debby Walker is."

CHAPTER FIFTY-THREE

The thudding sound repeated itself at regular intervals. At first, Debby figured it was part of her dream. Only, she realized she was no longer sleeping. The sound came from the front of the room. She counted the beats in between. When she reached ten seconds, it hit again. She dug into her pocket and pulled out the small flashlight and switched it on. She saw the wall shake a little on the following occurrence. Someone was breaking down the wall that imprisoned her.

She grabbed the last unopened bottle of water and headed toward the back of the room, cutting her light for the duration of the trip. By this point she had the layout of the room memorized, including knowing how many steps she had to take both walking and running. This time she sprinted. Her body crashed into the wall a half-step too soon, sending her falling back and hitting her head on the hard floor.

Any air in Debby's lungs escaped with the sound of a whimper. It felt like an elephant sat down right on her chest. Her head ached and her fingers ran along the back of her skull feeling for blood. The flashlight had become dislodged from her grasp. She looked to her left, then her right. She'd managed to switch it on before dropping it. The light rolled along the floor and settled against the side wall. She tried to get up so she could grab it. The pain in her chest and stomach kept her from doing so.

Another thud crashed against the front wall. Bits of the interior fell to the floor and bounced and scattered like someone had tossed gravel across the room.

Debby stretched her arms out as far as she could. Finally, when she thought she could last no longer, air rushed through her mouth and into her lungs. It hurt more than when they were deprived, but it allowed her to get up off the floor. She raced toward the light, grabbed it and aimed it toward the front of the room. She saw the little hole in the wall.

Who was out there? Could it be the cops or her mom and brother or anyone who wanted to save her?

"I'm coming for you," the man said. "Just sit tight you little bitch."

She realized that this was no rescue attempt. Debby fought off her tears. She swung the light toward the back wall. The hole she'd created looked wide enough to accommodate her slender frame. Surely, the man on the other side would not be able to get through. Although, he did have something, a sledge hammer perhaps. If he could get into the room, he could get through the wall. That didn't matter. Debby had to go through the hole and take her chances on whatever was on the other side. She'd yet to climb through, only managing to finish earlier that day.

She took a sip from the water bottle then tossed it through the opening. Her hands followed, bracing against the other side. It felt like needles jabbed against her palm at the spots where splinters remained. A cool breeze met her face as she stuck her head inside the hole. Did that mean that it led to a way out? There wasn't time to wonder about that. She jumped up and patted her hands further along the other side of the wall until she teetered against the opening at her waist. With her hands out in front of her and the flashlight in her mouth, Debby gave one last swing of her body and toppled through the opening. She tucked her chin to her chest and rolled through as her body dropped to the floor. Her feet came to rest against the far wall. She grabbed the flashlight and swung it to her right. There stood a wall. She looked to the left. The space extended out five feet or so, then curved around.

"Where are you?" the man yelled from the other side of the opening.

A beam of light penetrated the hidden chamber from the hole above her head. Debby gasped, rose to her feet and started to her left. She followed the curve of the room. The breeze hit her in the face. Freedom lay around that corner. She was sure of it. Her light hit the end of the passage, revealing not a wall, but a door. Freedom ahead, yes! Debbie picked up her pace. She hit the door going full speed, slamming into the handle.

It didn't move.

She bounced off the door and took a step back. She traced the outer edge of the frame with her light. There were no locks inside. She pushed against the handle again. It depressed fully, but the door didn't budge more than a few centimeters. "No," she whispered. She kicked at the door, slammed into it a few times, but nothing helped.

"There's no way out," the guy yelled.

Debbie turned and leaned back against the door. She cut the light. Her body slid down, coming to rest on the floor with her knees to her chest and her arms around her knees. This was where it would end.

CHAPTER FIFTY-FOUR

Roy Miller took his time inspecting the room. It was obvious where the girl had gone. Through the hole in the wall. He'd seen the plans of the water tower, though, and he knew that the space behind the room had only one exit. An exit that he'd locked himself. There was no way a child would break through that door.

He saw several full water bottles placed in a straight line in front of the wall to his left . He went over, grabbed one and opened it. As he lifted the bottle to his mouth, he realized it did not contain water. The girl had urinated into the bottle. He tossed it across the room. It hit the wall and fell to the floor, the first few splashes of urine against the floor were audible. The girl had been more resourceful than he'd realized. Perhaps he should speed this up.

"Come on, girl," he said. "I'm not going to hurt you. You and I are going to leave this place. Someone owes me something, and if they pay up, you'll be free."

Not to go, though, he thought. He only wanted his share of the ransom money. Brad McCree had stiffed him and fled. By taking the girl, Roy could threaten to implicate the man and state that he had been forced to take part. And look at the goodwill he'd show by returning the girl unharmed.

Thus worked the mind of a killer.

"This will be much easier on you if I don't have to break that wall down," he said. "So why don't you come on over and I'll pull you through."

The girl's soft cries echoed through the chamber. He smiled at the sound, waiting a few moments before proceeding.

"Okay," he said. "Have it your way."

He reached down and grabbed the handle of his sledgehammer. He used the heavy end against the floor like a cane, setting it out in front of him. It clapped against the concrete with an ominous warning. He stopped at the far end of the room and shone his light through the hole the girl had made. It was wide enough for him to stick his head through, but nothing else, and he couldn't see anything.

"Last chance," he said.

The girl screamed a curse word back at him. He smiled.

"Have it your way." Miller took a step back, lifted the sledgehammer and slammed it into the wall. He would not stop until the opening was large enough for him to slip through.

CHAPTER FIFTY-FIVE

Judging by the cloud of dust, we reached the water tower parking lot only moments after Bridget Dinapoli. Her government sedan was parked diagonally in front of the entrance. Its headlights lit up the front door, which stood wide open with Bridget heading toward it. She had on jeans and a blue FBI windbreaker. Her hair was pulled back into a ponytail that rose and fell with her steps.

I pulled to a stop in the middle of the parking lot. Beyond the water tower, the sky was dark except for a thin band of light blue close to the horizon. Sam and I stepped outside and rushed toward the entrance. The lot was empty aside from Bridget's car and mine. I presumed that she had not called this in either.

I yelled for her to wait for us, but she ducked inside the building anyway. I broke into a run and entered the tower a few seconds later. The room was dark, still and quiet. I flicked on my flashlight and slowly panned around.

"The other day," I said, "I thought this place looked different, 'cause of the light." I glanced in Bridget's direction. She stared at me. "But it wasn't the light."

"What was it?" she asked.

I directed my light at her, then to a spot on the floor. "There was a pile of bricks there the first time I was in here."

"Where are they now?"

I spun around, hitting the wall with my light and stopping at the gaping hole in the wall. Strewn about the floor were bricks, both whole and shattered. "There." We reached the hole at the same time. "Call this in, Sam."

He didn't, though. Instead, he was on my heels as we squeezed through the opening. I panned my light across the floor. So did Sam. There were bread crusts near a bunch of water bottles, some of which appeared to be filled with urine. The room smelled of feces and sweat. Our flashlights shone on the far wall at the same time, revealing another rugged opening. A shovel handle was propped against the wall. A muffled scream slipped through the hole.

I pulled my gun and sprinted across the room, reaching the opening first. Whoever had gone through had been much smaller than me. I stuck my right leg through, twisted and managed to get my torso through. The moment my head slipped past the wall, I had both arms out, aiming with the flashlight and my pistol. To my right, the small corridor dead ended. I headed left, following the curve of the wall. I saw Roy Miller-Michael Lipsky, his back against a door and his arms around Debby Walker's neck. It appeared that his only option for escape was to go through me or bust down that door. I wasn't going to let either happen.

"Not another step," he said. "I'll snap her neck, ass—"

I pulled the trigger. The bullet slammed into his forehead, knocking him back against the door, then forward. Debby wriggled out of his grasp and ran toward me. Sam pushed me aside and scooped up the little girl. His eyes were wide and he looked between me and the dead man on the floor.

"Okay," Sam said. "We found him like this. Someone had—"

"Sam," I said. "Don't."

Bridget said, "Get her out of here, Sam." Then she forced her way in front of me and turned around. "Mitch?"

I blinked a few times and then met her gaze.

"He threatened the girl, Mitch. You thought he had a weapon in his hand, and he was threatening her life. He said he'd kill her, and you swear that you saw the glint of a knife blade or the dull reflection off the barrel of a pistol. He moved to hurt her. You got that? You had no choice, so you fired your weapon to save the girl."

I reached back and grabbed a handful of my hair. I hadn't thought at all, I simply reacted. The thought that troubled me was that perhaps I had shot him willingly. I would have done so even if he'd stuck his hands in the air in surrender.

Bridget reached up and placed her hand on the side of my face. "You did what you had to do."

Sirens echoed through the small corridor. The flashlight illuminated the space. I looked directly at Bridget. "Did I?"

She nodded and wrapped her other arm around my shoulder, lightly gripping the back of my neck. She lifted herself up and into me, pulling me toward her. Her damp forehead met my sweat-soaked cheek. Her breath felt hot on my neck.

I grabbed her hands and pulled free from her grasp, taking a step back. "Bridget..." I didn't know what to say.

"I'm sorry," she said as she pushed past me.

I followed her out of the corridor and through the room where Debby Walker had been kept. Inside the main area of the water tower, a few members of Bridget's team gathered. Red lights bounced around the room. I glanced outside and saw an ambulance and fire truck in the parking lot on either side of the Boss. Maybe I shouldn't have left it sitting in the middle of the lot. Hopefully they hadn't scratched it. Two paramedics checked out Debby Walker while she rested on a gurney. I nodded at Bridget as I walked past her and through the door.

"You okay?" Sam asked.

I'd just taken a life. Never an easy thing to do, even when the life was already owed. "I'll be all right. I had no choice. He threatened the girl and I thought he had a weapon."

"I heard him say it, Mitch. He said he'd cut her neck."

"He said he'd snap—"

"He said cut, Mitch. I heard it." Sam dipped his head and locked his gaze on me.

I nodded. "Yeah, that's what he said." I turned my attention toward the girl. "How is she?"

"Hungry. Tired. No obvious injuries except to her hands. They're all cut up and blistered and full of splinters. She made that hole in the wall. At least initially she did. Apparently, Miller showed up a bit before us. She climbed through for the first time and found the door, but it wouldn't open. He busted through the hole she made and came after her. We arrived a couple moments later. Had we not, he'd have busted down that door and taken off with her."

I stared past Sam, past the water tower. My head shook involuntarily. "This whole time, she's been right here."

Sam walked past me. I followed him to where Debby Walker sat. "Mind if we talk to her?" Sam asked.

The medics nodded, rose and walked away.

"Do you know how long you've been in there?" Sam asked.

The little girl shook her head. Her eyes welled with tears and her bottom lip quivered.

"Think for me, Debby. How many times did you—"

I reached out and grabbed Sam's shoulder. He stopped mid-question and looked at me. "Not now," I said. Then I turned toward Debby. "What is it?"

"Did you find Beans?" she asked. She bit her lip, then added, "Did they kill him?"

I leaned over so that I was eye level with the child. "He's at home with his parents, Debby. And I saw your mom there, too. She was sad, worried, crying, and praying for you to come home to her."

She burst into tears, sobbing heavily. I imagined that the entire time she'd been staying strong for Bernard, and now that she knew he was safe, she could let go.

I straightened up and turned back to Sam. "There's plenty of time to question her. For now, why don't you compare those bricks in there to the ones we brought with us?"

Sam nodded and headed toward the Boss to collect the samples. Around that same time, squad cars started to arrive and I did my best to get out of the way. Soon enough they'd descend upon me. Technically, I had no business being out here. I should have never been in a position to discharge my weapon. I had a bad feeling this wouldn't shake out in my favor.

Bridget stood off in the distance, alone. I headed in her direction, organizing my thoughts along the way. What was there to say? Things had happened so quickly between us. There was no denying a connection existed, but how strong was it? Could it withstand any of this?

She turned when I got within five feet of her. "You doing okay?"

I nodded and leaned against the split rail fencing.

"I guess I owe you an apology," she said.

"For what?"

"Running out on you after we visited that woman. Turns out she was helpful."

I shrugged. "She might have just been lucky. Honestly, I should have noticed it before. Those bricks were on the floor the first time I was in there, and then they were stacked and mortared the second time. That shouldn't have been the case. This place hasn't been operational in years."

"You had no way of knowing that."

"I suppose."

"I'll go to bat for you, Mitch. If they try to press charges against you, I'll be a witness and stand up for you."

"Appreciate that." We both said nothing for a few minutes. Finally, I broke the silence. "So, what's next?"

She looked up at me with full eyes that began to water over. "I leave for Denver in two weeks."

"I guess I should offer you my congratulations."

This time she shrugged.

"What are your plans until then?" I asked. "I'm pretty sure I'm going to be free."

Bridget shook her head and took a step back. "I can't, Mitch. I'm sorry. I just can't do it." She walked away.

Fortunately, Sam spotted me and headed my way, preventing me from chasing after her. He held up two bricks and nodded.

"A match?" I asked.

"You bet your life it is."

"I guess we ought to go pay Lana a visit."

CHAPTER FIFTY-SIX

W e managed to leave the water tower without anyone following us. The drive to Lana's took only a few minutes. The windows of her house were dark and the shades still drawn. I knew she'd be up soon, though. I pulled into the driveway and parked behind her car. Though I didn't think she'd run, I figured I'd make it hard on her if she decided to.

Sam made it to the front door before I did. He raised a large fist to knock.

"Don't," I said, waving my keys in the air. "I can get us in."

Sam stepped aside to let me stick the key in the lock. The door opened with a creak. We stepped inside and stopped in the foyer. Envy the cat greeted us. I nudged him away with my foot. He stuck his tail in the air and walked off, perturbed, I presumed.

We walked through the entry hall toward the back of the house. Lana stood in the kitchen wearing a short silk nighty that barely covered her breasts and stopped several inches short of the cast that came up to her knee.

"Mitch?" she said. "What are you doing here?"

"We found the girl," I said.

Her eyes widened and grew wet, and she smiled. "Debby? She's okay?"

I nodded. Sam began walking toward the back door, cutting off the possible escape route.

"Where was she?"

"I have a few questions for you, Lana."

She set down her coffee mug and placed her hands on the counter. "What is it?"

"What happened to the bricks?"

"Bricks?"

"From the chimney." I nodded toward the back of the house. "There's a stack of new bricks, but half of the old bricks are gone."

"I don't... I..."

"You what?"

She started looking around the room and her hands felt along the counter top. She seemed to wobble a bit. I couldn't tell if she was going to make a break for it or pass out. Regardless, I could not relent.

"Why'd you do it, Lana?"

Her gaze focused on me and she steadied herself. "Why'd I do what?" Her voice was steady and calm. Had she rehearsed the line in anticipation of this?

"How much did they pay you to go along with it?"

"What? You don't think—"

"Where'd you hide the money, Lana? Did they give you all of it for safe keeping, or just your share?" I mirrored every movement she made.

"Mitch, I had nothing to do with this." Tears fell from her eyes. "Those kids mean everything to me."

"Dammit, Lana." I pulled my pistol and aimed it at her.

"Mitch," Sam said from behind me.

I ignored him and took a few steps toward Lana. She tried to step backward and lost her footing, falling back and catching herself on the counter. "Tell me what you did!"

She couldn't speak through her sobbing. Either she was guilty as hell, or scared to death. It'd be a few moments before she'd calm down enough to talk.

Sam came up behind me and grabbed my arm, pulling the pistol away. I'd already shot and killed one person tonight. I figured he worried that I'd do it again. Once he had my weapon, he pulled me back and said, "Get over there, Mitch."

I took a few steps back, grabbed a chair and fell back into it. I found it difficult to watch Lana struggle to stand upright, tears falling across her cheeks. Though it had been based on a lie, we had spent four months together, and, at one time, I thought she might have been the one to ease the pain Ella and I shared.

"Lana," Sam said. "I need you to look at me." She wiped her eyes and met his stare. "Look, we took Roy Miller into custody an hour ago."

Instinctively, my eyes darted to the side then back at her.

Sam continued, "He's in a room right now spilling his guts out and telling us everything about how this went down. If you are in any way involved, he's going to let us know. Now, if you tell me what I need to hear, we can work something out for you. But, if you decide to lie to me and he says something else, there's nothing I can do for you. You understand that?"

Lana nodded while looking at me. I rose and walked over. I held out my hand to her and she took it. I helped her over to the chair I had been sitting in.

Sam walked over and said, "What role did you have in all this, Lana?"

She shook her head. "I had nothing to do with it. I swear, nothing. I'd never seen that man prior to the week before when he started as the janitor."

"Okay." Sam took a deep breath. "Tell me about the bricks."

"What about them?"

"Why are the old one's missing?"

She quickly looked up at me and then shifted her gaze away. "Ben came over one day and he took them."

"Ben McCree?" Sam asked.

She nodded.

"Did he say why?"

"Um, he said something about needing to replace some at his house."

"Lana, we found bricks that match those at the water tower," I said. "They were used to cover up the opening to a room where Debby Walker was being kept."

"Oh my God," she said, a new wave of tears descending down the slope of her face.

"Again, Lana," Sam said. "If you've got anything to tell us, the time is now."

I marveled at how calm and convincing he sounded.

"A few weeks ago, when we were..." she paused and bit her bottom lip, looking at me. "When Ben and I were together, I mentioned that Bernard had told me his father had sold something to the government, and they were going to receive a lot of money. I mean, a lot, like ten or fifteen million. I thought it was a good thing, the boy could get all the treatment he needed and go to a school where he'd be accepted." She used her palms to wipe the tears from her face. "Oh, Jesus. You don't think Ben was involved do you?"

"Lana," I said. "Roy Miller had an accomplice. That accomplice's name is Brad McCree. Brad is Ben's brother."

"I thought he was an only child," she said.

I stared at her and said nothing. She met my gaze for a few seconds, then closed her eyes. Tears lined her shut eyelids. Whether or not she'd physically taken part in what happened, she now realized she'd indirectly caused it. She planted the seed by telling Ben McCree about the Hollands's windfall. The rest fell into place after that.

"We're going to have a car come by and pick you up, Lana," Sam said. "You'll need to give a statement at the station. It'll be up to them whether to hold you."

Sam followed me outside where we waited for an officer to arrive and escort Lana.

"You think she's innocent?" Sam asked.

I nodded. "Of some things." I turned to face him. "I think the guilt of knowing that she helped initiate this, even indirectly, will eat at her enough to make up for the rest."

"I'm sorry, man." Sam placed a hand on my shoulder and squeezed reassuringly.

I shrugged and looked up at the orange-tinted sky. The humidity had already kicked in and I felt sweat beading up on my forehead. "Not your fault, Sam. Hell, you probably warned me about her."

Two officers showed up ten minutes later. They escorted Lana from the house. She refused to look at me. Her sobs were the only sound I heard. It went quiet after they shut the doors to the car and took off.

I drove Sam home. We stopped off for breakfast, but didn't speak.

"Heading back to your place?" he asked as he opened the car door in front of his house.

I shook my head. "Heading west. Gonna pick up Ella."

"They're probably going to want to talk to you about what happened with Miller."

"I suppose they will."

"I know Dinapoli said she's got your back. You know I do too."

"I know."

"All right." Sam remained seated for a minute, door open, one foot in the car and one on the ground. He looked like he wanted to say something, but didn't. Finally, he got out without another word and slammed the door shut.

I shifted into first and made my way to I-76, heading west, toward Ella.

CHAPTER FIFTY-SEVEN

I spent a week at the campground with Ella. We fished and swam, talked and sang, and just enjoyed each other's company. Terrence spent his spare time with us accompanied by his own children, who were there a lot of the time anyway. I spent several hours on the phone with Huff, Townsend and Chief Warren. The latter two didn't sound too happy to speak with me. Huff was surprisingly supportive. The interviews had the air of formality more than anything else. Both Bridget and Sam had gone to bat for me. A knife had been found in Miller-Lipsky's possession, solidifying the story that had been told.

We left the campground amid a flurry of hugs and tears. Ella had had a great time there and made me promise that we would return for a few weeks next summer. I obliged. I figured I'd need it by then for one reason or another. From there we headed south to Williamsburg, Virginia. We spent a day wandering around Colonial Williamsburg, and then two days at Busch Gardens. A bit further up I-64, we stopped outside of Richmond and spent another few days at King's Dominion. Turned out Ella was something of a daredevil. Although she wasn't tall enough for all the rides, I managed to get her on them. Benefits of the badge.

Before heading home, we spent two days walking around D.C. It was Ella's first trip. She wanted to go to the White House and play with the President's daughters. I told her that might not happen. She didn't believe me. As we drove away from D.C., she went so far as to blame me for not trying hard enough to set up a play date.

I mostly managed to keep my mind off everything that had happened. It was easy to do during the day. Ella kept me occupied. But at night, when my brain needed to shut down and go to sleep, I had a hard time. I thought about Lana and the lie that made up the crumbled foundation of our relationship. I thought about those two children and wondered what the rest of their lives would be like. They'd need a lot of therapy to cope. Bernard's parents could afford it. Could Debby Walker's mom do so? Perhaps we could arrange it through the city. I made a note on my phone to do just that when I got back on active duty.

Time and again, my thoughts turned to Bridget. What was it about this woman that I only knew for a short time, and only a few days romantically, that made her so hard to get out of my mind? As crazy as it sounded, there was a part of me that wanted to try and make a long distance relationship with her work. Thank goodness my rational side was the strong one, because it told me to let it go. Let it go, and let her go.

We got home mid-afternoon after stopping near Center City for a couple cheesesteaks. I wanted to head to my room and crash, but knew there'd be none of that. My mother showed up a half-hour later with a bag full of things for Ella. Toys and clothes, mostly. I headed out back and turned on the grill. The patio table was covered in a fresh layer of fallen leaves. I left them there for Ella. She enjoyed brushing them off and watching them fall in spirals to the ground.

I threw four ribeyes on the grill. One for each of us, plus Sam who was on his way over. Ella came outside. She climbed up on one of the patio chairs and proceeded to sweep the leaves off the table with her arms. Her face had a gleeful look as she watched them fall.

"Go ask your Grandma for some plates," I said.

She smiled at me. I watched her run inside. I leaned back against the siding, enjoying the feeling of the wind as it blew in my face while the smoke from the grill wrapped around me. The smell of the seasoning I'd rubbed on the meat made my mouth water. The fire hissed each time fatty juice dripped off one of the grates.

Sam slid the back door open and stepped outside carrying a stack of plates and a six-pack of beer. We exchanged greetings while he opened two bottles. We all ate dinner quickly. Ella and my mother had plans for the evening. Sam and I waited for them to leave, and then he caught me up on the goings on of the past two weeks.

In the middle of him telling me that they had no leads on either of the McCree brothers, my cell phone rang.

"Bridget," I said, showing him the phone.

"You going to answer it?"

I shook my head and set the cell phone on the table, face down. It rang again. And again.

"Just answer it," he said.

I relented. "How's Denver?" I said.

"How soon can you get down to St. Croix?"

"St. Croix? I just had two weeks of vacationing, Bridget. I'm thinking I'm good."

"We just found the body of Brad McCree."

"The body?"

Sam looked up and leaned forward, setting his beer bottle down on the table.

"Yes, Mitch. He was killed, neck slit, body dumped in a trash receptacle."

"Fitting."

"Isn't it?" she said. "We think Ben is hiding out down here. If you want to be a part of this, get down here now."

"Okay," I said, and then I hung up. Looking at Sam, I asked, "Want to go to the Virgin Islands with me?"

CHAPTER FIFTY-EIGHT

I quickly filled Sam in on what Bridget had told me. The timing was perfect, as he had a couple days off for a wedding that he was only mildly disappointed he wouldn't have to attend now. At least, that's the way he made it seem. I had the feeling he was elated. His family, maybe not so much.

We caught a red eye to Miami and a non-stop on a 737 from Miami to St. Croix. We both buzzed the entire trip, hardly sleeping. Bridget Dinapoli met us outside the airport. She had a government issued sedan that looked like it had been built in the early '90s. I let Sam take the front seat and I got in back.

"Glad you could make it," Bridget said.

"No problem," I said. "Aren't we breaking a few laws here, though?"

She shrugged. "I'm responsible. That's all that matters. Okay?"

Sam and I nodded.

"Okay, guys, here's the deal. We tracked Ben McCree down. He slipped up and made a call to a known forger, some guy who's an expert at making fakes. He's trying to get a fake ID, passport, documents, and so forth. He's also trying to exchange over five million dollars to rands."

"Rands?" I said. "South Africa?"

"Yeah," she said. "Not sure what his plans are from there. Maybe lay low for a while, then move on. To where, who knows. I can't imagine him staying there, though, unless there is some kind of family connection."

"What about the rest of the money?" My thoughts turned to Lana for a second or two.

"We don't know. Hopefully we'll find that out."

"So what's the plan?"

She didn't answer, and any further attempts to find out were met with silence. We drove for another ten minutes and pulled into a hotel parking lot. Bridget kept going until we were behind the building. She pulled out her cell and made a quick call during which she said nothing more than yes or no. My stomach fluttered and I wondered if this were an elaborate set up not for McCree, but for us. What if Bridget had been involved the whole time? She subsequently put my mind at ease.

"Okay, we're going to go in and observe. Once the exchange goes down, we move in and bust him." She looked over her shoulder and smiled at me. "We're going to put an end to this, Mitch."

I relaxed momentarily while contemplating whether or not her words had double meaning. Earlier I couldn't help but think that her inviting me down here meant she wanted to also discuss our possible future. Maybe it was all meant to end here, though.

The opening of the car doors brought me back to reality. I got out, and the three of us entered the hotel from the rear. We stopped at room 127. Special Agents Vinson and Braden greeted us. They'd ditched their suits and ties and were both dressed in t-shirts and cargo shorts. Sam and I were dressed the same. We looked like a beach bum quartet. A third man sat on the edge of the bed. He held a controller in his hand and a keyboard on his lap. He fixed his gaze on the television screen.

Bridget joined him in front of the TV. She pointed at the screen. "That's him. He just entered the lobby. Follow him, Darrel."

The guy on the bed hunched over his keyboard. His fingers struck at the individual keys delicately. He straightened up and grabbed the controller. With narrow eyes and a half-opened mouth, the guy tracked Ben McCree's every movement.

"That's great," Bridget said. "He's seated now. Can you zoom in?"

The four of us joined her in front of the television. It was cramped. I found myself pressed up against her. She smelled good, like tanning lotion. The picture on the screen changed. The focus was on the man wearing a hat, seated alone at a table near the front windows.

"Do we have any other angles?" Sam asked.

"Yup," Darrel said, punching at keys with his fingertips. The screen went blank for a second before returning with a dead on shot of Ben McCree.

"Got you," Bridget said.

"Why don't we just take him down?" I asked.

"Because if we catch him in the act," Bridget said, "we'll have something that we know we can make stick. We've got nothing linking him to the kidnappings. The others are dead. He can say he was down here because he got a call from his brother saying he needed help, and then he can walk."

"That's a load of garbage," I said. "He's not going to walk."

"There's our guy," Braden said.

On the screen, a man with bushy hair and a long beard took a seat on the other side of the table. The guy had on a tank top and tufts of hair stuck out on his chest and shoulders. He had a bag slung over his back. He removed it and set it down on the seat next to him.

"Let's go," Bridget said. She stopped Sam and I. "You two wait here with Darrel."

"Like hell we will," I said.

Sam grabbed my shoulder. "Mitch, let them take care of this. I'm sure once they have him in custody, Bridget won't object to us coming out there. Isn't that right?"

"That's correct. We have to take him down, Mitch. If you're out there, it could compromise the operation."

"Fine," I said, knowing she was right. "Go."

She did, followed by Vinson and Braden. Sam and I remained behind, watching the television with Darrel. A tense few minutes passed. McCree stood up suddenly. The man opposite him leaned back and raised his arms in the air. I noticed McCree had a gun aimed at the guy. He reached across the table with his free hand, grabbed the bag and began to back away.

"You gotta let her know," I said to Darrel.

He tapped at the side of his head, then the com box on his waist. "It's dead."

I sprinted to the door, pulled it open, then raced down the hall. Only problem was I had no idea where it led to or how to get to the lobby and the entrance to the dining room. I did the only thing one could do in that situation and followed the numbers down. We were on the first floor, so I only needed to find the elevators to lead me to the lobby.

From my position in the hall, I heard a collective scream erupt following a gunshot. Who'd fired the gun, and had anyone been hit? I ran faster. Sam called for me from behind. I glanced over my shoulder and saw him running toward me. I didn't slow down for him. I reached an intersection in the hallway. I glanced to the left and saw more rooms. When I looked to the right, it was obvious that was the direction I needed to go. A throng of people headed toward me, and another group went in the opposite direction, toward the front doors.

I kept going until I stood in the lobby. The entrance to the hotel's dining room was to my left. Vinson and Braden stood outside it with their guns drawn. McCree came through the open doorway a few minutes later. He held Bridget hostage, using her as a bullet shield, pressing his gun tight to the side of her head.

It only occurred to me at that moment that Sam and I were unarmed.

Sam cursed under his breath as he came to a stop next to me.

McCree saw us and he smiled. He was missing one of his top front teeth. "Hello, Detectives."

"Let her go, McCree," I said. "You don't want her."

"I don't?" he said.

"No, you want me. You know it. Let her go and take me with you."

"Mitch," Sam said. "What the hell are you doing?"

I shook my head slightly and took a step forward. "Come on, man, let her go."

Ben McCree took a few steps backward, dragging Bridget along with him. I mirrored his movements, moving forward at a slightly faster and longer clip. He shook his head and aimed his pistol at me for a second. "Stop right there."

I lifted my shirt, turned in a circle, then held out my arms. "I'm unarmed." Two more steps forward. "Just let her go and take me."

He looked from me to Vinson and Braden. "Place your guns on the ground and then back away."

They didn't move.

"Do what he says," I said.

"No," Bridget said.

"Let me handle this, Bridget," I said. I looked at the two agents. "Drop them." Sam placed his hand on my shoulder. I wriggled free from his grasp and took a few more steps toward McCree.

"Far enough, Detective," he said. Then he removed his arm from Bridget's neck. In one fluid motion, he kicked her to the ground and swung his weapon toward me. "Don't move!"

I didn't. My gaze shifted from him toward the floor, where it settled in on Bridget. "You okay?"

Before she could respond, McCree fired at her. She screamed and collapsed to the ground while a dark red spot blossomed around her midsection. Vinson and Braden headed toward their guns. McCree shot at the feet of the men and they froze in place.

"Come with me, Detective," McCree shouted.

I walked toward him as calmly as I could. I had to control the situation. That meant getting McCree out of the hotel and onto the street. He'd be slightly disoriented and that would be my opportunity to take him down. Of course, I realized at that moment that Sam's training would have made him a better choice for this than me. Hindsight and all that. Nothing I could do.

McCree forced me to turn around. He placed the barrel of his gun against the back of my head. It was hot and singed my hair and my scalp. I clenched my jaw to keep from yelling.

"You best get me out of here before the other agents show up," I said.

He nudged me in the back and we started toward the doors. The crowd that had dispersed had knocked one of the doors off its hinges. It lay on the ground, shattered. We exited through the doorway. He pulled the gun away from my head and adjusted his grip on my arm. An effort to draw himself closer to me, I presumed. It was time for me to act. I whipped my torso to the right and drew my left arm up. I planned on driving my left elbow into his ribs, as close to his sternum as I could manage. I couldn't see to aim, but I had a good feel for where he was in relation to me.

"What the hell?" McCree managed to get out as I changed direction and started toward him. Gunfire erupted. My eyelids reflexively clenched shut. I waited for the searing pain, but never felt it. I did feel McCree sliding down my body. I heard him smack against the ground.

"Are you okay, Mitch?" It was Bridget.

I opened my eyes and looked over my shoulder. She stood ten feet away, clutching her pistol and holding herself up by leaning into the wall. In his haste, McCree had failed to disarm her.

"I had him," I said.

"Yeah," she said. "So did I until you came along playing hero."

I looked around at the faces staring back at me. McCree bled out on the ground at my feet. I leaned over him and watched as he drew in his last ragged breath. His skin turned ashen and I knew life had left his body. Bridget came toward me. She pressed against a blood soaked section of her shirt. I rushed toward her and offered her my arms in support.

"Turns out you're the hero today," I said.

She smiled. The color in her face started to drain. Her eyelids fluttered.

"Are you okay?"

"Flesh wound," she said, strained.

Behind her, an ambulance turned onto the street. I adjusted my arms and fully supported her. There was no doubt Bridget was a tough woman. She refused to go to the ground, instead choosing to stand victoriously over her assailant.

The paramedics took her from me and assisted her onto a gurney. She looked over at me and smiled. Before they placed the oxygen mask on her face, she said, "Will you come see me in Denver sometime soon?"

I smiled, nodded and lied. "Maybe, Bridget."

CHAPTER FIFTY-NINE

S am and I caught a flight home the following day. By six that
evening we were back in Philly. Good thing, too, because the
Eagles played that night. We decided to watch the game at my
house, figuring it'd help Sam escape the ire of his family, who
were pissed off he'd missed the wedding. There was time for him
to get to the reception, but after what we'd been through, he had
little interest. Besides, we could drink at my place and not be
bombarded with the Hokey Pokey.

Ella greeted us on the porch after we pulled up to the house.
She had a big smile on her face, oblivious to what her daddy had
just gone through. I wanted to keep it that way, too. My mother, on
the other hand, looked concerned. She had no trouble expressing
it either.

"Saw a report on the TV that the FBI woman on the case was
shot down in the Virgin Islands."

I nodded. Sam did the same.

"You two all right?" Momma asked.

"We're fine," I replied.

"All right, then," she said. "We've got some pizza inside."

"That's a first," Sam whispered to me.

Ella turned and ran to her grandmother, grabbing her hand and pulling her inside. She had on the custom jersey I'd purchased for her last Christmas. It had "Ella Kate" written across the top with double zeros for the number. She wore it all the time.

I crossed the porch and stopped at the front door. "Go on inside, Sam. I'll be right there."

He nodded as he passed by.

I went back through the screen door and stood in the middle of the driveway for a few minutes. The sun was setting and the sky turned several different shades of red, orange and pink. It felt refreshing and gave me hope that there was a chance for new beginnings, even in an old life.

I pulled out my cell and placed a call down to Savannah. Cassie answered on the second ring.

"I wanted to thank you, Cassie. Your tip paid off. We got the girl, and we caught the bad guys."

"Always happy to help, Mitch. How's Bridget?"

I paused for a second. "She's doing okay. On her way to her next post as far as I know. Anyway, any updates on that other thing?"

"Your missing wife and child?"

That's what I loved about Cassie. No hesitation. "Yeah, that'd be it."

"Sorry, Mitch. Nothing. If there ever is, I'll let you know."

I said goodbye and hung up. A gentle breeze blew across the porch. One of my neighbors was cooking steaks on their grill. Seemed like a good idea to me.

I walked over to the mailbox and pulled down the plastic door. There were a few bills and a couple coupon mailers. I hated those things. They never had anything I wanted. Buried at the bottom was something I did want, a postcard. My heart skipped a beat at the letter written in pencil. I ran to the porch and flipped on the light.

Hi Daddy! I'm having a great time on this vacation with Mommy. I sure miss you and Ella Kate, though. We've been all over, even through Texas. Too many of those blue stars there, though. I'm not allowed to tell you where we are right now, only that we are doing good. Mommy says I'll get to see you soon. She says that a lot, though. I miss you. Love, Robbie.

Through watery eyes, I searched the postcard for a postmark. It had been sent four days ago from Denver, Colorado. Soon, Robbie, I thought. I'll find you soon.

The End

MITCH TANNER'S story continues in Into the Darkness. Click here to purchase now, or read an excerpt below!

Sign up for L.T. Ryan's new release newsletter and be the first to find out when new Mitch Tanner and Jack Noble novels are published (and usually at a discount for the first 48 hours). To sign up, simply fill out the form on the following page:

http://ltryan.com/newsletter/

As a thank you for signing up, you'll receive a complimentary copy of *The Recruit: A Jack Noble Short Story*.

If you enjoyed reading *The Depth of Darkness*, I would appreciate it if you would help others enjoy this book, too.

Lend it. This e-book is lending-enabled where available, so please, share it with a friend.

Recommend it. Please help other readers find this book by recommending it to friends, readers' groups and discussion boards.

Review it. Please tell other readers why you liked this book by reviewing at your preferred bookseller. If you do write a review, please send me an email at contact@ltryan.com so I can thank you with a personal email.

ALSO BY L.T. RYAN

The Jack Noble Series

The Recruit (free)

The First Deception (Prequel 1)

Noble Beginnings

A Deadly Distance

Ripple Effect (Bear Logan)

Thin Line

Noble Intentions

When Dead in Greece

Noble Retribution

Noble Betrayal

Never Go Home

Beyond Betrayal (Clarissa Abbot)

Noble Judgment

Never Cry Mercy

Deadline

End Game

Mitch Tanner Series

The Depth of Darkness

Into The Darkness

Deliver Us From Darkness - coming soon

Affliction Z Series

Affliction Z: Patient Zero

Affliction Z: Abandoned Hope

Affliction Z: Descended in Blood

Affliction Z Book 4 - Spring 2018

MITCH TANNER 2: CHAPTER 1

He sought refuge under the canopy of the centuries-old live oak. The leaves couldn't stop all the rain, though. Thin and fat, drops passed through unscathed and pelted the top of his head. The Spanish moss hung low under the weight of the storm, whipping sideways in the gusts.

Thunder cracked and lightning lit up the land as it scratched down from the heavens and clawed up from hell to meet somewhere in the middle, revealing a sky the color of a week-old corpse.

The living avoided the graveyard tonight. Most places, in fact. Few were crazy enough to be out in this kind of weather. Samantha might be Category Three by the time she hits at the border of Georgia and South Carolina. Savannah would be hit, but Charleston would get it worse.

He didn't care.

Though the living refused to go near the graveyard, the souls of his victims were out.

In all, five of the women he'd murdered — although if one

were to ask him, he'd say they were liberated — were buried in the ground here. More than any other local graveyard. Of course, thirteen between the two port cities were still missing. The bodies of those dumped at sea had not yet washed to shore. And no one had come upon the women he'd dumped deep in the low country woods.

Nor had they connected those from his travels throughout the country.

Through the hammering rain he saw their translucent souls dancing, free and naked, relishing every time lighting and thunder ripped apart the silence and darkness.

As much as he fed on the energy, even he had his limits. After an hour of playing with the dead, he stopped to visit Lucille. He stood in front of her tombstone for several minutes. Like the other graves, he didn't need light to know what was written there.

For a man the police wanted badly enough that they devoted a team of detectives to finding him, he had lived unnoticed, right under their noses, for years.

Until they caught him.

It all started with a visit to Lucille, years ago.

"Lucille," he said. "Even in death, you're such a bitch. It was all because of you."

He dropped to his knees. With his eyes closed, he ran his hands through the damp grass, allowing each blade to choose a path on either side of a finger. Though cold, he imagined the liquid to be fresh blood pouring from his victim. A new one, perhaps. It had been so long that memories of those he had killed did little to excite him.

Except for one woman. The one who had bled on this very same spot. He'd stabbed her one time shy of enough. If only he'd plunged his blade once more, deeper, twisting and cutting and tearing until she faded, things would have been different. He would have been allowed to continue carrying out his work.

Ridding the area of the dark-haired whores who pervaded the streets and squares.

He could have carried his mission further across the country. More connections would have been made. He wanted to add to the five men who now helped to achieve his goal. His vision. His dream.

The wind died down to a breeze. The voices of the trees quieted. A lull in the storm engulfed him.

He lifted his hands from the earth, brought them to his face, and wiped the blood of ghosts on himself. He smelled it. Tasted it. The coppery sensation felt so real. His hands and fingers tingled. Something stirred in his stomach. A feeling that hadn't been there in months. Excited at the prospects of killing, his erect penis pressed hard against his zipper.

Tonight he would not discriminate. There was no time to plan.

He began his retreat as the storm resumed, leaving trails in the mud as he struggled to maintain footing while descended the small hill to the road leading away from the cemetery. The deserted road offered no refuge from the torrential downpour. Why would anyone visit the graveyard or anywhere else tonight? The storm was the reason he felt safe coming out of hiding.

Fifteen minutes later he walked against the wind toward the river on Skidaway. The streets were deserted and dark. He saw no traffic lights, street lamps, or house lights. The power had gone out. Preemptively, he presumed. Those lazy bastards didn't want to work during a hurricane. He was the only one with that kind of work ethic.

A car turned from East Anderson Street. The headlights caught him in a spot where he had no cover. The driver flashed hi-beams. He continued walking forward. The car cut across the street and slowed to a stop in front of him. He shielded his eyes from the rain as the driver's window descended, revealing a twenty-something brunette and her three companions. They were similar in looks, but none as perfect as the woman driving.

"You shouldn't be out here," she said. "Hurricane is going to hit soon."

"Got caught at the cemetery," he said, altering his accent and offering a slight smile. "Came all the way out from Kansas to see it."

The woman looked back at her friend in the passenger seat. They kept their voices low making it impossible for him to determine what had been said. They looked like the kind of intelligent women that presented the kind of challenge he enjoyed. But they would pull away without him. He was sure of it.

"Where are you staying?" She smiled while squinting against a heavy wind gust. "We'll give you a ride there."

He placed his hands on the windowsill and leaned forward so he wouldn't have to shout against the noise of the storm. "Stupidly, I got off the bus and walked right down here. Figured I'd be able to find a room somewhere along the river."

"You'll never find a place now."

He looked up into the rain, stood with his hands out, and shook his head. "I know, I know. You must think I'm the biggest idiot in the city, right?"

"Pretty much." The woman bit her lip as she looked him up and down.

There was nothing menacing about him. He went out of his way to make sure of it. Clean cut, short hair, polo shirts, tan chinos. His face was always clean-shaven. Fingernails manicured. Neat and simple looking. His frame belied his strength. Wiry, but not overly muscular. Plenty strong enough to do the job, though.

She gestured toward the back door. "Get in. You can stay with us. It's not the nicest place, but we've got a great couch."

"You sure it's wise to invite a stranger to stay in your house?"

Her grin widened. "Something tells me you're a safe bet. Now get in."

The rear driver's side door popped open. He saw the two women there scooting along the bench seat to allow him room to sit. He adjusted his bag so that it was on his outside shoulder.

The night wouldn't be as fun if they discovered the knife and handgun it contained.

All four women introduced themselves. But he only remembered Alice, the woman driving. He told them his name was Rick Harrison. A lie. He then wove a tale of growing up on a farm, then leaving home for the Army — special forces, of course — only to wash out because of a broken leg that hadn't healed properly. It had acted up again tonight while he fought the wind and rain.

By the time they reached the women's home on the other side of Forsythe Park, the women had let their guard down completely in front of the guy they perceived to be an idiot who came to Savannah in the middle of a hurricane with no place to stay.

Perfection achieved. Almost.

They stayed up for another hour or so, drinking wine and warm beer. Talking and even a little flirting. He heard their stories. In one ear, out the other. He didn't care what made them tick, what their life dreams were. Those dreams would end tonight. Only his dream could carry on.

He wished them all goodnight on their final night as they slipped down the hallway to turn in. He made note of which door each went into, then took thirty minutes to clear his mind. Meditation, it'll help you achieve your goals!

MITCH TANNER 2: CHAPTER 2

Two of the women bunked in the same room. He had to be quick about killing them. He hated being quick. A cockroach deserved a · quick death. Not a woman. For she was a play thing in her final minutes.

He stuck a pillow over the first woman's face, both hands over her nose and mouth until she stopped squirming. Her muffled cries for help barely reached his ears. Then, using the same pillow, he smothered the other woman's face, but only to stop her from screams from drifting out of the room. He took his knife and used it to cut her shirt from the bottom up. She railed against him. The blade sliced into the flesh of her abdomen.

"Damn you," he whispered as he cut her neck. Stupid whore. Covered him in blood. He couldn't surprise Alice like he had planned. He pulled the pillow off the dead woman's face. Her opened eyes glistened. "All you had to do was play along for a few minutes."

The floorboards creaked in the hallway outside the room. He stopped and leaned back against the wall. At the end of the corridor there were two doors. But he found himself unable to recall which one led to which woman. The whore's rebellion had thrown him off. Enter the wrong room, and everything was ruined. He'd have to kill Alice right away instead of playing with her first.

What a shame.

Alice tantalized him in all the right ways.

He continued down the hallway, walking close to the trim. It helped to reduce squeaking. He stopped at the end of the corridor between two doors. One to the right. One to the left. The house exhaled a steady hum, while wind and rain battered its shell. He closed his eyes, absorbed the sounds, and held his knife out.

"Oh show me the way, my steeled companion," he whispered.

When he looked down, the knife pointed to the left.

Of course, the door with the seashell sign hanging from a bent nail. Alice's room. She had said she grew up on the beach in Florida before attending the Savannah College of Art and Design.

SCAD, he thought. *What a silly name.*

He opened the door on the right. It smelled floral. Overly so. And it was hot. A sheet covered the woman. As he neared he noticed how tightly wrapped it was around her ass. She mumbled something indecipherable as she drew one knee up. He stepped into the room, spun in a half circle, and shut the door, holding the knob tight to the right to prevent the latch from clicking while he turned the lock.

At the side of the bed, he clawed for her face, but found her hair. He traced his fingertips along her body toward the foot of the bed. Felt the dip in her lower back. The shapeliness of her ass. His preference for her to be on her back diminished. The stomach would be even better. He wedged his fingers into the crease where her thighs met.

She tensed. Her leg snapped back and her thighs pressed tight together.

He snatched her pillow, wrapped it around her face. As he

straddled her back, he tied the ends of the pillowcase together. She thrashed underneath him, but all it did was arouse him. He worked his hands along her arms until each gripped a wrist. He wrenched them back until they touched. The pillow muffled her choking sobs. He held her arms in place with one hand, and grabbed the bed sheet with the other, which he used to tie her wrists together. She continued to thrash, her back pressing against his testicles. He went still, closed his eyes, cocked his head and listened.

Her moans melted into the howling wind and pelting raindrops. There was no way they slipped past the door. The door which he'd shut. The door which he'd locked.

He had time to get some of the vitriol@ out of his system.

Alice would appreciate that.

Using his knee, he wedged her thighs apart. She twisted and bucked, but couldn't force him away. He tore her panties down the middle. But then the sensations that stirred in the graveyard, and yet again while she fought underneath him, were no longer present.

As much as he wanted the release so that he would be in control when he went to Alice, that would not be the case.

"Shit. You stupid, stupid bitch. What's wrong with you?"

He hopped off the bed. The woman rolled over and retreated to the corner. The pillow slipped down, revealing her darkened eyes, nose and mouth. She could have screamed due to his idiotic decision to release her for a moment. But she didn't. Instead, she whined breathlessly.

"Please, don't."

Using the sheet he snatched off the floor, he wiped her friend's blood off his blade. Then he lunged forward and gagged her with the bloodied sheet. With her arms bound behind her, she could do nothing other than kick to defend herself. Not an easy feat with his weight bearing down on her thighs.

He rose up, one hand behind her head, pulling tight on her neck. The other holding the knife in front of his crotch, inches from her throat.

One way or another, he'd have his release.

And so he stabbed her over thirty times. The blade penetrated her face, neck, chest, abdomen and thighs.

He left her to bleed out, the knife buried deep in her stomach. The doorknob on the other side of the hallway felt cold against his flushed skin. He gripped it. Turned it. Cracked the door. Felt a rush of cold air that smelled like lavender wash over him.

"Hello, Alice," he said in his country accent. "I thought we might talk for a while."

She rolled over. Her form cut through the darkness as she sat up. She switched on a flashlight aimed at herself. He could see from her exposed breasts and erect nipples that she was happy he'd entered her room.

"I was hoping you'd join me," she said.

"I know you were, Alice." His voice had changed. "But this night is not going to go as you expected."

Available now - Click here!

https://www.amazon.com/Into-Darkness-Mitch-Tanner-Book-ebook/dp/B077YZJP8W/

ABOUT THE AUTHOR

L.T. Ryan is a *USA Today* and international bestselling author. The new age of publishing offered L.T. the opportunity to blend his passions for creating, marketing, and technology to reach audiences with his popular Jack Noble series.

Living in central Virginia with his wife, the youngest of his three daughters, and their three dogs, L.T. enjoys staring out his window at the trees and mountains while he should be writing, as well as reading, hiking, running, and playing with gadgets. See what he's up to at http://ltryan.com.

Social Medial Links:

- Facebook (L.T. Ryan): https://www.facebook.com/LTRyanAuthor

- Facebook (Jack Noble Page): https://www.facebook.com/JackNobleBooks/

- Twitter: https://twitter.com/LTRyanWrites

- Goodreads: http://www.goodreads.com/author/show/6151659.L_T_Ryan

Made in United States
Orlando, FL
20 January 2023

28859147R00209